D0677127

PENELOPE LEMON

Yellow Shoe Fiction
Michael Griffith, Series Editor

Also by Inman Majors

Love's Winning Plays
The Millionaires
Wonderdog
Swimming in Sky

PENELOPE LEMON

Game On!

INMAN MAJORS

LOUISIANA STATE UNIVERSITY PRESS ▐▐▐ BATON ROUGE

WITHDRAWN FROM
RAPIDES PARISH LIBRARY

RAPIDES PARISH LIBRARY
Alexandria, Louisiana MR

Published by Louisiana State University Press
Copyright © 2018 by Inman Majors
All rights reserved
Manufactured in the United States of America
First printing

DESIGNER: Michelle A. Neustrom
TYPEFACE: Whitman
PRINTER AND BINDER: Sheridan Books, Inc.

LIBRARY OF CONGRESS CATALOGING-IN-PUBLICATION DATA

Names: Majors, Inman, author.
Title: Penelope Lemon : game on! / Inman Majors.
Description: Baton Rouge : Louisiana State University Press, 2019.
Identifiers: LCCN 2018001224| ISBN 978-0-8071-6951-3 (cloth : alk. paper) |
    ISBN 978-0-8071-6950-6 (pdf) | ISBN 978-0-8071-6949-0 (epub)
Classification: LCC PS3563.A3927 P46 2019 | DDC 813/.54—dc23
LC record available at https://lccn.loc.gov/2018001224

The paper in this book meets the guidelines for permanence and durability
of the Committee on Production Guidelines for Book Longevity
of the Council on Library Resources. ♾

♥

To Betty Winton, my aunt who left us too soon.

PENELOPE LEMON

1

Penelope Lemon sat on the bleachers at her son's baseball practice, wondering if she'd still be married to her husband if she'd never seen him in his yellow kimono robe. The robe in question was a short little matronly number that came just to his knees and no farther. It wasn't actually a kimono, of course. It was shorter, for one, much shorter, and made not from silk but from the same poly-satin as most of her own undergarments. James was a tall, pale man with knobby knees, and she thought, then as now, that it was an odd sartorial choice for someone hoping to entice a woman into sexual dalliance.

It had been hard for her to have sex with him after an early morning sighting of the shorty robe, especially when he'd initiated the proceedings while still wearing it, his knees poking out so obviously, and the sash cinching his midsection in a way as to make him look paunchy above and bony below. On those bleak mornings, her first order of business was to remove the robe. Her second, as they were moving toward the bed, was to try to erase it from her memory. She could do this—most of the time, in fact—unless she happened to spot his cowboy boots lying about, but that was a whole other story.

She actually found James handsome when he wasn't wearing kimonos or boots. He had a fine head of black hair that had just been turning salt and pepper when they divorced and expressive brown eyes that reflected what he was thinking or reading, even what he was eating. A fresh grapefruit, purchased from the high school band fundraiser, could set his eyes to flickering and firing, and just one mouthful in, he could be discoursing on the hybridization of citrus, or the benefits of taking one thousand times the recommended daily dose of vitamin C, or even a roadside store in Florida with a chained bear and pecan rolls that he visited as a boy.

These discourses were predictable and frequent and Penelope tended to enjoy them, nodding her head whether actually listening or not. James had a deliberate, near-monotone way of speaking, and when he was off on one of his grapefruit jags she could go into a state of hypnosis, listening without listening, nodding rhythmically, thinking of all sorts of things besides bears and vitamin C and pecan logs. It was really quite relaxing, especially in the morning before her coffee kicked in.

The shorty robe was not predictable. She never knew when it might rear its silky smooth head. She did note that the donning of the kimono frequently coincided with amorous morning thoughts James was having. Perhaps the breeze coming in from below contrasted with the warmth and softness of the poly-satin in ways he found provocative. Perhaps longer robes didn't offer this same arousing juxtaposition. Did airflow cause blood flow to sensitive areas? Or did amorous thoughts precipitate a mad rush for his lingerie? It was definitely a chicken/egg situation.

Regardless, one day the mini-kimono disappeared. He only asked about it once, whether she'd seen it, and when she said, no, no, she hadn't, he let the matter drop. His morning passions waned for a while, but not for too long. He dutifully wore the full-length terrycloth robe she bought him, but bathwear was no longer an accessory or prelude to his lovemaking. She felt a little guilty about depriving him of his *mangligee*, but her peace of mind had been at stake, as had their love life.

James was smart. That was what had first attracted her. She was smart too, despite the fact that she'd dropped out of college to marry her first husband, who happened to be a huge, huge redneck. Basically, if you were from Hillsboro, Virginia, and weren't a doctor or lawyer's kid, you likely had a bit of red about the neck, no matter how well you did in school. Anyway, her first marriage had kind of made sense at the time.

Now here she was, a twice-divorced, underemployed mother to a nine-year-old son. That same son was currently taking his turn at bat as the coach did his best to look interested and hopeful as he lobbed in pitches from the mound. Penelope had been a good softball and basketball player as a kid, but Theo, poor thing, had inherited his father's limited athletic ability.

"Come on, Theo!" Penelope yelled after he had let the third straight ball go over the plate without moving the bat from his shoulder where it rested so comfortably. "You can do it."

Theo could not, in fact, do it, a truth that every parent around Penelope knew all too well. The coach's wife, sitting on the front row of the bleachers, offered a *Come on, Theo,* but it was perfunctory at best. Every parent in the stands and every child on the field knew that Theo generally refused to swing and would either strike out or walk depending on the accuracy of the pitcher. Oh, how Penelope longed for a walk when the pitcher had accrued three balls on young Theodore. And when that fourth ball came, and Theo had looked back to the sympathetic umpire to check that his luck had held, he would sprint headlong in his wobbly, storkish way (so like James, so so like James) toward first base where he would smile sheepishly and pretend he was like the other boys whose fathers had been working on their hitting, their pitching and catching, and yes, on their running too, since birth.

"Come on, Theo!" Penelope yelled again, though she was beginning to see the humor of the situation: a little boy who didn't give a rat's ass about hitting a baseball being begged and cajoled to do so by a group of full-grown adults. "Just swing it once."

At this the coach's wife turned and smiled. Penelope giggled and said, "Just move the bat a little."

The coach shot her a wry grin now from the field. He was a good sort, kind even to the lesser players, and nice-looking. It was too bad he was married, and married apparently to someone who loved youth baseball as much as he did, judging from her attendance at every single practice. WTH? Penelope would have paid good money to skip these biweekly two hours in the heat and dust. Nearly as much as Theo himself would have paid.

Theo seemed to sense the adults' levity at his plight and swung—like an unoiled robot—at the next pitch and then the next, whiffing badly at both.

"Good job," said the coach. "Good try."

"That's the way, Theo, that's the way to try!" Penelope yelled, clapping and smiling, fighting a hysterical urge to laugh as Theo trotted off, smiling himself, toward the dugout and his glove and then the comfort of deepest right field.

James didn't play sports growing up, seeing himself as more the rugged outdoorsman instead, a kind of overachieving individualist in the mode of Theodore Roosevelt, the old Rough Rider himself. James had been reading a book called *Theodore Rex* during her pregnancy. The book stirred him considerably, and he would turn to her in bed while reading and blurt out that *rex* meant king in Latin. She told him she knew what *rex* meant since she'd had two years of Latin in high school. A few minutes later, he asked if she'd ever had salmon tartare, explaining that *tartare* meant *raw*, and that it was a delicacy in the Pacific Northwest, and that explorers in that region, lone frontiersmen, had been eating it for hundreds of years, and that the Indians had eaten it for eons before that. He said that one day he'd like to go off into the woods of the Pacific Northwest with just a rifle and fly rod to see what that was like. Then he said, no, British Columbia would be better, more rugged, more *out there*. He asked if she'd read Jack London. She admitted she had, but that she'd grown tired of reading about dogs fighting and cold weather. When she said this, he nodded in a sympathetic way that suggested she wasn't of true frontier stock. He talked briefly of the first knife he'd had as a boy and of cooking bologna in the woods behind his subdivision. Then he said he'd like to name their son Theodore.

The next day he rose early and went to shoot beer cans at his uncle's farm.

She thought of all this while Theo, in the far outfield, stood flinging his hat up in the air and attempting—and failing—to catch it upon its return. Now he was trying to kick it off the ground and into the air so as to catch it. Penelope noted that her son's cleats looked shiny as tap shoes compared to the mud-caked ones of his teammates. His hat also looked newer and stiffer than those of the other boys, as if it refused to mold to his uninterested head on principle alone. But perhaps this kicking and flinging would make it appear played in, sweated in. Did Theo even sweat? He was often pungent, but she couldn't recall visually apparent perspiration. He was indoors most of the time. James claimed he didn't perspire due to highly evolved glands. According to him, modern man, the beneficiary of forced-air cooling and no longer having to make his way in the wild by dint of muscle and hustle, was losing the need to sweat. But this wasn't true, at least in James's case. A good western could lather him up plenty. His favorite gambit on these nights was to call her Miss Kitty, who he said was the kindly bordello keeper from *Gunsmoke* and rumored paramour of Sheriff Matt Dillon. Afterwards, their lovemaking did have a certain frontier flair, but that might have just been James's joyous shout of *yee-hi* at the culminating moment.

She considered yelling out to Theo, urging him to pay attention as the other parents did, the dads especially, but found she didn't really care if he paid attention or not. He wasn't frontier stock, no matter how many times James took him to the outdoors store to look at canoes. The only reason she'd signed him up for baseball was in the hope that he'd find some playmates. So far nothing had developed, though the boy playing second base had potential. He was smallish and had a bright, quizzical look about him, as if he too would enjoy talking about

Pokémon cards and Legos. Additionally, he wore tennis shoes and not cleats, and this, Penelope felt sure, marked him as an individualist—or his mother as one—and not the kind who would call Theo *Weird Turd* or *Fart Boy* as they did on the school bus each day. Perhaps she should introduce herself to the mother.

All the parents were up in the bleachers, the fathers who she guessed chose to be there, the mothers, many single like herself, because they had to be, the coach's wife being the perky exception. Only the mother of the individualist second baseman sat away from the crowd, behind the backstop in a foldout chair, reading and never glancing to the field.

She had to be cool if she read at practice.

Thinking this and feeling resolute, Penelope got up, smiled once just to be polite at the father of the hulking first baseman, who seemed to enjoy ogling her in between exhortations to his son to keep his elbow up, and made her way behind the backstop. Penelope stood just behind the woman, trying to get within her peripheral vision so that a conversation might start naturally when she turned a page or something loud happened on the field.

That moment was a while in coming, for the reading woman either hadn't noticed her or didn't want to talk. She sat in a cheap foldout chair, with thin tan legs sticking out of jean shorts and wearing a black T-shirt that Penelope couldn't see, but that she gathered was for some rock band. Penelope hoped so. She was a bit of a closet metalhead herself: Zeppelin, AC/DC, Metallica, etc. The woman's massive sunglasses had slipped halfway down her very tan nose and Penelope wondered why she didn't push them up. Perhaps her book was that engrossing. Moving up a few feet, as if truly riveted by nine-year-old baseball, Penelope slowly, slyly, craned her neck for a look at the cover. She couldn't make out all of it, but bursting bosoms and bare masculine chests were in no short supply. That these chests were heaving in front of an elegant desk and sumptuous leather chair suggested that executive-style hanky-panky was in the offing.

This gave her pause. She didn't object to books with tawdry covers, or to books with horny executives who saved a lot of time by using their offices as bedrooms. God no. She devoured them by the dozen. But wouldn't it be disconcerting to greet this woman when she was in the throes of an especially raunchy section? Enrique might just now be tying up Regina with his expensive silk tie and Penelope hated to interrupt.

It was then that the woman laughed in a scoffing way and said, "Oh give me a break, would you."

Startled by this, Penelope tried to give the impression of deep immersion in little-boy baseball, yanking her head toward the field and squinting in appraisal as the fathers often did. She nearly shouted for Theo to *Look alive out there,* but thought that might be laying it on a bit thick. She could feel the woman eyeballing her and realized she was standing closer than was the societal norm. There was no question she'd been caught spying.

"Have you read this?" the woman said, brandishing the book at Penelope and shaking it in a rough way that made her blond ponytail bounce. Her voice was deeper and huskier than Penelope would have guessed from her size, and her whole manner was like an aggressive small dog.

Penelope couldn't decide whether to maintain her ruse of engrossment or just cop to being a weird turd who stood too close to people reading inappropriate books at Little League fields. The woman was staring at her through the windshield of her spectacles and seemed so irritated by what she'd just read that she didn't care if Penelope was looming over her, only whether Penelope was the type of person to indulge in books like *The Tycoon's Dare.*

"Well, it's total crap," the woman said. "I can't believe my friend recommended it."

"I haven't read it," said Penelope.

This was a bald-faced lie. She'd read it two weeks ago, and the man's name *was* Enrique, only it wasn't Regina being tied to the credenza with a Savile Row tie, but Sabrina. She felt guilty now, and more than a little tawdry. She glanced unconvincingly toward the outfield to avoid the woman's inquisitive gaze, and saw that Theo was shaking his rear end, fast and furious, bouncing side to side like an old-timey washing machine. It was his Shakira dance. Until now, she'd assumed he restricted his diva dancing to the house, but apparently that wasn't the case. He truly was a Fart Boy, an unabashed Weird Turd.

The reading woman was glaring at her, but she didn't care. Theo was really moving out there. And now the centerfielder was gyrating a bit too, moving his shoulders and laughing, egging Theo on. Penelope could see the bleacher parents pointing and smiling. It was clear they found this behavior in character and they seemed, for the most part, to be amused by this break in the action.

Despite the scowling book snob beside her and the parents pointing at the spectacle that was her son, Penelope found that she was smiling. She turned to the woman and said: "That's my son."

"The one way out there?"

"Yes," she said. "The dancing one."

"Oh, is that what he's doing?"

"Yes. He really likes that Shakira song."

"Which one?"

Here Penelope sang the bit about her hips not lying and how things were starting to feel right.

The woman didn't reply, which Penelope found surprising. It was a good song and she wasn't a bad singer. She could feel the book being brandished at her as if she was the sort—the exact sort—to like such trash. She moved from one foot to the other, unsure whether to look at the woman or the book being waved like a disapproving banner. For some reason, she now recalled that James had once taken eleven months to read *Anna Karenina*. He would very importantly crack the book while in bed, sigh appreciatively every few sentences, then fall asleep four pages in. During the time of *Anna Karenina*, she'd finished forty-two novels, not all of them trash. She'd read the books everyone else was reading, *The Secret Life of Bees* and *The Goldfinch*, all those. At some point, tired of the huffing James did about her reading choices, she'd begun the tally of Books Read versus Books Started. When nearly a year passed and James was not quite to the halfway point of Tolstoy's masterpiece, Penelope began to tease him, gently of course, the only way possible to tease James, about their 42:1 disparity, with the result being that he spent all of one beautiful fall weekend racing through *Anna Karenina*, though Penelope was sure he was skimming huge chunks there at the end. Anyway, no one could ever say James hadn't read Tolstoy.

Snapping back to the present, Penelope took another gander at the cover of *The Tycoon's Dare*. On closer inspection, Enrique didn't look like a high-powered global executive who cut billion-dollar multinational deals. He looked more like a pro wrestler, super tan, all muscled up, and faintly dewy with sweat. Did this stop Sabrina's breast from swelling? It did not. That top was coming off and coming off soon.

"I actually have read that book," Penelope said, though not exactly sure why. Maybe it was Theo's honest interpretive dance on the field. Maybe because this woman, despite having a sensitive-looking son who didn't wear cleats, wasn't quite what she hoped her to be.

The woman didn't reply but did set the book on her lap. Penelope breathed a sigh of relief. For a moment she'd feared the snob was going to fling it at her. She had begun walking back to the bleachers when the woman called out: "I love this book!"

Penelope stopped in her tracks and turned. "Really?" she said.

"Oh, hell yes. I was getting all hot and heavy over here. I was just embarrassed you busted me. I figured my face was flushed or I was moaning out loud or something. Was I moaning? Tell me I wasn't."

Saying this, she broke into a strange laugh, like a small bird twittering and hiccupping at the same time. The nervous laugh didn't match the woman's voice or demeanor, and Penelope felt sure she was in the presence of a complicated person.

The woman stood now and knocked her chair over backwards in the process, the folding part snapping onto her bottom until she had to squat, still hiccup-laughing, to try to shake it off. She was laughing and breathing hard and trying to say something now. Then she reached into her pocket for her phone. With the chair still stuck on her rear and the romance novel clumped on her stomach, she tossed the phone to Penelope.

"Take a photo, quick. My friends will love this."

Penelope did as requested.

"Take a bunch. I do this sort of thing about twenty times a day and my friends post them on Instagram. I don't do that teenybopper crap, but apparently I've got quite a fan club. My name's Missy, by the way."

"I'm Penelope."

The boys in the field were staring at them and the coach had turned to see what the commotion was about. Missy's son at second base was shaking his head, more in a knowing fashion than an embarrassed one, as his mother tried to extricate herself. Even Theo had paused mid-shimmy in the outfield.

"Do you mind pulling this chair off my ass?" the woman said. "I seem to be stuck."

Penelope walked toward her, feeling certain she'd made a new friend. The T-shirt the woman was wearing was Van Halen, one of her favorites.

2

"So practice was fun?"

"Yeah, I guess," Theo said from the backseat, where he was doing something hectic with his handheld gizmo. His face was angry, brow furrowed, mouth twisted, the way James's often was when watching the History Channel or reading about volcanoes.

"I was glad you swung at some today. You'll hit one pretty soon, I bet."

Theo made no response to this but grunted rhythmically with his game.

"Don't you think?"

"Yeah, I guess."

In the rearview she could see her son, his face still holding some baby fat, though it looked, judging by his feet, like he would end up tall and rangy like James. Penelope was shortish and had been told on more than one occasion that she resembled a soccer player. She guessed this was a compliment, but wondered if people were suggesting her thighs and butt were wide. Whatever. She was strong for her size. Both her first husband and James had found that out during bedroom wrestling matches. Did all men like to wrestle women for fun? Or was this just a ploy, as these bouts generally led to messing around? Anyway, the grappling had been fun even if both ex-husbands, caught in the death grip of her leg vise, would resort to tickling, which she considered beneath her and not worthy of a true combatant.

Oh why couldn't Theo have inherited her legs, her strength, her athletic ability? Her whole side of the family could throw and catch and hit a ball. Also run without wheezing or flopping your head around like James did. She studied her son some more in the mirror. He did have her eyes, wide and blue and a little surprised-looking, as if just pleasantly startled by good tidings. And his thick dark hair, wavy and untamed, was a carbon copy of her own. He wasn't a Weird Turd. He was a neat kid, once you got to know him. But what about this Fart Boy stuff? That sounded specific, the kind of name with some backstory.

Did Theo toot frequently on the bus, so much so that he was known by both eye and ear on those early mornings when all was sleepy and quiet? Or had it been just a single gastric explosion, epic and historic, that had sealed his etymological fate forever more?

Who knew?

Maybe Fart Boy was a character from a cartoon or video game she'd never heard of, one who was funny and well-liked, but a little gross at times like all boys were. Just a silly, popular, occasionally flatulent, animated what-have-you. This thought appeased her briefly, but only briefly.

"How's your stomach, Theo?"

"What?"

"How's your stomach? Has it been upset lately?"

"No."

"What do you eat at school? Do they serve chili?"

She'd had his attention momentarily but now he was back on his game. The question went unanswered.

"Do they?"

Again no answer, but she did glimpse a triumphant smile. Something menacing had been destroyed or evaded.

"Will you talk to me for a minute, Theo? You're at your dad's all weekend and I'm not going to see you again until Sunday."

He sighed as James did when asked to take a pause from deep concentration. She might as well have been asking her ex-husband to take a break from his archery magazine to empty the trash.

"They serve chili sometimes. Why? That's a weird question."

Penelope should have been expecting this. Her days of seemingly innocuous queries to glean information about his life had been over for a while. She felt nostalgic about how easy it had been to trick him into telling on himself back in the good old days. He was getting savvy as third grade came to a close. The only way to stay in the loop was to improve her detective skills. She gave this some thought before proceeding.

"I was just wondering."

Theo smiled. He seemed to understand the advantage was now his. "Just wondering about chili?"

Penelope laughed. "Yes. I'm interested in your diet."

"You're wondering about the Fart Boy thing, aren't you?"

"No," Penelope said, trying unsuccessfully to stifle a smile. She was a terrible liar.

Grinning and going back to his game, Theo said, "Right."

"Well, why do they call you that on the bus?"

"It's not everyone. Just Alex and Ty. And sometimes Jason." He paused. "And also Sondra and Madeira."

"Girls?"

"Yeah, so?"

"I don't know. When I was in school, girls didn't talk like that."

This was another lie. Girls on the bus back in her day had talked pretty nasty sometimes, at least the ones Penelope hung out with. Just not where the boys could hear. She considered the fact that she wouldn't see Theo for the next forty-eight hours. Why end their week together on a sour note?

"Theo, do you toot on the bus or something?"

It was out before she could stop herself.

Theo, who had been looking at her through the rearview, now gazed out the window.

"Theo, just tell me. I don't care. I'm just curious. Are you ripping big juicy ones on the bus or not?"

"No more than I do at home."

"Theo, you toot all the time at home. You're like a walking whoopee cushion."

Theo smiled at this but said no more.

"I think you might need to go to the doctor."

"No, I don't."

"You can't be farting all the time on the bus. The kids will tease you if you do."

"They usually laugh."

"Yes," Penelope said, "and then they tease you. What, do you like being Fart Boy?"

Still looking out the window, he said, "I don't mind."

"I think you do. Or else you wouldn't have told me about it. Does Ms. Dunleavy know about this?"

"I don't think so. But please don't call Ms. Dunleavy. There's only three more days of school. It's not a big deal."

"What's to stop them from calling you names next year?"

"They'll probably forget by then. Please don't make a fuss. I'll hold them in these last few days."

"Why didn't you hold them in before? That's not really something meant for public consumption."

"I told you. The kids thought it was funny. I was just goofing around."

Farting for attention. Could there be anything sadder? Perhaps James had been a publicity-seeker as a boy. She tried to picture him in his youth, on the bus, but couldn't fully conjure the image. The best she could do was a frowning boy, wearing a short robe and holding a plastic dinosaur. The little James in her mind looked as if someone had just questioned his theory on the evolution of pterodactyl flight. He didn't seem like a Fart Boy. A Weird Turd, sure. But that was no surprise.

Nearing her ex-husband's new house, Penelope wondered about

her attraction to the Weird Turds in life, the redneck ones who tried to set the record for household items—apple/flashlight/thermos/deer antler/Christmas ornament—turned into pot smoking apparatus, and the academic ones in kimono robes who were aroused by biographies of Teddy Roosevelt. Maybe her friends were right. Her track record with men didn't hold up under close scrutiny.

Speaking of men, a little church bell had just chimed on her phone, the signal that someone was contacting her on her new dating app. It was called Divote, *For Modern Christians on the Go*, and was a fortieth birthday gift from her mother. It wasn't what she would have chosen for herself, but she was too broke to afford a different one and beggars couldn't be choosers. She wasn't even sure she was ready to date again. Yet here she was, her Christian dating app tinkling away like the tiniest and most wholesome of churches.

The whole concept made her feel unworthy, as if by signing up she was guilty of false advertising. And the chiming bells didn't make her feel less Jezebellish. Regardless, she wasn't going to even look at who had contacted her until Theo was out of the car. It would be perverse to engage in cyber-whatever while chauffeuring her nine-year-old. That was simply a bridge too far.

She glanced in the rearview, feeling proud of her self-restraint. Theo was back to his game, thumbs careening on the keyboard, face twitching with the thrill of competition. A quick glance wouldn't hurt anyone. On the other hand, it wasn't that perverse. Who wouldn't look? Moms were curious too. And Theo wouldn't know anyway.

Feeling like an international spy, she snuck her phone from her purse, set it surreptitiously on the seat away from curious eyes, and took a peek. The man who'd rung church bells in her honor was handsome and smiling in an ironic way. His name was BrettCorinthians2:2.

The picture was so small that it was hard to tell much about this fellow, but unless her eyes were mistaken, there was definitely something afoot. Glancing once in the mirror to see if the coast was clear, she raised the phone close to her face. What she discovered was that she'd seen what she thought she'd seen: BrettCorinthians2:2, modern Christian on the go, was shirtless.

Penelope found this odd and also interesting. He was pretty fit. Very fit actually, and under thirty. Wow. Her first ever contact on a dating app was a young, hot guy who lived within forty miles of her. She made a note to look up Corinthians 2:2 when she got home. She'd been a regular churchgoer all her life but had never really thought of bare-chested men from The Good Book. She assumed they all wore robes or cloaks or some kind of flowing garment, other than Goliath or maybe Samson, who she could see strutting around with their shirts off. Who did this BrettCorithians2:2 think he was?

On the other hand, his Likes, signified on Divote by tiny wedding cakes, included many of the same TV shows she watched. That was big. Finger hovering over the screen, Penelope pondered. A swipe left would mean no thanks. A swipe right and PenelopeGenesis2:1's Easter bonnet was in the ring. She knew what her friends would say, that she needed to be less concerned with dating and more concerned with discovering exactly who she was and what she wanted out of life. Her friends seemed pretty hung up on the two-divorce thing, much more than Penelope herself was. It wasn't like she was racing toward a hat trick of "I-Dos" in the next week or anything.

But tell that to her happily married busybody friends.

Then again, her own mother had gotten the dating app for her. To swipe left or right? Did she want to date or not? Would Theo care? Had it been long enough since the divorce?

From the backseat came a shout—a triumphant war cry—that shocked Penelope so that she instinctively hit the brakes, the result being that her phone, perhaps still showing a shirtless young Samaritan unfamiliar to her son, flew out of her hand and over the seat.

"Good God, Theo. You scared me to death."

"I just kicked Gorzomo's butt."

"Congratulations. Still, I wish you wouldn't shout like that when I'm trying to concentrate on the road. You almost made me wreck."

Theo didn't reply, but did reach across the seat for the phone. He scooped it up and looked intently as Penelope watched in the mirror. From the scowling face Theo made, it was clear that BrettCorinthians2:2 was still smiling out at the world, and that his ironic look displeased her son.

"Who's this guy?"

"I don't know, Theo," Penelope said, stretching her arm backwards over the seat. "But please hand me my phone."

Theo did as asked, but with a knitted brow. "What's Divote?"

In her hurry to be rid of the shirtless hottie, Penelope tossed the phone across the front seat, where it slid like a tiny sled to a stop against the passenger door before clunking down on the floor.

"What's Divote?" Theo said again.

"It's an app," Penelope answered, feeling caught in the act.

"Why do they misspell *devote* on purpose?"

"I don't know, Theo. Why did they name the guy on your game 'Gorzomo'?"

This was a mistake. Theo now went into a lengthy synopsis of several games and creatures, the upshot of which was that Gorzomo was both an evolution *and* an amalgamation of other creatures. Apparently this was rare and impressive, for when he finally stopped for breath, he gazed toward Penelope with a look of sophisticated bliss, as an English professor might after a well-delivered lecture on Derrida.

"Wow, I didn't know that," said Penelope, nodding as if she'd understood. She felt sure this must be connected to Pokémon but knew better than to ask. Theo would talk to a stop sign, and at length, about Pokémon.

The good news was that during his seminar on Gorzomo he seemed to have forgotten about BrettCorinthians2:2, who, now that she thought about it, had been staring pretty knowingly at her. That horny little Christian dog.

"So who was that guy?

Penelope came to. Her head still felt a little woozy from Theo's taxonomic lecture, which had covered everything from kingdom to phylum, genus to species. He really liked Pokémon.

"What guy?"

It was an idiotic response, but at this point she was stalling. Theo locked skeptical eyes with her in the mirror.

"Divote is sort of like Facebook," Penelope said. "All kinds of people come across your page. He's probably some friend of a friend."

Theo gave a nod to this, less satisfied with the answer than antsy to get back to Gorzomo and the struggle for universal dominion.

Penelope felt as if she'd simultaneously dodged a bullet and taken one. The divorce had been final for four months as of this week. The notion of dating hadn't come up before with Theo, but sooner or later she'd have to get back in the game. Had James talked to Theo about the prospect of his parents dating?

On one hand, she hoped so. She thought boys were less bothered by their fathers dating than their mothers, and if James brought up the subject, maybe it would temper things a bit. On the other hand, James's discussions with Theo were infamous for going into a lot more detail than a child would need: *Now your mother and I may one day begin to see other people. Adults have urges. You'll understand that some day. Lovemaking—sexual intercourse—is a natural thing. And now that Mommy and Daddy are no longer together . . . The man's penis becomes erect . . . Erect means standing straight and stiff. Yes, like a soldier about to salute. And then the man . . .*

Oh God, it would be even worse than that, a weird mix of physiology and Darwinism and James's brand of gentle romance. She felt sure some combination of these words and phrases would be used: *Beautiful shared ecstasy, vulva, spermatozoa, The Origin of Species, stimulation, zygote, coital union, climax,* and *Galapagos Islands.*

She'd once pointed out that *coital union* was redundant, and this had spoiled his post-coital mood. But that was beside the point. All he'd really needed to say to their son was what Penelope now said:

"Theo, you know that one of these days I may have a date, right?"

Theo didn't look up, but said, "Yeah, I know."

"Well, let me know if that bothers you."

"It doesn't bother me."

"Really?"

"No. Dad's already had a bunch of dates."

3

Penelope pondered the dad-dating information as she entered Meadow Creek, James's new subdivision. When they'd split, their old house, the cute little Cape Cod in the quaint neighborhood, had been sold and the money divided. There wasn't much to divide, unfortunately, as they'd bought high and sold low. Penelope considered the real estate market as she drove through her ex-husband's new neighborhood, as well as the financial claims he'd made during arbitration, and discerned a certain tension at work. All the houses here in Meadow Creek had that fresh, hopeful look of the young newlyweds who'd just moved into them. Penelope thought it was a surprisingly tony place to live for someone who'd cried so poor during the divorce.

Then again, she was currently living with her mother and stepfather, so any tent in a field was starting to look good.

But James was already dating? He'd taken the divorce hard, even though he was the first to show his displeasure with the state of their matrimony. His strategy had been to be as mopey and lethargic as possible until no one on God's green Earth would want to keep disappointing him with their presence as Penelope apparently did. She'd ultimately been the one to propose splitting up, two full years after Mopey Boy had emerged.

The moping had always been there, of course. It was part of his makeup. But where once it had been balanced with a kind of hyperactive intelligence (*Did you know that a baby opossum only weighs 1 ounce at birth? They can literally fit onto a teaspoon! I just find that awesomely cool*), for the last years of their marriage the moping had been juxtaposed only with ennui, the ennui accompanied by bouts of constipation. She thought at first that the constipation was psychosomatic, or just something for him to blame his hangdog look on (*I'm a little, you know . . .*). If that was the case, he'd gone all in, for the next thing she knew the pantry was chock-full of Craisins and prunes and weird little fiber tablets. And the juicing! Dear God, the juicing!

James was dating someone.

And now he was standing in his new yard with his new garden hose and looking as if he was whistling a jolly tune, more than likely the theme from *Shaft*, his go-to when feeling frisky and alive.

She parked and Theo bolted without a backward glance.

"What do you say, Sport?" James said. "How many homers did you hit?"

Any other father asking a boy like Theo such a question would seem sadistic. James had seen him play, after all. But this was just James being whimsical and came with a palm for high-fiving and a wide smile. Then he was tousling Theo's hair and play-wrestling him, hugging him more than anything, as Theo giggled and copied his father's mock face of intensity.

Penelope sat in the car, her fingers on the door handle, witnessing this scene with mouth ajar. Smiling James? Tactile James? James in a fit of whimsy? What the hell?

She opened the door and stood behind it, some part of her convinced that Whimsical James would bear-hug her if she came nearer. This despite his professed dislike of the hug, and the European cheek kiss, and any other gesture that put him in contact with a fellow human being. For him it was a starchy handshake or a firm cowboy head nod. The exceptions to this were the moments when he was berobed or otherwise in a preconjugal state.

"Penelope," he said with a rakish grin as he crouched and continued to engage Theo in horseplay. "How in the world are you?"

"I'm fine, James," she said, surveying the scene before her: the smiling stranger roughhousing—like a mechanic or an insurance salesmen or any other normal man—with their son, the hose dropped behind him, water spraying willy-nilly, after being kicked in their athletic (athletic!) maneuvering. How many times had he lectured her about the length of her showers? Or dropped the water bill with a disapproving stare onto whatever book she was reading?

All five of her senses were alive now and it took only an instant for them to uncover the hidden truth behind this smiling James, this touchy-feely James, this normal-man James. There could be no doubt. Kimono silk was thick in the air, wafting silkily and with a hint of jasmine through the open window of his new living room. Her nose was fairly aflame with the scent. Nothing else could account for the jovial display before her. She felt an urge to rush past him and hell-for-leather to his bedroom where she would throw back his closet door to discover that slinky bit of yellow nothing.

Even standing in the driveway with no hard evidence before her, she wanted to shout, *Aha!* in the worst possible way.

So who exactly was this new strumpet of his?

She shook her head clear, having decided that what she needed was a glass of wine, and quick.

"Okay, fellows," she said. "I guess I'm off now. I'll see you Sunday around five, Theo."

James stopped wrestling now and simply stood Theo upright from his former upside-down position. He'd been threatening in a ringside announcer's voice to pile-drive the boy. Penelope felt dizzy. Where was the man who bemoaned the emphasis on sports in American society, the one who thought the only sport worth watching was archery because it had a practical application? That is, if/when society broke down, an experienced archer could still find his own food, in ways that even a man with a gun couldn't, bullets eventually/inevitably becoming scarce over time.

Maybe she should have a Cosmo instead.

Now speaking in the voice of a gruff but gentle father as often seen on TV, James said, "Go give your mother a hug good-bye, son."

She almost lost it with that "son" bit. But summoning all her self-restraint, she threw on a thankful smile befitting every wonderful matron she'd ever seen on television. She had the sudden desire to sing, *the hills are alive / with the sound of music,* but managed to fight off the temptation.

Kissing Theo on the cheek, she climbed into the car and was preparing to get the hell out of Dodge when James trotted over, calling out as he did, "Theo, why don't you run in the house and make yourself a snack? I want to talk to your mother for a second."

Penelope watched her son climb the front porch steps, passing en route two planters with fresh pansies. A ceramic gnome had been placed beside the door and bright window treatments added to the living room since last time she'd dropped Theo off. James had always been a stickler for just the right kind of window treatments.

"I'd like to give you this," James said, standing at the car door and reaching into his wallet for a hundred dollar bill.

"I don't want it."

"I know. But I figured you could probably use it. Just till you get your feet under you. I know you've got to be looking for your own place by now."

Penelope thought of the times when James had offered her money, unasked for and unprompted, even when they were married. Those times added up to zero. She felt flummoxed and off-kilter, and it didn't help that the gnome was giving her a pervish smile. That's why she didn't like garden gnomes. They didn't look cutely mischievous, as James argued, but like lusty little trolls, eager for a skirt to scurry up or a calf to sniff.

"I don't want it," Penelope said.

"Just take it. Go out to dinner this weekend. Take Sandy and Rachel with you. Buy something. I don't care. Just please take it."

This was beyond strange. What was his new girlfriend doing for him? His-and-Her shorty robes? The high-heel, bra-only plus cowboy-kerchief thing that was his favorite? Or maybe even that roping lasso number he'd once suggested, with her in Indian moccasins, beaded necklace, and nothing else.

Her mind reeled at the possibilities of James's quirky, complicated mind and someone willing to indulge a good portion of it, even the portion that revolved around James Fenimore Cooper.

The fact was she could use that hundred like nobody's business. She'd yet to chip in on the bills at her mother's house and that was starting to drive her crazy. After the cell phone and credit card and buying shoes for Theo, who needed a new pair every week it seemed, she went through the child support and the tips she made waiting tables in a flash. The notion that she was anywhere close to looking for her own place was laughable. As was the fact that she was a forty-year-old waitress living with her mother.

"No thanks, James," she said. "And sometime this weekend, maybe on Sunday, we need to talk about Theo and what's happening on the bus."

"The Fart Boy stuff?" James smiled at this in a way she found irritating. "It's just idiot boy stuff. It's not a big deal."

She almost said, *right, Strange James,* but that would have been a low blow. The confession he'd made about his middle-school nickname had come out of the blue one night after an episode of *The Sopranos*. She was trying to figure out whether the new bad-guy rival of Tony's was as good, as hateable, as the one previous when James had made an unexpected lunge toward her pajamas. *The Sopranos* often got his blood flowing. She'd reacted with a start and a shriek, the end result of which was the deflation of gangster-fired James and the arrival of the dreaded Mope Boy.

Feeling guilty and trying to get over the awkward moment of being groped without preamble, she'd offered that she loved all the nicknames on *The Sopranos*. It was a throwaway line, a stall to try to get herself in the mood should the moping man beside her suddenly morph into a confident, post-apocalyptic archer. Already, however, James was wearing his constipated face. A wheat-germ smoothie looked imminent.

Then, from nowhere, out came the admission of his schoolboy sobriquet.

She'd not known what to say while her husband brooded beside her, other than something about how mean boys that age can be. Eventually, she'd given him a vigorous handjob just to move on from the subject of Strange James.

But back to the present nickname situation.

"What if I do think it's a big deal that kids are ganging up on my son and calling him names?" Penelope said. "I'm considering talking to Theo's teacher."

"I don't think that's necessary. The year's almost over. Let's just ride it out. His teacher can't do anything this late anyway. If it's still going on next fall, then yes, definitely, we take action."

"I want to think about it some more this weekend."

"Okay," said James, as if everything in his life was kimono-new. "We can talk Sunday if you like. And I'll see what I can get out of Theo about it. Frankly, he doesn't seem too bothered by it."

"Exactly," said Penelope, and pulled out of the driveway.

4

Penelope was now at her friend Sandy's house, slurping down a glass of chardonnay at the kitchen table. She'd decided against the Cosmopolitan even though Sandy had offered, but had no regrets about her choice. She found chardonnay both medicinal and delicious. Though Penelope had dropped in without warning, Sandy needed no encouragement to join her, all but ripping the cork out with her teeth when Penelope came in. It was Friday afternoon, which meant a two day respite from cracking the whip to get kids fed, dressed, and out the door for the bus without resorting to corporal punishment. They'd earned this glass of wine and more where that came from. Almost in the same instant of opening the bottle, Sandy had called Rachel, her next-door neighbor and another of Penelope's pals. Now they sat, long-stemmed glasses in hand, feeling better about things than they had only moments before.

"And now he's got this garden gnome in the front yard," Penelope said, finishing up her opening remarks on the recent meeting with James and his zippity-do-dah ways.

"On top of everything else, he has lawn statuary?" said Sandy. "Well that just takes the cake."

Sandy was smiling as she said this, as if she found Penelope a trifle unhinged. Penelope realized she'd been talking for a long time and felt a little out of breath.

Thinking she should eat something, she went to the counter where Sandy had set out pretzels, cheese, and crackers. Behind her, she knew her friends were swapping looks. A pep talk was in the air, she could feel it. Since the divorce, the topic of how Penelope might improve herself and her life always came up during these impromptu get-togethers. Usually it took a while to get there, but the last few weeks Sandy had been impatient to dive right in. Penelope didn't mind. Sandy was a good gal and as loyal as they came. They'd met six years ago during children's story time at the library when Theo got kicked out for incessantly requesting *Thomas the Tank Engine* during the stern librarian's read-aloud session of the *Berenstain Bears*. Sandy and her three boys got the boot not long after, and the two moms found themselves laughing together in the stacks about their shared ignominy. She met Rachel that same week.

Penelope came back with a handful of crackers and plopped them on the table.

"We have plates," said Sandy.

"I know," said Penelope, "but I'll just eat these real fast."

"You obviously have no idea what my kids put on that table."

Penelope didn't like the thought of this so she didn't dwell on it. "Oh, and James is dating someone."

"What?" said Sandy. "Who in their right mind would date James?"

"I have no idea," said Penelope. "Theo just let it slip when I was dropping him off today."

"Why was Theo talking about his dad dating?" said Rachel.

Penelope weighed telling her friends about the flying phone and Theo getting a look at the shirtless man of faith. They already thought she was something of an outlier as a suburban mom, and that was before her current incarnation as a middle-aged waitress.

"Well," said Penelope, crunching a cracker and gulping it down with a sip of wine. "I have this new dating app on my phone, and this guy popped up on the screen today when I was driving to James's house. He wasn't wearing a shirt."

"Wait. What?" said Sandy.

"Just hold on," said Penelope. "Anyhow, my phone ended up flying over the seat and Theo saw the guy who had candied me."

Her friends were looking at her as they did when she told a story too quickly or in a fashion they found incomplete.

"Anyway," Penelope said, waving away their quizzical looks with the nub of a cracker, "one thing led to another and I thought it was as good a time as any to mention to Theo that his father and I might date other people someday, and he just says, *Oh, Dad's already had lots of dates,* or something like that."

"Someone *candied* you?" said Rachel. "Did I hear that right?"

"Yeah, if someone's interested, they send you an icon that looks like a little box of chocolates. That means you've been candied."

Rachel laughed at this, putting her head on the table in the process. Sandy glared in disgust.

"Candied?" she said. "That's gross. What is this thing?"

"It's the Christian dating app my Mom got me."

"LoveSynch?" said Rachel, smiling that cheerleader smile that could fool anyone who didn't know her well.

"No, that's the online dating thing. Mom sprung for both of them. So I have a dating app for my phone, Divote. And also the online dating service. That's LoveSynch. I think me being single on my fortieth birthday really bummed Mom out. Anyway, if you're interested, you candy them back."

"Please stop saying that," said Sandy. "I'm not sure I'm prepared to know everyone you give your candy to."

She and Rachel laughed pretty heartily at this. Penelope had been trying to explain in a manner that didn't make it seem ridiculous, but realized that was unlikely to happen with these smart-alecks.

"Every single dating app should be named Booty Call," said Sandy, laughing. "I mean, who's kidding who?"

"No," said Rachel, smiling in her most insincere manner. "This is Divote. You only get devoted guys. Guys who want to give you chocolate and roses all day long. As long as you live nearby and can meet up in like five minutes."

Penelope smiled at this. Rachel had been raised Baptist, after all, and Penelope knew she had some experience with the set of boys who couldn't, or didn't, drink/smoke/curse. What was left for them to do but think about girls?

Sandy got up huffily from the table and Penelope's mind wandered back to the one straight-laced boy she'd dated in high school. Poor, sweet Dale Mercer. Who would lead her shyly down to his basement, put on a James Taylor soundtrack, then dry-hump her till the cows came home, dry hump himself to climax, she was pretty sure, with the framed photographs of Jerry Falwell and Ronald Reagan cheering him on from the mantel. Afterwards, Dale would talk about their fallen state and about the fallen state of man. Sometimes he'd turn to the Bible for guidance, often while still flushed and breathing hard.

Thinking of those nights now, Penelope realized she hadn't felt particularly fallen, hadn't felt fallen at all, even the next morning at church. What she had felt, keenly and distinctly, was zipper-sore after Dale's hunchathon on her Levi's.

"Okay," said Sandy, sitting back down with a newly opened bottle of wine. "Back to these good Christian boys who are looking to Divote themselves to you."

Penelope smiled and offered her glass for a refill. She normally wouldn't have a third drink, especially before sundown, but the thought of heading home to her mother and George and whatever crappy programs were on TV kept her arm extended and her happy glass calling for more.

"The only thing about Divote," she said, "is that I feel like I'm false advertising. I go, but I'm not super-churchy. I'm pretty sure I'm not the type these guys are looking for."

"Sure you are, sweetie," said Rachel in a wry tone that conveyed the exact opposite of what had just come out of her lips.

"Anyway," said Penelope, "it's just too much pressure. Those guys want a hot supper on the table every night and about fourteen kids. They're just too lusty and good."

"Lusty Christians?" asked Rachel, still feigning ignorance. As if she hadn't been dry-humped by a million Dale Mercers in whatever Georgia high school she'd attended. That little cheerleader smile wasn't fooling anyone at this table.

"Yes, *Rachel*," said Penelope. "Lusty Christians. That's why they all live so long and have such good skin. They don't do anything that's bad for them, other than eating steak about five days a week. Just fuck night and day. I'm starting to think I'm too old for that shit."

Dropping the f-bomb at the table where Sandy and her husband and kids would soon be having their nightly nourishment seemed to act as a catalyst, or maybe it was just the new bottle of wine. Regardless, they were now on a true laughing jag, one which Penelope *divoted* herself to entirely.

5

"Okay, back to the unfathomable idea that James is dating."

Penelope must have frowned without knowing it, for Sandy said: "I know he was your husband, but don't look at me like that. We're all sure you were hypnotized or something. You really have no idea who the new tart is?"

"No idea," said Penelope.

"You've got to be curious though, right?" Rachel said.

"I don't know. I guess. I suppose it's only natural to be a little curious about who your ex has taken up with. I'm not going to get all hung up on it, though."

Sandy looked at Rachel and said: "Seriously, who in the hell would date James?"

"All I know is that she must be a doozy," said Penelope. "He offered me a hundred bucks today."

Both friends reacted strongly to this. James's skinflint ways were known far and wide.

"He's berobed!" said Sandy.

Rachel nodded, saying, "He's found himself a cowgirl."

"No doubt," said Penelope.

"You took the money, I hope," said Sandy.

"No way."

Sandy looked at Rachel and said: "Her mopey ex-husband screws her over in the divorce, and she won't take a hundred dollars when he offers? This is the same guy who used to time her showers. Unreal."

She turned to Penelope now and said: "He's living in a brand new house, despite his claims to being broke, so either he hid money from you and your worst-ever lawyer during the arbitration, or he's won the lottery, or his parents—who are rich, by the way—are helping him out. And you're living with your mother. Give me a break. Take the stinking money."

"I'm not taking his money," she said, "just because he feels guilty. I don't need it that bad."

"Yes you do," said Rachel.

"A hundred dollars wouldn't change anything," Penelope said. "Why bother?"

"She's not even mad at Mopey Boy," said Sandy, again addressing Rachel.

"You know her," said Rachel. "She never gets mad. Or not for long. And she can't hold a grudge at all. It's just not in her makeup."

"Well, it drives me crazy," Sandy said, throwing back the last of her wine and reaching aggressively for the bottle, which they were no longer even pretending to keep refrigerated.

"I'm sitting right here, you know," said Penelope.

Rachel smiled. "You can't help it, can you, honey? You just don't have a temper."

"Seriously, what's wrong with you?" said Sandy.

"I don't know," Penelope said. "I had a teacher in second grade who called my mom because I smiled all day in class and it was freaking her out. I didn't even know I was doing it. I've just always been kind of laid-back, I guess."

As her friends continued to talk about her temperament and laissez-faire approach to the vagaries of life, Penelope thought now was as good a time as any to head to the bathroom.

When she returned to the table, her friends were on several simultaneous topics. The need for Penelope to find her own place. The need for Penelope to find a half-decent job. The need, the apparent urgent need, for Penelope to spend time alone without the company of a man.

"When was the last time you didn't have a man in your life?" Rachel asked.

"You mean besides now?"

"Yes, besides these last four months."

Penelope swirled the wine in her glass and considered. She'd taken up with the huge huge redneck (the HHR) her senior year in high school and had married him, in true redneck style, before she even graduated college, so hot was their passion for cohabitation and take-out pizza and arguing over how many largemouth bass he could mount on the wall.

But there had been a lot of boyfriends before the HHR.

"I don't know," said Penelope. "Maybe third grade."

"What?!" Sandy shouted. "So you had a boyfriend in fourth grade, and from then on you haven't been without?"

"Fourth grade wasn't really a boyfriend," said Penelope, smiling at the memory. "My friend Debbie and I would chase these two boys home from the bus after school. And about every other time, they'd trip on purpose so we could catch them. Then we'd hop on their chests, wrestle a bit, then end up kissing them."

"That sounds like assault," said Sandy.

"I told you. They tripped on purpose. We never could have caught them otherwise. Tim Newton was the fastest kid in the class. Eventually I'd let him flip me over and he'd yell *I'm too hot to handle and too cold to hold!* and take off running."

"What?" said Sandy.

"It's Macho Man Randy Savage," said Penelope. "All the boys loved him."

"Macho who, macho what?" said Sandy.

"The Macho Man," said Penelope, trying to jog Sandy's memory. *"The tower of power, too sweet to be sour, ohhh yeah!"*

Rachel nodded. She knew the reference. Sandy's upbringing in New Jersey had obviously been vastly different from the southern gals at the table.

"He was a pro wrestler," said Penelope. "But for the record, I was a better wrestler than Timmy Newton. If I'd wanted to, I could have held him down and smooched the day away. He was kind of shrimpy. Fast but shrimpy."

Sandy and Rachel exchanged looks, amused that Penelope was proud of her grappling ability. But now that she thought of it, maybe she could teach Theo some moves. Next time one of those mean kids called him Weird Turd, he could get a little of his own with a casual sleeper hold. Perhaps an old-school suplex. That might make those smarties reconsider a nickname or two.

"Seriously, I was a good wrestler."

"We believe you," said Rachel. "But what about your friend Debbie?"

"Oh, Debbie. She wasn't much of a wrestler."

This made Sandy and Rachel laugh really hard. Penelope took a sip of wine and let them. Fourth grade had been a really good year.

They eventually calmed themselves, and Penelope could see Sandy trying to stiffen her face after the laughing jag. She was suddenly all knowing head shakes as Penelope recounted her afternoon at baseball practice with Missy, the smutty book–reading mom.

"I'm just suggesting," said Sandy in a weary tone, "that you're in a vulnerable spot right now. And that when you're like this, when you're feeling at loose ends, you seem to attract kooky people. Just an observation I've made."

"Well I've got to have someone to hang out with," said Penelope. "And now you're saying this new gal is out because she's reading the exact same book you guys did. You know, y'all want me to spend time alone, without a man, but that gets old after a while. And you two aren't available that much. You have husbands. And kids. What do you suggest I do when I'm by myself on the weekend at my mom's house?"

"We thought you'd just read raunchy books 24/7," said Rachel, smiling. She was looking at Penelope as if afraid she might cry.

"That doesn't make you want to avoid men," said Penelope. "The exact opposite, in fact."

Both friends were smiling at her and Penelope realized she'd made them feel bad. A pep talk ensued. Penelope nodded at appropriate times but stopped listening almost immediately. She was sure it followed the standard script, which went as follows:

1) Warn Penelope off of men.
2) Suggest a hobby or something enriching that she could do alone or with other sober-minded women. Knitting/scrapbooking/quilting—all that old lady stuff.
3) Suggest jobs better than the one she had.
4) Adamantly suggest how much better she'd feel once she had her own place.
5) Remind her that she was only two years away from a college degree and offer a few updates on distance-learning.
6) General suggestions for mental, physical, and spiritual well-being, including biographies of various Tibetans and assorted shamans, and also *The Kite Runner*.
7) Another, mercifully shorter, spiel about the joy of macramé.

Finished, her friends smiled warmly at her, glad she wouldn't be reduced to tears by her own sad existence, an existence, frankly, that she didn't find quite as depressing as they did. Her mother had reminded her at nearly every meal about the starving children in India, and it was of them she thought when feeling glum about her nominally middle-class life, as she was now—just a little—thanks to this rousing pep talk from her friends.

6

Penelope pulled up to her mother's brick rancher, hoping against hope for an empty house, but both cars and George's old pickup were parked comfortably—smugly even—in the driveway. She was SOL. Why couldn't the senior citizen dance be every Friday instead of just twice a month? Better yet, why couldn't they take two-stepping or canasta lessons every single night of the week? Didn't seniors need to stimulate themselves via museum trips and group jigsaw puzzles or risk brains turning to gruel? Shouldn't they be performing weight-bearing exercises well into the night?

She visualized the house she was walking into: George, her stepfather since she was twelve, would be in his recliner watching the Western Channel at ear-blasting level, the six-shooters banging this way and that amid the heavy tread of a stampede. Next to him, on the loveseat, her mother talking over the gunfire and whooping Indians to her friend Bernadette about the cesspool of intrigue that was the Hillsboro Garden Club.

In short, a cacophony of gunfire and subpar coneflowers, dance hall pianos, and the need for *fresh fund-raising ideas.*

Man, she needed her own place.

She grabbed the two bags of groceries she'd bought on the way back from Sandy's, meanwhile tallying her checking account and average weekly earnings at Coonskins Frontier Steak House. How much would she need before committing to an apartment? One thousand? Two? She continued her intricate and hopeful calculus as she came up the front walk. By the time she stepped into the carport, she understood that after health care and car insurance payments, she would be able to move out at the earliest possible date of:

NEVER.

And that wasn't even counting the oil light in her car that had been a steady nagging yellow for a week now, the engine suffering from some jungle fever, some mysterious mechanical bile. She had no idea. Damn James and his cheap-ass ways. Damn her early redneck marriage. She should have a regular career by now. Waiting tables at forty—what the hell? At the very least, she should have kept working at Doctor Kirby's office after she got married. The pay wasn't great but at least she'd have benefits now. Yes, she enjoyed being home with Theo when he was little, but she could have gone back to work once he started school. Or gone back to finish her degree. James hadn't encouraged either, the opposite in fact, but who cared what he thought? She'd just gotten too complacent, too sure the life she had in the suburbs was the life she'd always have.

Her mother and George were nowhere in sight when she came into the kitchen, though she could hear their bedroom blaring. Yes, George was surely riding the open range at this very moment. And if she listened closely, she'd hear her mother on the phone with Bernadette, plotting a tulip bulb coup against the wildflower freaks in the garden club.

Typical old-married-people stuff.

Feeling not in the least old or married, and not particularly hungry, she unloaded her groceries and snuck down the stairs to the basement. It was time for a little investigative reporting to see if she might discover the mystery woman who'd put her ex in such a jolly, generous mood.

She settled into the smaller of the two downstairs bedrooms, which George had converted into his office. Theo preferred to sleep upstairs because the basement aggravated his asthma. Asthma, my God. Was there a single white-person ailment Theo didn't have? Of course James had them all too: allergies, asthma, motion sickness, tight hamstrings, nearsightedness, burned skin in the summer and a flaky scalp all winter long. James, who loved all things evolutionary, claimed he'd have no physical problems at all if he'd never been moved from the Scottish bog of his forefathers. But weren't bogs wet and damp? Wouldn't that environment—the mold specifically—trigger asthma, allergies, and a host of other snotty things that usually left him bedridden and crying out for the Nyquil?

Scottish bog, her ass.

While she waited for the computer to boot up, she took in George's cute little man cave. In the corner, the assortment of walking sticks that he fashioned in the carport. On a far shelf, his medley of hats: darling plaid tams that he'd purchased on a trip to England, the lucky bowler he wore to poker games at Judge Wyatt's, and finally his favorite, the sturdy dust-colored (of course!) cowboy hat he broke out in the fall whenever he was going to build a fire. Maps of colonial Virginia and books on American wars and founding fathers completed the quintessential old-man refuge, cozy as a wool cardigan. Good old George. What a sweetie.

The computer had finally come on, so she quickly clicked on the browser. Unfortunately, thoughts of Scottish bogs reminded her of James's family coat of arms—the one with the swords and the apples and the lion—that he'd insisted on hanging in their den. She was brooding about having to look at that thing every time she wanted to watch TV when a pop-up appeared. This wasn't uncommon, as George's computer was powered by small mice racing on a wheel under the desk. She was lost in a Scottish daze, wondering if those really were apples in the coat of arms or some fruit/vegetable native to the moor, and paid no heed to the pop-up. It was either an advertisement for gold buying in the coming financial meltdown or salves to soothe George's aching joints.

The motto on James's family crest is as follows: *Ictus Leonis Et Non*

38

Pet, which translated to: *Neither Stroke Nor Pet The Lion.* She didn't miss that coat of arms.

And now she didn't miss the pop-up either. There, inches from her face, was a woman, nude save for black stockings and super-high heels, with the biggest breasts she'd ever seen. The woman was winking and holding a finger to her mouth, indicating that whatever Penelope decided to do with her naked buxom image would be their little secret. She'd never tell. The banner above her head read *Boobie Bungalow* and offered unlimited access to films and jpegs of the highest ppi for only $7.99 a month, with the first month offered free of charge and without further obligation.

Penelope contemplated those boobs. They were artificial, of course, now that she looked at them closely. And bigger than the average pumpkin picked for a Halloween jack-o-lantern.

How in the name of God could the poor woman even walk on those two skinny stockinged legs of hers? You'd think the heels would just flatten like pancakes under mammary overload. The breasts didn't seem physically possible, even with the aid of modern science. Did they just keep filling the implant up like kids with a water balloon on the hose, giggling and daring to see how full they could get it? Were they going for a world's record?

It occurred to her that pop-ups of this sort didn't happen out of the blue. Read some article about a return to the gold standard and up popped advertisements for end-of-times investing. Do a search for naked women with giant ta-tas and what was likely to pop up was ye olde *Boobie Bungalow.*

But George? Sweet little George with his plaid tam and his Hush Puppy shoes? Patriotic George with his fighter plane models? As she contemplated the source of unwanted computer advertisements, the phrase *pop-up* took on a new, sad, and gross meaning. Did her mother know that George still had urges, that his was a lion that wanted to be stroked and petted by clans of absurdly buxom bimbos?

Whatever. It was his office, he could do what he wanted. Her mother wouldn't know or wouldn't care, so busy was she preparing for the garden club fund-raiser. Penelope could practically hear the envelopes being licked and stuffed from here. Nodding at the Middle American familiarity of this, she clicked the naked woman of the aching back off the screen and raced to James's Facebook page. She planned on being thorough in her cyber-snooping and discovering how it came to be that he was dating and living in a nice new place and humming the theme from *Shaft* when she was in her mother's basement, alone, on a Friday night.

She started with the ABOUT section:

Chief Financial Officer at IndiCo.
I.e.: accountant.

Studied business and history at The University of North Carolina.
Majored in looking serious while in cowboy boots and holding a shotgun (see timeline).

Lives in Hillsboro, Virginia.
In a cute little dollhouse. Without his parents. Unlike his kind and lovely ex-wife.

From Asheville, North Carolina.
God is a Tarheel. Sky is Carolina blue. Look Homeward, Tarheel. Tarheel arts and Tarheel crafts. Tarheel this and Tarheel that.

In a relationship with A Very Special Lady.
Gross her out the door. Seriously. Right out the door.

But who was this enigmatic vixen? Penelope was just moving to James's *Likes*—he was notorious for updating those in tune with his mood and how his day had gone—when up popped another big-breasted lass. Under a banner proclaiming *MMM: Melon MILF Mélange* stood a topless middle-aged woman with two actual cantaloupes in each hand. She seemed by the pose to be indicating how paltry melons grown from the good Earth were compared to her own. Penelope looked closer. This woman was also in heels and stockings, though hers were red whereas *Boobie Bungalow*'s were black. Another difference was that these boobs looked real, amazing as that was. She wished now that she could go back to the *Bungalow* picture to compare. Her money was still on the artificially enhanced woman, but her heart was pulling for the lady before her, choosing the nature over science side of the debate as was only proper.

Regardless, George was a horny dog. While her mother was busy with garden club mailings, George was eyeing the History Channel with unbridled lust in his heart. The Battle of the Bulge indeed.

But now it was time to get back to her search for the Very Special Lady in her ex-husband's life. She was prepared to spend the whole evening investigating and was glad to have a purpose. Friday night TV really was the worst. So, bidding a somewhat fond and admiring adieu to MMM and the mysterious bounties of nature, she returned to her mission.

His FRIENDS and PHOTOS were unchanged since she'd checked last week, so she moved down to PLACES. She thought this was likely a waste of time even as she did it, for James had his go-to locales which rarely changed:

Asheville, North Carolina, birthplace of Thomas Wolfe.

Brixham, England, where William of Orange had first come ashore.

Arbroath, Scotland, where lions, poor things, would receive no physical affection, not even a friendly pat on the head.

To these standbys of Scots-Irish Protestantism and Tarheelian fetish, a photo had been added of Jackson Elementary, the school that Theo attended.

Penelope considered this addition but could make nothing of it. She moved on to MUSIC, which was, per usual, heavy on the southern rock and alt country: *Wilco, Uncle Tupelo, The Avett Brothers,* and his guilty pleasure, *.38 Special.* Penelope noted, however, a significant addition: Van Halen's *1984.*

This gave her pause. James liked Van Halen okay, but had in the past accused her of being a fan because of their association with boys she'd made out with in the backseat of muscle cars. The accusation was founded, of course, and she was perplexed as to how James knew. Maybe she reminded him of girls he knew in high school who did the same. But that was beside the point now. James had Van Halen front and center on his Facebook page, and that was no accident.

She thought of the woman at baseball practice. She was wearing a Van Halen T-shirt. This had to be more than coincidence. The universe was whispering in her ear.

Feeling hot on a new trail, she moved down to MOVIES, skimming over his kitschy favorites, *Roadhouse* and *Point Break;* his western classics, *High Noon* and *Shane;* his ode to sensitive boyhood and hunting; *Where the Red Fern Grows,* and stopping, aha!—on the new addition here: *Mr. Holland's Opus.*

Mr. Holland's What? With Richard Dreyfuss? Of course James did love the word *opus* and used it whenever discoursing on a favorite long book. For example, Thomas Wolfe's *Look Homeward, Tarheel* was an opus. She'd heard him call it that many times.

But what was the story line of *Mr. Holland's Opus?* Oh yes. Richard Dreyfuss as an inspirational teacher.

Her brain was a well-oiled machine. The eureka moment was at hand. A photo of a school. A movie about a teacher. And Van Halen's classic *1984.* Like a detective with that one nagging clue that doesn't add up, she feverishly entered the relevant information into the search engine: *Van Halen, 1984, song list.*

Only to be delayed by another smiling, naked, monstrously bosomed woman popping up on the screen.

"Damn it, George," she said, wondering if there was nothing besides unnaturally large breasts that he liked. Her mother was reasonably flat-chested. Men were weird. She clicked off the banner for *Titty Tavern* and was back on point. The search had hit home and she was soon on the Wikipedia page for the album. Trusting her gut, she arrowed right past all the history, etc. and settled on Track Listings:

Side one: 1984, Jump, Panama, Top Jimmy, and Drop Dead Legs.

Side two: Hot for Teacher, I'll Wait, Girl Gone Bad, and House of Pain.

There it was, as plain as the bulge in David Lee Roth's tights: James was dating a teacher. James was dating a teacher at Stonewall Jackson Elementary. James was dating Theo's teacher, Ms. Dunleavy.

Granted, her mind was racing and she was jumping to conclusions the clues didn't necessarily point to. He was dating a teacher. Any idiot could see that. But how did she know it was Ms. Dunleavy? She didn't know, but it was. Her whole body was tingling with the factualness of this. Was this the real reason James didn't want her to broach Theo's bus situation? His ex and his current having a conversation would surely put James on edge, especially if he was trying to keep the identity of his Very Special Lady a secret. She glared one last time at the computer, then marched upstairs with Van Halen drums pounding in her brain.

7

In the kitchen, she opened the refrigerator door though she still wasn't hungry. She shut the door. The bottle of wine she'd bought beckoned her, but then she thought of tomorrow's shift at Coonskins and reconsidered. The lunch shift was bad enough without a raging hangover, and it was her turn to load the salad bar and have her hair smell like ranch dressing for the rest of the day. And those stupid bacon bits that always spilled everywhere. Maybe one of the guys would trade rolling silverware for salad bar. It was worth an ask.

Not sure what else to do, she poured a glass of water from the sink and gulped it down. James was dating Theo's teacher. Was that even legal? Teachers could just date the fathers of their pupils? She knew they were banging their students left and right these days, but didn't know the dads were in play as well. Wow. What a world they lived in. She was contemplating this, and trying to recall exactly how Ms. Dunleavy looked, when she heard the bedroom door open and then footsteps in the hall.

She hoped it wasn't George. She'd be fine to see him in the morning. But not now, not after she'd just been run over by the melon truck. In fact, she rather hoped it was her mother. This was not a sensation she often experienced of late, this wanting to discourse with her mother. Mommy Dearest was just a little too interested in how Penelope was faring with *modern dating on the Net*. But at the moment she couldn't wait to talk about James and his Very Special Lady. Her mother would be even more riled than she was.

A weird clicking sound was coming down the hall, one Penelope hadn't heard at first for the TV blaring from the bedroom. And then her mother joined her in the kitchen. Penelope was about to launch into her recent discovery, planning on sparing no detail about her intrepid investigative work, but something stopped her short.

Her mother, a look of surprise on her glowing face, stood before Penelope in a short kimono robe as once favored by James. She'd not bothered to cinch the silk sash and it hung wantonly to either side.

Penelope was in the kitchen with her naked mother. Her naked mother who was wearing black heels and stockings as favored by the *Boobie Bungalow* lady. That was the clicking she'd heard. Her mother, in no hurry, casually fastened the kimono sash, but not before Penelope saw what she wished she hadn't.

Her mother flounced to the refrigerator and stood there in her stockinged legs and high heels, without a care in the world.

This was the woman who brought her into this world, who changed her diapers and gave her Band-Aids and read her bedtime stories. And despite herself, Penelope had to admire both her still-firm legs and her fighting adventurous spirit. Her mother was humming a tune now that sounded like "California Dreamin'" and reaching for Penelope's bottle of wine. The garden club seed and bulb sale seemed far from her mind.

Penelope noticed her phone on the counter, took it from the charger, and texted Rachel:

My mother shaves her bush now.

Rachel texted back immediately: For the garden club?

Penelope: No. HER bush.

Rachel: what?

Penelope: you heard me.

Rachel: you mean like trims it up? So what?

Penelope: no. all the way. BALD.

Her mother came toward where Penelope was texting about her nether regions. Penelope realized she was standing in front of the drawer where the corkscrews were and moved out of the way.

"You don't mind if I have some of your wine, do you?" her mother said, reaching into the drawer.

"Of course not," said Penelope. "Help yourself."

Rachel: Bald?

Penelope: Bald.

Rachel: OMG.

Penelope: Got to go. The bald eagle is standing right here. She's wearing a kimono btw.

Rachel: Like James?

Penelope: Hers is pink. But yes. Having bad flashbacks.

Rachel: Was James a shaver too? Maybe it feels silkier that way.

Penelope: Got to go. You're making me sad.

Her mother had poured herself a healthy glass of vino and now took a long, satisfied sip. Simultaneously, a familiar scent came wafting down the hall and tickled Penelope's nose. George had lit his pipe. All in all, the upstairs portion of the house seemed pretty pleased with itself.

"How was your day?" her mother asked, leaning against the counter, wine in hand, tapping a high heel on the linoleum, the sash loosening, devil-may-care, as she spoke. She was moving her shoulders too as if dancing in place.

"Okay. Normal. Tips were decent for lunch."

"And how was Theo's practice? Did he hit the ball?"

"Of course not."

"Did he swing at least?"

"He did swing," Penelope said.

"Well, that's a start," her mother said, turning and reaching toward the cabinet where they kept the prescriptions and first-aid items.

"Can't forget George's heart medicine," her mother said, pulling down a small bottle.

"No," said Penelope with meaning in her tone, "you'd better not forget that."

Her mother smiled and winked at this. Then she was swishing out of the kitchen, the sash of the kimono trailing coquettishly to either side in her wake.

Penelope was back in the basement, watching a bad reality show and trying her best not to think of what had just occurred in the kitchen. She was also pondering her interest in her ex-husband's dating life and his suddenly sunny perspective, and telling herself that she shouldn't care. She wasn't in love with James and she wasn't hung up on him and if he'd asked to get back together, she would say no. So who cared that he was dating and tactile and even smiling these days?

She did, actually. After all, he'd spent the last two years in a non-stop brood and all but saying she was the source of his displeasure in life. She was nice, she was fun, she was smart. When things got a little stale, she'd played along with his western-themed sexual fantasies, his Scottish Highlands fantasies. She'd not complained when he shouted out, *Sweet Pocahontas, this teepee is hot!* Or to lovemaking in matching kilts.

So what if she'd snatched his shorty robe?

She'd stopped flipping channels on the Home and Garden Network, where a handsome couple about sixteen years old was complaining about the paint scheme in the million-dollar house they were being forced to buy.

"Paint!" Penelope screamed at the television. "Just buy the color you want and paint it yourself. It will take like three hours!"

Now the man was saying something about the tile being dated. Soon he'd wax rhapsodic about open floor plans. Penelope switched the channel. Tonight she could do without arguments about the ocean

47

view versus the awesome natural light in the master suite, walk-in closets as opposed to his-and-hers Jacuzzis.

And what was up with that guy's fedora?

She sat in the darkened basement for a moment, contemplating life in sunny California with men in vintage hats and tank tops. She'd never lived anywhere but Virginia, and other than her two years of college, her whole life had been spent in Hillsboro. She'd rarely left the state, much less traveled to some exotic place like Santa Barbara.

Reflexively, not really even aware she was doing it, she pulled out her phone and went to Facebook. Friday nights alone were the pits. She wondered what Theo was doing. Something fun, no doubt. Go-Karts or mini-golf or a movie, all the things that felt like a luxury to her in her current financial straits.

On her newsfeed were the usual mixture of parents complaining about, bragging on, and making fun of their kids. The same people who always posted recipes that she would never try had posted recipes. The people who posted funny animal videos had stayed true to form. Two people she knew vaguely had posted vacation photos of beachy Edens she would never visit: lean, tall husbands with colorful drinks in hand. Wives with big sunglasses in bright sarongs by the pool. A joke, perhaps a loaded one, about couples yoga. A brief mention of a massage to die for.

Fuckers.

She sat there imagining these slender, rich-looking people doing all the things these people did on vacation. Windsurfing and scuba diving. Dining alfresco. Making athletic love without all the snuffling sounds James used to make on her neck. Without the hint of deer entrails from the HHR. Just the smell of cocoa butter and a salty breeze through the billowing curtains of the private cabana. The word *prawns* popped into her head though her whole life all she'd ever had was shrimp. Were they the same thing or not?

She clicked out of Facebook. Good for them, she thought. Good for those fuckers and their buttery prawns.

She went now to her LoveSynch page, thinking that this was a safer choice than checking out the hot dude on Divote again. Some older guy in a cardigan had messaged her. She was too tired at the moment to read over his profile, but he looked nice enough. She hadn't had her account long and had never replied to anyone before. But what the heck. She messaged back:

Hey, how are you?

At least he had his shirt on. She went down the hall toward her bedroom, thinking that she really did need to work a double the next day. Maybe someone would give up their night shift. If she worked every double she could, the money would eventually start to accrue. That would mean less time with Theo, but getting their own place would be worth it. She had to think long term.

In her room, she found a letter waiting on the bed. The letter had been typed on the official stationery of the Hillsboro Garden Club. Communication of this sort always signaled official business, and this was no exception.

Penelope,

Aunt June and Doozy confirmed that they will come as planned June 28 and stay through July. I was afraid you might have forgotten about their visit and wanted to remind you while it was fresh on my mind. We seem to keep different hours these days and I'm being run to death with the fund-raiser. Remind me to tell you what Gladys Deerfield proposed (hand-sewn seed baskets, as if we had the time. Ridiculous!).

June said they could bring the camper and sleep in the backyard, but I nixed that. Can you imagine that big thing in the yard? We'd look like trailer trash, as if we don't already with that old truck of George's in the driveway. June is worried about Theo's asthma and refuses to take his room upstairs. She's also worried about imposing on you, but I don't see any other options. It looks they will bunking with you downstairs. They offered to take the fold-out, but with Doozy's back, I don't think that's a good idea.

I know this isn't ideal timing for you, but June says Doozy isn't sleepwalking nearly as much since he started the hypnosis sessions. The snoring, unfortunately, is the same. We'll get you a fan and some earplugs and just hope for the best.

Love,

Mom

Penelope perused the letter several times, hoping that somehow the words on the page would be different on subsequent readings. She recalled the Fourth of July weekend spent in the RV, with Doozy pacing up and down, dead asleep, calling out menu options as if he was still a mess-hall cook. Apparently succotash had been often on the menu at Fort Benning and the soldiers were none too fond of it. Doozy would bark at the grunts to put a sock in it and keep the line moving. If some private back-sassed the slumbering sergeant, they were brusquely reminded that he could use his spatula for more than swatting flies.

His snoring, even before he deviated his septum via a night-walking collision with a grandfather clock, had been epic, voluminous, cacophonous, and comprehensive, shaking the recreational vehicle from steering wheel to chemical blue toilet water. It was the heavy logs being sawed, even more than the bossy cook with the spatula, that had frightened her as a sixteen-year-old.

She visualized the three of them—Aunt June, Doozy, and herself—cohabitating in the basement, the snoring and the sleepwalking and the commands to keep the line moving. Then she realized that not only would they be sharing a sleeping area but also the lone bathroom. The RV toilet shared with Uncle Doozy was a memory she'd suppressed until now.

She took the note and wadded it tightly before flinging it into the wastebasket.

She had indeed forgotten about the long-planned visit of her aunt and uncle.

On her way to Coonskins, Penelope took in the ambience of her hometown, the Walmart and Applebee's and Target that had replaced the local employers of her youth:

Santeramo's Pizza, where she was a smiling, eager hostess who could wear what she pleased.

The Sweet Scoop, where she dished out soft-serve waffle cones in a red and white T-shirt and cap.

The Pirate's Cove, where she served seafood in a saucy black skirt and white blouse tied at the navel.

Even *Jackie's Gym for Ladies,* where she'd folded towels and checked the pH level in the hot tub, was gone, left vacant in a deserted strip mall with the ghost echoes of synchronized clapping still ringing in the jazzercise room.

Oh, where art thou, little Richard Simmons?

Penelope's current work uniform consisted of a denim skirt, white Coonskins T-shirt, and the black cowboy boots she'd had since high school. Her hair was pulled into a perky cowgirl ponytail and she knew if James could see her now, he'd be firing his peacemakers in the air and asking if she would *mosey on to bed, little Pilgrim.* She had to admit that she liked how easy the uniform was to throw on, how fast she could go from ignoring the fact that she was about to wait tables at forty to actually doing it, but there was no getting around the fact that the skirt flattened her butt. Why did everyone love jeans turned into a skirt? Who cared if they went with everything? Did you want a butt or not? Penelope did and made no apologies about it. Hers was powerful and firm and, thinking of it now, she gave it a couple of flinches, tightening one cheek and then the next in rhythm with the song on the radio. Yes, it was still there, despite the girdle all her friends swore by. Why couldn't they face facts: the denim skirt could turn a pumpkin into an ironing board.

She arrived in the parking lot, got out of the car, and walked toward the entrance. She realized that her mind was on a weird topic—ironing boards and pumpkin butts—to avoid thinking about the shift to come and this one customer who always sat in her section and spent three hours on a Cobb salad and about four hundred glasses of sweet tea. She could see him now, shaking his glass at her as she walked by with a tray of ribeye sandwiches for another table, the last little chives and bacon bits stuck to the sides of his bowl, the lone remaining egg slice nestled against a fragment of avocado, all to be savored one dainty bite of Roquefort at a time.

She paused to look at herself in the glass door, wondering how she'd gotten to this point. How exactly. But here she was. There was no getting around that. And if she wanted her own place and to avoid Uncle Doozy and his somnambulant mess hall, she had to start making—and saving—some serious money right now. Maybe she wouldn't need two thousand. Maybe fifteen hundred would stake her to a new place. Even a thousand. Feeling a tad better about things, she stuck out her tongue at the fretting reflection, took a deep breath, then reached around for a quick backside adjustment. It was time to earn some dough.

❤ ❤ ❤

"You know that's my section," Barbo said.

"Yes," said Penelope, "I do. But they told Carrie they wanted me as their server and she accidentally sat them with me. You know she can't remember the sections."

"Well, that's my section. Has been for eight years."

"I know that, Barbo. I couldn't care less if I wait on them. I'm just telling you they asked for me."

"I'm window section. That's my section. I don't mess with other people's sections."

Penelope was about to say that she didn't mess with other people's sections either, especially not the gold mine that was the window section, but knew she was wasting her breath. Barbo wasn't a conquering dictator, but what landmass she'd won fair and square after eight years of Coonskins battle, she planned to keep. Penelope could respect that.

Unfortunately, the restaurant was bursting at the seams—a girls' softball team had de-bussed in the parking lot and a young couple with a little girl was just sitting down in her section as well. Penelope felt she was in some danger of getting in the weeds.

"How about this?" she said. "You take the table but explain why."

Barbo shook her graying hair to this.

"Okay, I'll take the table and you get my next one."

"I don't work the floor."

It's floor up there too, you dingbat, Penelope wanted to shout. But she knew that in Barbo's mind, those three steps up to the window section, where customers had a once-in-a-lifetime view of the parking lot and the traffic on Lee Highway, were not to be trifled with. And now Cobb Salad was raising his tea glass for the third time, smilingly, but raising it nonetheless, and Carrie had just seated a softball family of five in her section and they were hungry-looking people.

A large portion of her wanted to tell Barbo to stick it. The other portion weighed the fact that Barbo was pushing sixty and still waiting tables and a creature of adamant habit.

"Okay. I'll handle it. You take the table and I'll tell them why."

This answer appeased the Coonskins veteran and she whisked off to the kitchen for the necessary basket of peanuts.

How Penelope hated those stupid peanuts. Or, more specifically, the shells, which customers were encouraged to gleefully throw all about the floor. This was what customers liked best about Coonskins. Apparently, if you decorated the walls with coonskin caps and a few replica flintlock rifles with names like Old Betsy and Old Tick Licker, then scattered stuffed raccoons and foxes on every available ledge, what you ended up with was a veritable frontier roadhouse smack dab in the middle of a strip mall. And nothing, nothing at all, said roadhouse like a shitload of peanut shells all over the floor.

So kicking a few out of her way en route, she grabbed a pitcher of tea off the ledge where it had been guarded by an albino fox, topped off Cobb Salad with a smiling *sorry to keep you waiting,* and went to Barbo's window section where the only two guys in suits in the restaurant were sitting. They were out-of-towners and had tipped her twenty bucks on a fifty-dollar tab two days before. Why Carrie couldn't remember whose section was whose was beyond her.

"Hey guys," Penelope said. "Sorry I can't wait on you today. This isn't my section."

"Yeah, but we asked for you," the silver-haired guy said.

"I know. But our hostess gets a little distracted sometimes. You know how teenagers are."

Saying this, she glanced over her shoulder to the hostess stand where Carrie was currently texting and chomping gum and ignoring the elderly couple waiting to be seated.

"Which one is your section?" said the other fellow. "We're not in a hurry."

Penelope pointed down below, where the famished-looking softball family, all five of them, had turned to glare at her. She really needed to get a move on. Cobb Salad would need more croutons any minute now.

"Where those ladies are leaving?"

Penelope looked. Sure enough, her two-top was standing and shuffling the last of their peanut shells from the table to the floor, as if this was not just roadhouse custom, but the polite thing to do.

"Yes," said Penelope, "but I have to run."

"We're going to grab that table," said the silver-haired dude, rising.

This was trouble with Barbo, Penelope knew, but she had to go. She refused to get swamped this early in her shift.

"Okay," she said. "I'll see you down there."

♥ ♥ ♥

"How bout some more peanuts," said the burly, pink-faced father of the softball family, fairly shoving the empty basket, their third, into Penelope's midsection.

The restaurant was teeming now, with ten or so people waiting to be seated. The softball players had mostly pushed their plates to the middle and were now talking or texting or refixing their ponytails under their caps. It was a cap-heavy crowd to be sure, with fully every softball father and about half the mothers donning the requisite Coonskins headwear.

Unfortunately for this softball family, the kitchen had lost their order, and they were none too pleased about the missing steak sandwiches or the AWOL curly cheese fries ordered a full thirty minutes before.

"I'll fill this right up," Penelope said. "And ask the kitchen to try to hurry. I'm really sorry about your order. They're usually pretty on top of things."

"That's what they all say," said the mother, who was wearing a T-shirt that bragged *Elkton Softball Girls Go Long*. The father smiled gruffly through his beard, and the two softball girls rolled their eyes and took long straw slurps of their Mello Yello. The youngest at the table, a boy about Theo's age, threw a full peanut right past Penelope onto the floor then glanced around the table, smirking, as the rest of his family made a show of pretending to stifle laughs.

"I'll be right back," said Penelope, turning to leave.

As she did, a peanut hit her right on her denim-flat booty. The little pipsqueak in the Jeff Gordon hat had just plonked her, much to the amusement of his family. One of the girls sounded like she'd sprayed

Mello Yello snorting at his antics, but Penelope didn't turn to look. She couldn't get rid of this family fast enough.

As she walked into the kitchen, one of the line cooks hollered out: "Eighty-six steak sandwiches."

What? How did a roadhouse run out of steak? It was like running out of mixed martial arts on the seven televisions jammed in every cranny not occupied by a stuffed North American mammal.

"What do you mean?" Penelope said. "I've got five people who are already pissed waiting on them."

"We're out of the small sirloins," the cook said, keeping his spatula on the grill and flipping other cuts of beef in a way that would have made sleepwalking Uncle Doozy proud. Penelope looked closely at the young cook and realized he looked less stoned than usual, maybe not stoned at all. And his hat was nearly straight on his head. Penelope found both these developments odd.

"Can't we just use other steaks?"

"Nope. Not according to Marty. It's burgers or a full-price sirloin for the rest of the day. Sorry, P."

So saying, he slapped meat on several plates and turned up the volume on the country song playing on the radio. His strangely clear eyes were forlorn and Penelope knew he was dearly missing his work buzz. She checked the other two cooks, and they too looked sad and straight, just like the caps on their heads, which were usually jauntily askew. What was going on? First no steak sandwiches and then un-stoned cooks? Maybe that was why they'd misplaced her order. Their work brains were all fuzzy with sobriety.

"You can have these three, P," said the cook, placing three steak sandwiches on the grill. "Last three in the house."

"Thanks," said Penelope. "But I need them quick."

"They ordered them medium-well."

Of course they did. Penelope wanted to bemoan the missing two sandwiches and to complain about the softball family, but knew the cooks didn't give a rat's ass about the customers. They were just faceless food-gobblers, never seen, never considered. Penelope was starting to think maybe the cooks had it all figured out.

It was then that a tiny tap came on her shoulder, and she turned to find Carrie, the hostess, standing behind her.

"Derrick said you could have his night shift. He's got a date. With me."

"That's great," said Penelope. Saturday nights were usually good for a hundred to one-fifty.

"I know," said Carrie. "He is so hot."

Penelope ignored this and was estimating just how badly her hair was going to smell after a double when the following question was asked:

"Hey, do you know where I can get some pot?"

This brought her out of her meditations on stinky follicles. Did she know where Carrie could get some pot? Of course she did. The HHR lived in a cannabis jungle, where the grow lights burned Vegas style, 24/7.

"No, don't be ridiculous," Penelope said. "Why do you ask?"

"Because the whole town is dry."

"Well, I assumed that. By why did you think I would know about weed?"

"I don't know. You just seemed like you were one of those cool moms who maybe smoked a little sometime. Maybe because you said you liked the idea of me getting a septum ring. My mom would never say that."

"I don't remember saying that. I thought I said it sounded painful."

"No, you said it would be cool and adventurous."

Penelope doubted this, but maybe she had. Carrie often followed her around while she tried to work, and she found herself nodding to things without really listening.

"My mom was pretty pissed when I told her you thought the septum ring was a good idea. She asked if you were a pothead or something."

Carrie laughed at the irony of this, both she and her mom thinking of Penelope as a ganja queen when that evidently wasn't the case.

"Listen, Carrie, I'm in the weeds. I don't have time to talk."

"In the weeds, I wish."

"You have to let me work."

"Okay, that's cool," said Carrie, walking over to tell the cooks that even pot-mom Penelope wasn't currently holding. When she got there, she reached into a basket of cheesy curly fries that was up on the ledge— the softball family's cheesy fries—and took a big goopy handful. Then she seemed to remember something and turned, smiling, to Penelope:

"Oh, and Barbo's really pissed at you."

9

After delivering hot fudge sundaes to the couple with the young girl, Penelope stood at the grill, waiting for the steak sandwiches and thinking about her many tables and their levels of satisfaction. She'd also been turning over a phrase Carrie had used: *cool mom.*

At first she'd been pleased, despite herself, emphasizing in her mind the first of the two words. But now it was the second word that kept rearing its ugly head. Cool MOM? Didn't that just equal uncool? Weren't cool moms the ones who kept trying to dress like their daughters? *Mom* by itself was bad enough. Did the whole restaurant staff think of her as *mom-ish?* Like Barbo, basically? The two old warhorses of Coonskins?

To heck with that. She was cool, no qualifier needed. She could find pot in like five minutes if she needed. The HHR never went dry. And shirtless young men were contacting her out of the blue, as were older ones in cardigans on LoveSynch. Cool mom, her ass. She was straight cool.

She had just about talked herself into feeling hip despite the denimed butt and the hair smelling of cheesy fried etcetera when she felt another tap on her shoulder. She turned to find a motherly face that no one in the world had ever asked for pot.

"We need to talk," Barbo said.

"I can't right now," said Penelope as she reached for the third steak sandwich, which had finally appeared in the window. "I have to get these out to A-9."

"Those guys in suits moved out of my section."

"I know, Barbo. I'm sorry. But that was thirty minutes ago. Why are you just now mentioning it?"

"I was doing my job, taking care of my customers, and I just now got the time. Those guys should have been mine. They were in the window section."

"Barbo, I'm sorry. I really am. You can have my next table if you want it."

"I just want the tables in the window section. I don't mess with other people's sections."

"I don't either," said Penelope, picking up her tray and trying to maneuver around her aggrieved colleague.

Unfortunately, Barbo made a quick countermove, like a wily boxer cutting off the ring. This sudden movement, quicker of foot than one would have imagined from the gray-haired doyenne, caught Penelope off balance and she let the tray lurch for a moment in her haste to be around Barbo and rid of the peanut-throwing softball team. Off slid the medium-well small sirloins packed onto buttery French bread. Off slid the curly cheese fries recently pawed by Carrie. All to land in a clutter at Barbo's lizard skin boots.

"Damn it, Barbo, damn it to hell," Penelope said, flinging the now-empty tray sideways, where it clattered on the floor. "Look what you made me do."

"I didn't make you do a thing, thank you very much. But I will talk to Marty about being cussed at by a junior waitperson."

Penelope stared at the mess in front of her, saying without realizing it: "There are no junior waitpeople. We're all just servers. And no one cares about that stupid window section but you."

Barbo flinched when she heard this, then turned in a huff and clickety-clacked her way to Marty's office.

Now the cooks were gaping at Penelope, and Carrie's eyes were bugged wide. Penelope wasn't sure if the shocked reactions were because of the profanity directed at the respected elder of the staff or the comment about the sacrosanct window section, but apparently she'd entered uncharted Coonskins territory. She knew this because the song "Country Boy Party" had just come on the radio and not one person had hollered to turn it up.

She stood amid the broken plates and spilled beef, wondering whether she should clean up the mess first or go back out to her tables. Maybe Marty would comp the softball family's lunch for the botched order. She started to walk toward his office, but there was Barbo waving her hands and jerking her head back toward the kitchen. Ray, one of the cooks, came from behind the line with a broom and dustpan. His pale face in the straight-billed baseball cap looked especially young and unstoned up close, and Penelope had a vision of him helping an old lady down the aisle in church.

"I'll get this, P," he said, starting to sweep but unable to look Penelope in the eye.

Penelope realized that she was in for it and felt a twang of poignancy for the young cook in front of her, so sweet to be cleaning up for her. On the radio, "Country Boy Party" was just getting going:

> Pull down the tailgate and ice the keg
> Them rowdy boys got some hollow legs

But Ray, the cook, wasn't singing along like usual. He was truly mourning his lack of a workday buzz. Perhaps she should call the HHR on his behalf—on behalf of the whole kitchen staff. It was like a morgue in here, like an accounting office, and she hated to think of them going weedless behind the grill for another day. What would Kid Rock think if he walked into the kitchen right now and saw all those baseball caps facing stiffly forward like they were a bunch of country club brats? Talk about loss of street cred.

Dancing Daisy Dukes, swaying Elly Mays
They won't ask for your dossier

No doubt about it, her mojo had been off from the moment she walked past the first stuffed raccoon at Coonskins. Whether it was James being hot for teacher that was to blame or the encounter with her mother's trendy box, she didn't know. Either way, there was nothing to do but face the music out in section A. She thanked Ray with a pat on the shoulder, grabbed a fresh basket of peanuts, and walked out of the kitchen to the chorus of "Country Boy Party":

Yes it's a risqué soiree
Kissing au francais
Country girl parfait
Look at them sashay

The softball family was shooting her daggers when she came through the swinging doors and Cobb Salad was waving his empty glass for a refill, but it was the businessmen's table where she headed first. After clearing their plates, she grabbed the pitcher of tea and veered toward Cobb Salad, wondering, not for the first time, about the vastness of his bladder. As she approached, pitcher in one hand, conciliatory peanut basket for the softball family in the other, a nut came flying across her face. She flinched but refused to look. Out of the corner of her eye, she thought she'd seen the mother cock her arm and fire, but couldn't be sure. It might have been the daughter. They both had pretty good angles on her. Regardless, there was no doubting the throwing arms of Table A-9. The flying nut had whizzed by with velocity to spare before knocking the window in Barbo's section with a solid thud, loud enough to startle a few customers who'd been intently watching the television over the bar, where one man in his underwear was applying a chokehold to another man in his underwear.

"Hey waitress!" someone behind her shouted.

It was the softball dad. The moment had come. For once she regretted not having more tea to fill for Cobb Salad, six more croutons to make his salad absolutely perfect. She made her way over with the fresh basket of peanut ammo like an anchor on her arm.

"I have some bad news," she said, placing the basket as close to the edge as she dared. She was hoping for a head start before the live rounds flew in earnest.

"I told you, Rex," the mother said, nodding at her husband. "They screwed up our order."

"I'm afraid so," said Penelope. "Believe it or not, we actually ran out of steak sandwiches."

"How in God's name does a steakhouse run out of steak sandwiches?" asked the woman.

"Actually there were three left, but I accidentally spilled those."

The woman smirked at her husband now. This admission had won her a point from an earlier discussion, likely about the quality of their server. But why had she admitted her mistake? Actually she knew why. She was constitutionally incapable of not owning up to her miscues. It was a weird pathology of hers. Damn her pathologies. They were always getting in the way.

"You spilled them?"

"Yes. And I'm sorry. Let me talk to the manager about comping your lunch."

"We ain't got no lunch to comp," said the father, and this got a wry chuckle from the table.

Penelope could see his point.

"I really am sorry for the trouble," she said.

"Honey, why don't you just run along and get us that manager," said the mother. "Our team bus is due to leave in ten minutes, and we're the only ones here who haven't been fed. We're starving."

"I'll go get him now," said Penelope.

She turned and strode to the kitchen, feeling as if things had gone

64

better than expected. One peanut hit the back of her head, but it was only a glancing blow. Several others flew wide of the mark. Penelope found these wayward shots surprising, but assumed low blood sugar was beginning to affect their marksmanship.

The door to Marty's office was open and Barbo was nowhere to be seen. Penelope breathed a sigh of relief and hurried in, only to find Barbo sitting in the manager's chair, the rolling one with side-arms, and Marty on the uncomfortable plastic one where servers had to sit when they were checking out. A bad sign. In the background "Country Boy Party" was coming to its close.

> Well, Sunday comes and they're off to church
> Monday comes and they're bound for work
> But right now let the good times roll
> Cause it's Friday night—Hell Yeah!
>> and the beer is cold!

Penelope had always found this stanza a little touching, the way the cooks would shout out the *Hell Yeah* part, even when it was Friday night and they were still at work and not attending some awesome raucous field party that kicked the shit out of anything the big city had to offer. But she couldn't dwell on that, for Marty was now bestowing his infamous disapproving stare.

"There you are," he said, his lips pursed and trying to look older than his twenty-six years by way of knitted brows. His attempts at establishing Coonskins order via the stare down were legendary comic fodder for the staff.

"Marty, A-9 wants to talk to you."

"That can wait," said Marty, grimacing and speaking in a weird husky whisper, like a television detective.

Penelope felt like she was looking at a cross-eyed, slightly bald baby bird. Marty wasn't actually cross-eyed, but such was the effect of the laboring brows.

"No, it can't, Marty," said Penelope. "We ran out of steak sandwiches and then I spilled the last three and these people are pissed and hungry. They have to board a bus in like ten minutes and everyone else in their group is finished eating. Can I just ask the kitchen to throw five full sirloins on right now? I'll pay for them out of my pocket if I have to. They've been firing peanuts at me for the last twenty minutes."

"We don't allow peanut throwing at Coonskins," said Marty. "Shells should be discarded on the floor, either in the aisle or under the table. I can't imagine they actually threw peanuts at you. That sounds far-fetched. People don't just waste peanuts."

"Well, they did waste peanuts, a lot of them, by throwing them at me, but who cares? Will you please go talk to them? They look like they really need some red meat. They look hungry as shit."

"See," said Barbo. "You heard profanity right there. Right in front of the manager. I told you she had a gutter mouth."

"I seriously have to go," Penelope said.

"Your customers can wait," said Marty. "Barbo here says you cursed her and also that you took one of her tables."

Penelope had a number of thoughts running through her head at once, all of them jumbled and irritating. First off, Marty was the f-bomb king. End of story. As for the pilfered table issue, she could blame Carrie for the initial confusion, but that would just get her in trouble, and she was already in the doghouse for a number of hosting offenses. Right now, Carrie likely had her hand on the smallest and most delectable onion ring on a saucer, or was licking a curious finger recently plunged into the choicest meringue of a key lime pie. Everyone knew about Carrie's car payments. So that line of defense was out.

"Yes, I said something like, *damn it to hell, Barbo* after I spilled those sandwiches. I'm sorry about that. I really am. But I didn't steal anyone's table. Those guys just got up and moved on their own."

"Yeah, after you talked to them," said Barbo, drumming her fingers like the older cop who only weighed in when the younger one got off course in his interrogation. But Marty jumped in now, voice huskier than ever: "Is that true, Penelope?"

"That I talked to them? Yes. I said they weren't in my section and then they moved."

"I told you, Marty," said Barbo.

"Listen," said Penelope, "I can't stand here all day talking about this. Barbo, I'm sorry I cursed at you. I didn't steal that table. And Marty, are you going to talk to A-9 or not?"

"Not till we settle this," said Marty, glancing once at Barbo to show he wasn't giving in too easily.

"I've got to get these softball people a basket of fries or something to tide them over. I think the mom wants to fight me as it is."

"Stop being dramatic," said Marty.

"I'm the one being dramatic? Are you kidding me?"

She found that her heart was beating fast, and a decision had to be made. Barbo and Marty were exchanging eyebrows, gray and skeptical meeting blond and confused somewhere in the middle distance of Marty's office. Actually, their gazes seemed to touch just over the filing cabinet where Marty kept the forms used when he had to *write-up* someone for a disciplinary matter. Penelope saw how this was going to shake out now and smiled despite herself.

"I'm going to have to write you up," said Marty. "You've admitted your offense. You leave me no choice."

"Okay. Do what you have to do. I'm going to get some food for those softball people before they turn cannibalistic."

"No, you'll wait right here."

But Penelope was gone. Two baskets of fries and a massive fried onion meant for sharing had just come up in the window and Penelope grabbed these posthaste.

"I have to have these," she said. "I'm sorry. Apologize to whoever I swiped them from."

"Sure, P," said Ray. "Just take them. For those steak sandwich people?"

"Yeah. And go ahead and throw five sirloins on for them, medium-well. I need those on the fly. Microwave them if you have to."

"Will do."

"Thanks," said Penelope. Then she headed out the door, wondering if the write-up would cost her the night shift she'd been counting on. She'd never been written up before and didn't know the protocol. And what if Marty made her pay for the sirloins? Was it possible she could lose money by working? That she could be further away from getting her own place than she was just three hours before?

Yes, it was definitely possible.

10

Penelope charged toward the softball family, sure of foot and feigning good cheer, the baskets of fried vegetables as the lamest of peace offerings. Before she even arrived, the mother called out: "And what is that?"

"Just some appetizers. On the house."

"No. I mean that big pile of something."

Penelope set the baskets of fries down first. Then, realizing what the woman was pointing at, she said: "Oh, this is our Funion Platter."

"Your what platter?"

Penelope hated to repeat the name. In normal situations it made her laugh anytime someone ordered it. *Riblets* had the same effect. But she soldiered on: "Funion Platter. It's like a huge onion ring that everyone can share."

She smiled as she said this, to show she didn't find the woman's tin ear for wordplay off-putting. In the meantime, the woman had grabbed the basket before Penelope could set it down and said to the table in a harsh voice that showed what she thought of puns in lieu of ordered entrees: "Anyone want a *funion* ring?"

"What I want is the steak sandwich I ordered thirty minutes ago," the father said.

Penelope noticed he had pulled his baseball cap extra low, as if trying to squeeze thoughts of food out of his mind before passing out. Or maybe to suppress burgeoning homicidal impulses. His beard looked thicker as well, though maybe it just shone a bit more from peanut oil that had been transferred from hand to face during his turmoil.

"What I want is the manager," said the mother as both girls rolled their eyes beneath the bills of their caps and the son snuck a peanut under the table. "The manager. Like right damn now."

"I've ordered five full sirloins," said Penelope. "They're going to be comped."

The woman waved toward the parking lot, where several team members and parents were milling around the bus and patting their stomachs in a satisfied way. Penelope wished they wouldn't do that. They seemed to be rubbing it in to the disappointed five-top in front of her.

The woman said: "We ain't got time for steaks, free or otherwise. We're about to load up. Is this the manager here?"

"Yes, I'm the manager," Marty said, appearing at Penelope's hip. "How can I help you folks?"

She and Marty were standing side by side one moment, and then, through some subtle maneuvering that he'd likely picked up from Barbo, Penelope found that he'd edged in front and she was out in the aisle. In her peripheral vision, she noted Cobb Salad lifting his tea glass up and down as if it were a dumbbell, and beside him the family with the sundaes, standing and flapping their tab at her. These were weeds extraordinaire.

"We've been here forty-five minutes and never got our food," the mother said. "And that woman there is the worst waitress I've ever seen."

Penelope shuffled her feet, fighting an urge to defend herself. Everyone knew she was the best Coonskins had to offer. Cobb Salad had tried out several servers before landing on her, simply because she was the fastest and the most efficient at keeping him hydrated and full of croutons and extra radishes or whatever his salad obsession of the day was. Worst waitress? That was a joke.

Marty turned briefly to give her the same sad-boy brow he had a month before when she declined to meet for a *quick brew* after work. Then he was back facing the table.

"I'm sorry to hear that," he said. "And I'm sorry about the confusion with the steak sandwiches. But what can I do now to make y'all feel better about your Coonskins experience? Your lunch will be comped. And I can get something out of the kitchen to go in about five minutes. Five full-sized steaks are on the grill right now with your name on them."

Cobb Salad was standing up now and doing a sarcastic little dance number with his empty glass. Several tables were gawking at him and seemed to find his antics amusing. She glanced away and found herself staring at a framed poster on the wall that signaled the start of Barbo's section. It depicted a wood carving that had once appeared on a tree in Kentucky:

D. Boon CillEd A. BAr
on tree in the YEAR 1760

Penelope felt this to be a bad omen.

"Well, what about that waitress?" the mother said, pointing at Penelope.

"I don't understand you," Marty replied.

"What. About. That. Waitress. The one who screwed up our order. Probably intentionally. I swear to God, she's the worst waitress I've ever had in my life."

A loud clatter came from the kitchen and Marty jerked in that direction. As soon as his head was turned, a flying legume popped Penelope flush on the cheek. It was the first shot she'd taken that actually hurt. That sucker had been thrown with real heat. She looked to Marty, hoping he'd seen the peanut projectile, but he'd missed it. He was now gawping at her, in full eyebrow mode, trying to divine her potential for order sabotage. That, or he was stalling for time. Marty was used to confrontations in the kitchen with his underlings, not out here in the open restaurant frontier.

Reflexively, Penelope put up a hand to rub the spot where she'd been struck. It really did smart. It was the boy who threw it, she knew, but everyone at the softball table was smiling. The accurate volley had been well received. He might make a pitcher after all. Penelope was not even looking at Marty and his nervous caterpillar brows, but at the woman who'd just called her the worst server she'd ever had. That claim was beyond the pale and Penelope brooded on it considerably.

As she brooded, Derrick, the waiter whose night shift she was supposed to have, walked toward a table just being seated. Penelope saw a hand reach into the basket of peanuts Derrick held. The hand looked far away from her, disembodied, but she knew on some level that it was her own. The boy who had flung the stinging peanut had an unusual expression now, perhaps because Derrick had stopped in his tracks to see what was about to happen. Perhaps because of the way Penelope, with a fresh, full nut in her hand, was sizing him up. Whichever the case, his recent pleased smile had vamoosed to parts unknown and been replaced with a look both quizzical and expectant.

In her day, Penelope had been a pretty good softball player, a shortstop with a good arm. She raised that arm now, sized up the target before her, and fired a volley as hard as she could just as the boy was about to duck.

Too late. The peanut had connected with a satisfying pop on the boy's nose. The mother had just opened her mouth, no doubt to push for Penelope's immediate termination, when Penelope walked to within a foot of her scowling face. One of the computer games Theo played would shout, *Game On!* whenever a new round was about to begin, and that was the phrase going through her head as she leaned down and popped the softball mother smartly in the forehead from approximately six inches away. *Game On!* she thought as she grabbed the basket from Derrick and flung the entire contents into the startled faces of the softball family. *Game On! Game On!*

She felt sure everyone at the table had taken at least one direct hit, but she didn't have the luxury to fully assess the damage before she was tackled to the ground by the irate softball mother.

Using a quick reversal, not unlike something she used to pull on Timmy Newton before kissing him back in fourth grade, she soon found herself sitting atop the woman. She used her knees to pin the woman's arms, and as the woman screamed in fury about *suing her ass off*, she scooped all the stray shells she could find from the floor. Using a rapid-fire motion, like someone feeding an infielder in a game of pepper, she methodically bipped the angry woman in the face from close range. The words that came out of her mouth were ones she'd never before spoken: "Say Uncle."

"Kiss my ass, you crazy bitch."

This was not the correct response, so Penelope groped around for more ammo, scraping the peanut-dust-covered floor with both hands as the woman struggled mightily to get free. Penelope found it surprising that the family didn't intervene. In fact, unless she misread the round, galvanized faces that looked down at her, they seemed to be thoroughly enjoying the bout. The father had even pushed his cap up to get a better view.

Penelope looked at the gaping, appreciative onlookers and said: "*The tower of power, too sweet to be sour, ohhh yeah!*"

"That's Randy Savage," said the father, first to Penelope and then to his family.

"Yes, the Macho Man," Penelope said, nodding at the father and thinking how impressed Timmy Newton would be if he could see her now. She was totally dominating.

But now Marty, Derrick, Ray and two other cooks were peeling her off the still struggling woman. Back on her feet the softball mom took one wild swing, and then Penelope was marched away by Ray and Derrick before anything else could happen. In the swinging door to the kitchen, she and Barbo passed going in opposite directions. Barbo held Funion platters in both hands.

Ray said: "That was awesome. You kicked her ass."

Penelope nodded. She had indeed. She was shaking now, and her legs felt suddenly boneless, and her laughter had begun to sound a little like crying. Someone shouted *take her to the office and sit her down*, and this request was obliged.

Someone brought her water and when Marty came in, she was herself again, though her heart was still beating swiftly. The recent episode seemed distant as a dream. Her brain was clearing when Marty spoke: "I have to fire you."

"I know."

"We might get sued," said Marty.

"I doubt it," said Penelope. "She started it. And I wasn't lying about the peanuts. They were throwing them at me even before their food was late. They were just assholes, Marty. I wouldn't worry too much about it."

She realized it was odd to be comforting the man who'd just fired her, but she could tell Marty was worried for his own job. He had yet to sit at his rolling chair, as he always did when conducting serious business, and couldn't really look Penelope in the eye. From where she sat, she could see the write-up for the incident with Barbo on his desk. Her full name had been written in Marty's deliberate block style, and some offense, from a list of infractions, had been circled below it. Looking closer, she saw that two items had actually been circled, and below that Marty had added a few follow-up notes. She knew these forms were to provide proof for firing someone with cause and wondered just how often Coonskins got sued. Peanut allergies might just be the tip of the iceberg.

After pacing aimlessly around to gather his thoughts, Marty went to the desk and grabbed a fresh write-up note, then scribbled for several moments. During the scrum with the patron, Penelope's ponytail had broken free, and now a few locks of wayward, sweaty hair kept falling in her face. The hair smelled of ranch dressing and A-1, and Penelope luxuriated in the thought of how good a shower would soon feel.

Marty handed her the write-ups and asked her to sign both. What she hadn't realized before was that these forms were on carbon paper, so after she signed, Marty briskly tore off the top copy for her, retaining the second for himself.

"Is this a souvenir?" Penelope said.

"What? No. It's for your records."

"Could I get one for my mother too? She keeps a scrapbook of my accomplishments."

Marty's brows were inquisitive and a little concerned, as if she was in the midst of a psychiatric episode.

"I'm kidding," Penelope said, taking her copies of the forms and tucking them into her denim skirt.

"I'm really sorry to do this."

"I know. Don't worry about it. I need a better job anyway."

Marty frowned as if Penelope had said something insulting.

"I didn't mean it like that," she said. "I just need something with benefits and more regular hours. For my son, you know."

Marty blanched at the mention of Theo. Everyone in the restaurant knew just how broke everyone else was, and Marty looked now to be computing Penelope's short-term financial straits.

"I'll give you a great reference," Marty said. "I know today was just weird. You've been an excellent Coonskins employee."

Despite herself, Penelope's eyes watered a little at this. It was a nice counterargument to the softball woman's comments. It had been that gibe about her capabilities as a server, the wrongness of it, much more than the tossed peanuts or anything else, that had made Penelope willing to wrestle another adult in public.

Penelope wiped her eyes with her T-shirt, then stood up.

"I'll have to ask you to turn in your apron," Marty said, unable to meet her gaze.

Penelope reached around to untie it. She looked at the motto one last time: *Coonskins: Where Fun Meets Frontier!*

She handed the apron to Marty, waved quickly at the cooks on her way past, then exited the restaurant through the back kitchen door.

11

Penelope was back at her mother's house after being fired. She felt some better after a marathon shower, though she was convinced a funky smell remained in her hair. Looking in the mirror, she pulled a big handful to her nose and took a whiff. Yes, it smelled of apricots and pineapple and whatever other fruity delights were in her shampoo, but there was also a hint of a stray onion ring, a rogue cheese fry. Maybe this smell would stay with her forever like some mark of Cain because of her unkind feeling toward stuffed raccoons and peanut shells. It seemed an odd fate, but then again, oddness sometimes had an affinity for her.

She entered the room where she'd slept these last four months. It still looked like every other guest bedroom she'd ever been in: a print of a flower arrangement; a print of a Revolutionary War battle waged by Virginians; curtains and bedspread from the 1970s, and no skimping on the pastels either. The only things she could claim as her own were a few photos of Theo on the dresser, her latest smutty novel— *The Stranger Within*—and the clothes draped on all available surfaces. Looking around for her robe, she noted one more thing that technically belonged to her—the denim skirt on the floor—and gave it a violent kick out into the hall. That restraining device was heading straight to the trash. She considered donating it to Goodwill, but couldn't do that to some unsuspecting soul sister out there.

Feeling like a patriotic feminist, she dug around in a pile of dirty clothes until she found her robe. Thus garbed, she headed to George's office, ready to start the job search anew. Getting fired was a setback, so she really needed to hop to. Doozy and his spatula would keep strict martial law in the confined space of the basement. It would be *Nightmare in the RV* all over again.

She sat down in George's swivel chair, thinking about jobs and stinky hair. When she returned from Coonskins, all the vehicles were in the driveway, so she'd crept around back and let herself in through the basement door like a thief rather than face a long Q-and-A session with her mother about what had just transpired. She'd never been fired from anything. And her mom would be chock-full of tips for employment. She might even recommend cosmetology school again.

Man, did she ever need her own place.

Her last venture on George's computer hadn't been erased from memory, but it was just easier to see things on the desktop than her phone. Plus, she could take notes at the desk about job openings, should any catch her eye. So what if George loved preposterous monster bosoms? They were likely in short supply on a Western Channel cattle drive.

The computer, powered by a single wind chime on the front porch, was still taking its sweet time to load, so she dialed James's cell phone, hoping to talk to Theo after his baseball game. It was always around this time on the weekend when she started to miss the little Fart Boy and thought a quick word with him might cheer her up.

"Hey Mom," came Theo's unusually peppy greeting.

"Hey honey. How'd the game go?"

"I hit the ball!"

"What? Seriously? That's fantastic."

"It was just a foul, but I did hit it. My bat hit the ball."

While she was engaging in urban warfare at Coonskins, Theo had made his first-ever contact with the ball. It didn't seem fair.

"Who cares if it was a foul, Theo? I am so proud of you. Now you'll have to do it at your next game so I can see it."

"That's a lot of pressure, Mom. I'm just glad I hit it once."

"Me too, sweetie. And no pressure at all. Did you all win?"

"I think so. Dad, did we win?"

Penelope strained to hear James's reply, hoping, just to irritate herself more, that he'd still be using the solid TV dad voice he'd employed the day before, but his reply came back muffled and sounding faraway.

"Yeah. Dad says we won."

"Well, what a day. I am so sorry I missed it. I'm going to try my best not to miss any more of your games."

"I have to go," Theo said. "Dad's taking me for ice cream to celebrate the hit."

"That sounds great. Eat as much as you can. You deserve it. And we'll do something special tomorrow night as well, okay?"

"Do I have to come home tomorrow? Dad and I are having a lot of fun, and I was wondering if I could maybe stay an extra night."

Penelope hadn't seen this coming and took a breath before replying. And then a few more. "Honey, you've got school on Monday, remember?"

"I've got clothes here. Dad bought some so I wouldn't have to worry if I ever forgot something."

Penelope felt panicked. She'd heard stories about boys of divorced parents asking to live with Dad when they got to be teenagers but didn't think she'd have to worry about that so soon. Who knew what James had at his house? He had plenty of room for that zipline Theo had wanted forever. How could she ever compete with a zipline?

She wanted to just speak truthfully, to say that she missed him and simply didn't want to spend an extra day without him, but that was a guilt trip she couldn't lay on a nine-year-old.

"Let me think on it, okay? It's probably fine, but let me sleep on it overnight. I'll call you after church and we'll talk about it then, all right?"

"Great. Thanks, Mom," Theo said and then hung up, forgetting as he usually did to say good-bye.

She stood from the desk and walked into her bedroom without

knowing why. It was a beautiful spring day and she was alone and now her son was asking to spend more time at his father's place. Grabbing her phone, she texted Sandy and Rachel: I got fired today. Want to do something?

She knew this was a lost cause even as she typed. Weekends were family time. Sandy was at some youth sporting event, and Rachel was hiking or wine-tasting or doing something else romantic and irritating with her husband. Damn their intact nuclear families. And damn their husbands too. Especially their loving and interested husbands. Who was she supposed to hang out with for the rest of the day?

After throwing her phone back on the bed and kicking again the denim skirt in the hall, she went back to George's office. The computer was buzzing along now and Penelope raced to James's Facebook page, intent on locating a zipline or a trampoline or some other super-awesome inducement to woo Theo.

But nothing had changed. No new photos of the two of them doing something fun in the backyard or in James's cute little house. It was still Hot for Teacher all over the place. No, wait. *Dangerous Minds* had been added to the movie likes. Was that the one where Michelle Pfeiffer played a teacher who instructs her tough-nut students in karate? Oh, this was too much. Hot teachers plus karate? Gag her with a spoon. James and his martial arts fixation knew no bounds. Did he think she'd forgotten Sad Karate Night? Or the whole Manhood Reclamation Project she'd been forced to initiate just to get the moping back to a manageable level afterwards?

She could picture him later that night, sexting in his shorty robe to his Very Special Lady, his pale legs keeping time to the *Roadhouse* soundtrack playing in the background. How James loved his bad boy southern rock when feeling frisky and alive.

Then she snapped out of it. No more obsessing about James and his possible recruitment, intentional or otherwise, of Theo. No more feeling sorry for herself. What she needed was her own place. And to manage that, she had to have a job. Doozy would not, absolutely would not, be bossing her around in his sleep about the succotash. She was getting out of that basement and into a cool new place for her and Theo, come hell or high water. Simple as that. She'd hunt for jobs right now. Just after she checked in—ever so quickly—with her LoveSynch account. She'd messaged that older guy in the cardigan right before work and maybe he'd replied. Who knew, maybe other men had contacted her as well—men closer to her own age and wearing a shirt. A girl could dream, after all.

Before she could get to the dating site, however, a fresh pop-up appeared. It was not, to Penelope's surprise, another topless gal in stockings, but instead an advertisement for *RhinoShaft*, which touted itself as *the unsurpassed male prolongater on the market*. She clicked the pop-up from the screen, only to see it replaced by another for something called *Cyclopenis*. This came with a colorful cartoon of a happy-looking Cyclops, his one proud eye glaring defiantly from the screen. The source of his cocksureness seemed to be a steady diet of catuaba bark. Thinking that many of Theo's drawings were better than this overconfident Cyclops before her, she clicked off the page. Immediately, another appeared. This one was for *Steel Cobra*, and to hell with catuaba bark. If you truly wanted to be serpentine between the legs, what you needed was yohimbe bark. Just ask the serious guy in the lab coat with the clipboard beside the snake. He was all about the yohimbe bark.

Penelope took her hand from the mouse, staring for a while at the smiling, lengthy cartoon snake and the fake scientist next to it.

Was George taking boner pills?

Surely her mother wouldn't allow it with his heart in its current compromised state. Maybe he was taking them on the sly and her mom was just the lucky beneficiary of all this bark ingestion. Then again, after last night's nudie show, maybe it was her mother who was pushing for rhino-cyclops-cobra satisfaction, and damn the fallout for her frail, sweet husband. Whichever the case, Penelope felt duty-bound to inquire. She loved old George and didn't want him to kick off anytime soon via exotic herb overload. He was a Virginian, for Christ's sake, not some Kama Sutra overlord.

She was now on the LoveSynch page and spent some time flitting, as a bumblebee in a picked-over flowerbed, around the assortment of single men who lived within her forty-mile dating radius. It was a sad affair, frankly. The men mostly left her with a poignant feeling, as if life hadn't been one big Country Boy Party like they'd hoped. She recognized several from high school and felt weird reading their biographies, which seemed truthful to the point of masochism. Sure, there were guys here and there claiming to be early forties when they were well into their sixth decade, and yes, it was damn irritating that nearly every single man, even the saddest-looking, said he was looking for fit/slender/athletic women from 21 to 39. Yeah, of course. And she'd like to date Brad Pitt on Monday and Matt Damon on Tuesday, so long as they lived within forty miles of Hillsboro. Now do your thing, LoveSynch! Work your matchmaking magic!

Okay, she was depressing herself now. Feeling like an expired carton of milk in the world of Internet dating, she went to her **Portnal** (portrait + journal). She studiously avoided the My Way (bio) she'd written, the Enthusiasms checklist, and the Mr. Write narrative about what she was looking for in an Internet dream man.

Everything she'd revealed about herself made her blush, and she'd revealed very little, just a mix of TV shows and movies she liked, a compilation of places she'd never visited but sort of insinuated she had, and some nonsense about wine tastings, though she'd only ever been to one. She'd dashed off the entire **Portnal** in less than an hour and had tried to sound casual, self-deprecating, and most of all not desperate. She'd left the personal income item blank and told a white lie about exercise frequency, counting her intentions to exercise as the real McCoy. The most time had been spent debating how to respond to the education question or whether to leave it blank. In the end, she'd written *Some College*, which felt like the worst thing of all. She'd submitted one photo, a selfie taken in this very chair while filling out

81

the application. The photo made her look a little tired, a little wan, but generally cheerful. She thought it the most honest part of her **Portnal** and the one thing that didn't make her cringe.

The LoveSynch stats sheet said she'd received two new *blends*, seven *flirts*, and three *Eiffel Towers*. Though she'd never bothered to figure out what these things meant, it seemed like a pretty decent haul. She felt cheered that so many of the sad local men had found her *blend-*, *flirt-* and *Eiffel Tower*–worthy. Perhaps the day would turn out better than it had started. But first things first. She'd replied to the cardigan dude without closely reading the message he'd sent. Maybe she ought to have another look at it:

My Dearest TheosMom75,

    I must extend, even before introducing myself, my heartiest congratulations to your parents for their foresight in giving you such a unique and fitting name. As soon as I saw your photo, I said to myself, there, if ever I saw one, goes a TheosMom75. In fact, the name was so apt, I wondered (aloud, I must admit. Brief segue: I sometimes talk to myself when expressing profound surprise or admiration) if your parents were even human. Perchance, thought I, this mysterious, lovely woman was taken in by mischievous woodland animals as a babe in swaddling clothes and raised as their own, free of spirit and unfettered by convention. Such was the effect of your symphonious name on my ear and imagination.

    I found your Portnal listings inscrutable and fascinating and spent many hours considering how first to approach you. Should I send a *flirt*? No, fireworks rather hurt my ears, even as a boy, and I thought you might feel the same. Well, it's an *Eiffel Tower* then, says I. But no. Paris and its trappings have always struck me as a rather bourgeois notion of romance. And the French, if you'll pardon my French, are just a right pain in the bum. So I decided to be rash—damn the *flirts*! Damn the *Eiffel Towers*!—and "message" you directly.

I am not sure I exist in anyone's Mr. Write profile. But I too enjoy tasting wine (though usually my own bottle at my own humble abode). And I too consider London one of the very best places on this lovely orb of ours.

Please write back. I feel, for reasons I can't explain, that we might be something of a *blend*.

Yours most sincerely,
Fitzwilliam

Below this was Penelope's return message from earlier that morning:

Hey. Nice to meet you. Off to work.

She stared at her message, feeling it dwarfed and inadequate compared to the missive that preceded it. Who was this freak? And why did his name sound familiar? She read over the note again, then clicked on his **Portnal**. Feeling shallow for doing it, but doing it nonetheless, she sought out his photos first. Like her, Fitzwilliam had only posted one shot, the one where he wore a cardigan. She studied the photo for a while and eventually decided that he was more oldish than just straight old, and could be anywhere from fifty-five to sixty-five.

He had left a number of entries blank on his **Portnal**, including those asking about age, income, and height, not that any of these mattered greatly to Penelope. Her own page was about as forthcoming. Better to reveal too little than too much. She could respect Fitzwilliam's restraint. Here is what he had to say for himself:

Places: Pemberley; Derbyshire

Occupation: Gentleman

Enthusiasms: Yes!

MyWay: Is not the way of the 21st century, alas.

Ms. Write: Will write! And often, I hope.

Education: Varied, sundry, and somewhat autodidactic in nature (also a PhD).

She compared this page to the others she'd perused on LoveSynch and found it notably lacking in mentions of bass boats, camo, duck calls, and a touch more about fishing. And not a word about watching sports. This gave her pause. Did this guy even live in Virginia?

No, if his **Portnal** could be trusted, he was from Pemberley by way of Derbyshire or the converse. English? In Hillsboro? It seemed unlikely. She threw both place-names into the search engine and soon had her answer. Of course. She thought that name rang a bell. Junior year in high school, she'd all but memorized the CliffsNotes for *Pride and Prejudice* for Mrs. Sketchin's midterm. And the movie wasn't bad either. Good old Mr. Darcy and his country estate, Pemberley. How could she have forgotten that? She still had the occasional nightmare about Mrs. Sketchin.

Feeling that one mystery had been solved, she went back to her LoveSynch page, ready for message two from Fitzwilliam Darcy.

12

Dear TheosMom75,

What a lovely, gnomic message you have sent to brighten the inbox of my day! I read it numerous times, and studied it, initially, as if coming across an unknown free verse classic by Dr. William Carlos Williams. On closer inspection, however, I thought I discerned a certain (if understated) formalist aesthetic. Says I: activate scansion mode, Mr. Spock.

Pulling out the trusty pencil and marking (as some out-of-fashion New Critic might) stress/unstress to your rhythmically impeccable line of poetry—*Hey. Nice to meet you. Off to work*—I experienced an exquisite flash of *Eureka!*

Archimedes sitting down in his warm tub and realizing that water was being displaced by his volume had nothing on my discovery that your words, your elegant, sphinxlike words, were (drumroll, please): iambic tetrameter!

As a lover of poetry, I must insist that you not reply again while the pen of opportunity is affording you verse such as this. But should your beneficent Muse

need a well-deserved respite from her (his?) efforts
sometime in the not-too-distant future, I hope you will
grace me with another of your lyrical efforts.

      Yours in the traditional poetic foot—
      F. Darcy

Penelope read this through several times. This Fitzwilliam dude was definitely messing with her. That was obvious. On the other hand, the ribbing seemed good-natured and pretty funny, and she felt flattered that he'd taken time to compose two long messages. No one she knew could just dash off something like that. This matter of time raised the question of why F. Darcy had so much of it, and now the voices of Sandy and Rachel popped into her head, reminding her of her weakness for smart, quirky, and underemployed men.

She considered this. The argument had merit. Of course they also said she had a weakness for huge, huge rednecks. In fact, Sandy had once suggested that her life had been one long yin and yang journey from smart boys in short robes to HHRs in duck blinds, a continual yo-yoing from one to the other then back again, ever seeking the opposite of what she'd just left. But was Sandy alone on a weekend? Had she wrestled with a softball mother at a frontier roadhouse? Penelope thought not. And was Sandy a medically certified psychologist? Again, no. Hell no, in fact.

Deciding to let those who are without sin cast the first psychoanalysis, she banished the disapproving voices of her friends and replied:

Dear Mr. Darcy,

    so much depends
    upon
    a red wheel
    barrow

```
but if that doesn't work

beam me up, Scotty!


Sincerely,

Elizabeth Bennet
```

She was proud of herself for remembering the William Carlos Williams poem and gave a grudging salute to the draconian but efficient Mrs. Sketchin for that bit of recall. Waffling for several minutes about whether to sign off as TheosMom75 or as the love interest of Fitzwilliam Darcy in *Pride and Prejudice,* she eventually threw caution to the wind. Who cared? It was Internet jive talk. She wasn't asking to be whisked away to the heath or whatever of Pemberley at Derbyshire. She wasn't sure she was ready to date anyway. Of course, James was dating already. But was she in a competition with her ex-husband?

No. Absolutely not. That would be just too high school. Okay, forget dates and men and Mrs. Sketchin too. Time to focus on finding a job. How could she consider dating when she lived with her mother? Talk about high school.

It took approximately three minutes to canvass the skimpy offerings in Hillsboro and its environs. Waitresses and dishwashers and day-care workers about covered her options. She had moved on to reading a list of the biggest jerks in Hollywood that took ten times longer than it should have because you had to switch a page for each new entry when another pop-up appeared for something called "Paybacks Are ~~Hell~~ Heaven!"

A quick perusal revealed this to be a website that featured snapshots of women in various states of undress, if various meant naked but with shoes, socks, bra, or hat on. What struck Penelope immediately was the amateurish quality of both model and photographer. These were snapshots, pure and simple, taken, if the first few were any indication, in dorms, hotel rooms, or trailers. One showed a Rolling Stones poster in the background, another a Jamaican flag with a marijuana leaf in the middle. Most included bedside tables loaded with beer cans, as if both photographer and model had recently been chugging a few. A few women were middle-aged, but most looked in their twenties, goofy with youth and lack of cellulite.

One photo of a girl with red hair drew her attention especially. It was the tan lines, those two big strips of white against the girl's brown skin. Everyone else looked the same color all over, as if they either never went out in the sun or only went out completely nude. The picture that caught her eye was old, a Polaroid, and the girl looked sleepy in a pleased sort of way under her wavy red hair. There was a gravity bong on the table beside her and a mounted fish above the waterbed, which she lounged upon as if it was the finest that the Taj Mahal had to offer. Penelope thought she looked like the sweetest, prettiest idiot she'd ever seen.

Which made her mad when she looked again at the website name and fully registered the word *payback*. This was one of those places where guys sent in photos of their ex-girlfriends and wives. Losers. Jackasses. Creeps.

Truth be known, way back when, she'd posed for some reasonably tasteful nudes for the HHR. She remembered the day perfectly. They'd gone out to the lake with Paulie and Theresa and done flips off Paulie's dad's pontoon boat despite drinking about two cases of Bud Light between them and smoking weed Rastafarian style for the duration. Afterwards, she and the HHR had gone back to his apartment. She was in her sophomore year of college and the HHR had started his lawn business. He was rolling in dough, at least compared to everyone else they knew, and had his own place with no roommate. They were just about to mess around. The HHR was standing at the sink, naked save for his high-top sneakers and the Lynyrd Skynyrd bandana he always wore at the lake. He was draining his fifteenth beer of the day while singing "Gimme Two Steps" and dancing in a comic way. Basically the big goof was performing a nudie Texas Two-Step.

She had to admit the HHR could dance. And he was funny. And

yes, handsome too. His curly hair was blondish brown and lay casually in Cupidesque rings beneath his bandana. His body was lean and muscular and he was good in bed.

She was on the waterbed, laughing at his antics, feeling frisky and ready for come what may. Smoking pot had that effect on her sometimes. Most of the time, actually. And earlier in the week, she'd dyed her hair red, just for the heck of it. She wished he'd get a move on. This would be her first time making love as a redhead, and she was curious if it would feel different. If he wanted to try out his new Polaroid, she was game.

Penelope paused violently in her recollection, the weird nostalgia for the early days with the HHR fleeing as suddenly as it had come.

Polaroid? Waterbed? Redhead?

Her eyes darted to the computer screen and the smiling, pretty idiot with the wavy red hair.

OMG, OMG, OMG.

What if George saw this when he was down here searching for behemoth bosoms? What if he already had? What if her mother saw the photo and offered tips on modern personal grooming? Or if James saw? Or Theo? Or any of those bullies on his bus? Or Fitzwilliam Darcy after they exchanged Eiffel Towers or whatever the hell it was that indicated you were ready to go on a date? Or anyone else in the whole world who owned a computer? Her preacher, her former teachers, that shy bag boy at Kroger?

This was her first reaction.

Her second reaction was to compare her memory of the photo session with the proof now staring her in the face. There was nothing remotely tasteful about the way she was sprawled there on the HHR's beloved waterbed. In her mind's eye, her legs had been decorously closed, with just a hint of peek-a-boo, like one of those old burlesque photos. But the stark evidence before her showed a full-on splay. She'd even raised her hips a bit, surely at the HHR's prompting. The coup de grace, however, to the memory she'd nurtured of herself as an *artistic model* was a hand caught mid-motion, finger curling toward herself, beckoning the photographer to hurry up and come sample the tasty wares. God, she was a complete tart back then. Even the largemouth bass above her could tell that. His plastic eyes were practically goggling at the spectacle below. And the bong in the background? Classy. Child services would be calling any minute now. Forget Theo spending an extra night with James. He'd be living there permanently if this got out.

This wasn't erotica. Not close. No, it was a straight beaver shot as featured in every magazine the HHR had managed to steal out of some trucker's garage. She might as well have been hiking a leg over a Harley Davidson.

There were other details of life with the HHR in the Polaroid: the faux-wood paneling of the back wall, the Black Sabbath sticker on the headboard, the sock drawer that the HHR never once in four years closed. And there on the floor, her cute little white two-piece of that summer, looking too shy and delicate for the sordid scene taking place on the bed.

And then the depth of the HHR's betrayal began to sink in. He was a lot of things, most of them stoned and shiftless, but he'd never before been a sneak, nor mean, nor vindictive. Yet here was proof that he was all these things. He swore that he'd burned those photos, and she shuddered to think what the others might show. She seemed to recall trying out several poses, and even had a hazy recollection of visiting the pipe while the HHR was still snapping away. Yes, now that she thought of it, she had definitely posed nude while hitting a bong. The bong was green. Her name was Tinkerbell.

Recalling all this, Penelope spent a moment wondering if she was really meant for life in the middle class.

Then she grabbed the phone and dialed. She knew the HHR's number because it was the same landline he'd had back in his freelance photography days. The HHR didn't trust cell phones, believing both his liberty and his sperm count to be imperiled through their use. Simply put, the HHR wanted to mow lawns and smoke weed without government intervention. And he wanted his full allotment of spermatozoa. Thus the landline.

Yeah, and he also wanted to send in naked photos of her without her permission just to be a perverted loser of a jerk. The HHR, doubtlessly searching for his phone among the taxidermy equipment that littered his domicile, took about fifteen rings to find the receiver but finally answered with a: "Yello."

"Don't *yello* me, asshole."

"Oh hey, Penelope. How are you?"

"And don't *oh hey, Penelope, how are you* me either, asshole."

"Hey now, you already called me asshole once."

"That's because you are an asshole."

"Now that's three times. And that seems like about two too many. We aren't married anymore, Penelope, in case you forgot."

Her bimbo self was still smiling at her from the screen. She seemed to think that Penelope should just chill. Maybe get reacquainted with trusty Tinkerbell. This younger version of herself, caught for all eternity in her serene horniness, really got her going now.

"Asshole, asshole, asshole. Why did you send in that picture of me? God, I can't believe you. I can't believe you'd do that to me."

No response came from the HHR, other than a long intake of breath that was followed by a minor coughing spell. The idiot was smoking dope as she ranted.

"Are you smoking dope right now, you asshole? I mean right this very minute?"

"That's immaterial. And frankly, inadmissible."

"What?"

"If I ask if you're taping this conversation, then by Virginia statute, you have to say yes or no. So I'll ask you: Are you taping this conversation?"

Penelope replied with the full extent of her profane vocabulary, the lion's share of which she'd learned while in the HHR's company.

"So," said the HHR after another long intake, another coughing bout, "you confirm that this conversation is not being recorded by any device?"

"I just told you no, idiot."

"Then yes, I am smoking marijuana, Penelope."

"Why did you send that picture in?"

"What picture?"

"That naked picture, you idiot. You dumbass. You asshole. It's on Paybacks Are Heaven."

"Really? That site is pretty raunchy."

"Oh my God. You sent in a picture of me."

"Penelope, I still have no idea what you're talking about."

"Maybe because you're stoned out of your gourd."

"Again, immaterial. What is your point?"

"You sent in one of those Polaroids you took of me NAKED that day after we went to the lake with Paulie and Theresa. And you told me you burned them all. You lied to me. You betrayed me."

"I did burn them. You saw me do it, out in the firepit."

"Yes, I saw you burn some photos. But you obviously didn't burn them all or else half the world couldn't see me naked on the Internet right now."

The HHR didn't answer. She heard a lighter being flicked, another gulp and swallow. Then the phone was set down and minor shuffling could be heard in the background. A minute passed and Penelope's ire grew. Then a truly massive, though still muffled, coughing attack could be heard. Penelope was just about to get her car keys to confront the HHR in person when he came back to the phone.

"All right," said the HHR. "I am now online and looking at the Paybacks Are Heaven website."

"What took so long, damn it? You seem pretty casual about all this. I'm really pissed."

"I got a new hookah—or a *chillum*, as it's called in Uzbekistan—

and thought I should clear my head before addressing your very real concerns."

Oh my God, thought Penelope, he's in his clear-headed phase now. This was a plateau only the HHR could reach, where if he just smoked enough weed he could power through his buzz and come out the other side, ready to philosophize and solve the minor problems of the world. This state was inevitably accompanied by precise language and a soothing monotone.

"You see the picture, jackass?"

"Indeed I do. And let me say first off, Penelope, that you look absolutely smoking hot. You're like the second hottest chick on there. Other than that gal pulling off her yoga pants. So frankly, I'm not sure what the problem is. You are simply in the natural state, the same way you came into this world. The same way all of us came into the world."

"I'm arching my back, you asshole."

"Yes, I see that now. You are a sexual being. No shame in that. The Creator meant for us to be sexual, else He wouldn't have made lovemaking so pleasurable."

"You sent in that picture, you big fat liar."

"I did not send in that picture, Penelope. That would be an invasion of your privacy and you know where I stand on that issue."

"How did it get on there then?"

"That I do not know."

Penelope paused. She could tell the HHR was truly in his philosopher mode now. She was getting sleepy just listening to him. Looking back, she wondered if it was his soothing stoned voice that had induced her to marry him in the first place. She'd always felt slightly hypnotized in his presence, such was his ability to get her in a relaxed state. It had probably been his stoned-philosopher voice that had talked her into posing nude as well.

"Okay, Plato. I saw you burn about ten photos out in your firepit. So here is a simple question. Did you burn every one of them?"

"I did not."

"Aha!"

"I couldn't. I had to keep one for sentimental reasons. You know you were my first real love."

This was likely true. He'd been married three other times since their nuptials, but she was his first blushing bride. She began to feel a little sorry for him.

"And," said the HHR, "some memories just can't be trusted to the spank bank. I had to have one visual. Come on. That was a rocking night."

"Spank bank? Seriously?"

"My memory is not what it once was. You know I'm nostalgic."

This was true. The HHR was nostalgic. He found it impossible to throw out any bong or pipe that had once treated him in a righteous manner and kept his former companions scattered about the apartment like decorative lamps he never turned on. He also had a whole shed full of antiquated leaf blowers that he'd spent many an enjoyable afternoon with, including his first one, which he'd named Calypso.

"So I did mislead you," continued the HHR, "about burning all those pictures. I apologize for that. I kept the one. But I'd never send it to any website. You know I wouldn't betray you like that. That was our private moment. I didn't even know it was missing from my drawer."

Penelope wondered if this was the same sock drawer he preferred left open, but thought better of inquiring. She found that she wasn't as angry anymore and that kind of made her angry too. She said: "Well, it got on there somehow."

This elicited another flick of the lighter and the turbulent sound of water rushing through intricate tubing. Then the HHR said, in his clearest, smoothest voice yet: "Hey, I bet I know what happened."

13

Penelope waited for the explanation that was forthcoming, but the HHR had gone silent. He did this sometimes when winded after working himself into the philosophical state. Penelope could see him now, gazing off to the horizon, or else staring, rapt, at one of the lunging, open-mouthed fish mounted on his wall, pondering the Grecian Urn thrill of the never-ending catch. Or just too stoned to stop gaping. Finally he resumed speaking:

"Penelope, I stand corrected. You are the hottest babe on this site. I think the gal in the yoga pants is a pro pretending to be an amateur, so she's disqualified. Damn, you look good in that picture."

Penelope took no pleasure from her coronation as Ms. Paybacks Are Heaven. She'd listened to his non sequiturs plenty back when they were married, but didn't have to now. She found that her anger had returned.

"How did it get on there, if you didn't do it?"

"Oh yeah. I zoned out for a second. I got broken into about three months ago and the dude took all my money, all my girlie magazines, and all the weed he could find.

"I don't care about your stupid weed. What about that photo?"

"The guy was a perv. He left one magazine on the waterbed opened up to the centerfold. Like he was trying to embarrass me or something. I felt a little violated."

Penelope would have liked nothing better than to violate the HHR with a hookah to the head. She was about to let him have it when he whispered huskily, *smoke break.*

Penelope could do nothing but wait. The HHR moved at his own maddening pace. How had she ever been married to this guy? Granted, nearly all her friends had an HHR somewhere in their past, a fun, good-looking guy who was relaxing to be around. Of course she was the only one who'd felt compelled to walk down the aisle with hers.

The HHR announced his return from the incommunicado state by declaring:

"The perv who ripped me off sent that photo in, I guarantee it. I had it with my other erotica. He's a weird dude, I'm telling you, and likely sexually stunted. I could see him sending it in just to be spiteful."

"You really got ripped off?"

"Since when have I lied?"

This was true. The HHR got a lot of things wrong—facts, history, just about everything having to do with metaphysics—but he wasn't a liar. Up till now.

"You lied about burning all the photos."

"And I'm ashamed of myself for that. That was out of character."

Penelope could tell that the HHR was about to quote something about character or forgiveness from Duane Allman or Blue Oyster Cult.

"Okay, I believe you. But what am I supposed to do now?"

"I'll get Weasel on it."

"Weasel? I thought he was out in Colorado being a river guide."

"No. He hit his head on a rock and fell in the river. Ended up with hypothermia. He's only got like six toes now, Penelope. You should see him in flip-flops. He looks like a bad ear of corn. Anyway, he's fine. He's one of my mowers now."

"What's Weasel gonna do? One of his stupid prank calls?"

"Exactly," said the HHR, as if the problem was not only solved but trifling to begin with. He had the air of someone disappointed that his abilities had been so lightly tested.

"That won't work."

"Do you remember that lawyer he used to impersonate? Where he'd get all worked up and start saying *affidavit* and *deposed* and mess like that? He's still watching all those *Law & Order* shows. I can't believe you've forgotten how good his aggrieved attorney is. It might be his best persona."

It was an idiot's plan spun by an idiot. Yes, back in high school they'd spent many an afternoon drinking beer and listening to Weasel make prank calls to local businesses. To their ears, he'd sounded like the greatest character actor and voice impresario of all time.

Penelope could see this was the best she was going to do for the time being. And now, despite it all, she was feeling nostalgic for high school, and picturing the HHR with his Cupid locks and thinking about how free and easy things had been way back when. Soon he'd ask if she wanted to come over, and she knew that it would be fun and relaxing and that the sex would be good. Time to get off the line before she agreed to something she'd later regret just because she was feeling lonely and vulnerable.

"Okay," she said. "See what Weasel can do." And with that she hung up.

She took one last glance at her young self lying on that waterbed. She did look fairly smoking hot back then. A bit untamed, granted, compared to her mother's splendid sheen, but those were Afro times, weren't they? Nodding to this, she stood up and tightened a few of her more important muscles. She was a bit thicker, perhaps, than the gal on the waterbed, but she was still firm where it counted, still strong in the right places. She still had it. Definitely. That didn't mean she wouldn't like to kill the dude who posted that photo on the Internet. Seriously, what the hell?

She left George's office with a jumble of emotions running through her, but desperation to get out of the basement was paramount. It was time to get going, time to find that next awesome job in Hillsboro for a woman without a college degree. Cash was what she needed, and cash was what she was going to get. She could use her phone for that and not have to worry about any more surprises on George's debauched computer.

She entered the bedroom and roughly swept aside the Coonskins T-shirt she'd flung on the coverlet earlier. Underneath the shirt was something she hadn't seen before in her mad dash to rid herself of everything having to do with frontier roadhouses, another note typed on official Hillsboro Garden Club stationery. Serious business was again afoot.

```
Honey,

    I was afraid I'd miss you if you worked a double
tonight, but I talked to June again this afternoon
and thought I'd pass on some information. The very
good news is that Doozy is hardly snoring now, so
the earplugs might not be an absolute necessity
after all. The not-so-good news is that he has cured
himself by use of something called a Neti Pot. Doozy
saw an ad for it in Modern Maturity a few years back
and had one sitting in his closet all this time
(don't get June started on all the doodads he buys
and never uses. QVC is no longer welcome in their
home). From what June says, this is some device you
use in the shower to clear your nasal passages. A
saline solution, I think. June says it sounds like an
angry flock of geese when Doozy is going at it in the
shower, but it's worked miracles. June slept through
the night for the first time in years.

    June was so excited about this development that I
didn't have the heart to ask about the shower cleanup
```

afterward. We'll figure something out. Thanks for
being a sport.

Xxxxoooo

Mom

Thirty minutes later, Penelope was still lying on her bed, trying her best not to fret about Uncle Doozy and his flock of geese in her shower.

Or about some concerned citizen who'd called social services about a local unfit mother who enjoyed posing in the nude for amateur photographers.

Instead, she was daydreaming about what life would be like with a sophisticated gentleman, perhaps one from Pemberley at Derbyshire, when she heard noise from the floor above her. Her mother or George was laughing. And then one of them must have leaped for the bed, because there was a harsh squeak, followed by a scuff that might indicate legs of a bed moving unwillingly across a floor. Penelope froze. For a moment there was silence. She waited for the sound of gunfire and stomping horses, hoping against hope that the Western Channel could save the day. But then there was a loud clunk, as if a high-heeled shoe had roughly been flung from foot. And then another clunk, louder and cockier and sluttier than the first. There was no doubt about it now. Shoes were being flung willy-nilly in the room above her. Penelope fought against it as hard as she could, but her mother's elderly stockinged legs came firmly into focus. Still she held out hope. She could not be about to hear what she thought she was about to hear.

But hear she did, her ears as alert as a deer on the HHR's back forty during hunting season. Poor ears. Poor unfortunate ears. For now the bed was squeaking forcibly as one person above grunted softly while the other shouted orders like a captain on the bridge during a heavy storm.

"Right. Right. Right there George. Yes George. You are doing it George. You are doing it! Steady now. Steady Georgie Porgie. Steady."

Whether it was catuaba or yohimbe or some special blend just for seniors, George was definitely hitting the penis bark, and hitting it hard if her mother's vocalizations from ten feet above could be trusted. Who would have guessed she'd be so vocal, or so bossy, or so particular about tempo? In the last minute, she'd moved from storm-tossed sea captain to square-dance caller:

"Slower. Just a little slower. Yes. Yes. Like that. Now harder George. Harder. Harder and faster. Faster and harder. Yes George. Yes, yes, my curious George. Yes, yes, yes."

Penelope realized she currently inhabited some dystopian universe where sex-crazed fogeys gave full play to their bark-induced libido while their woebegone children were forced to listen.

Throwing on jeans, sandals, and the first T-shirt in the drawer to hit her hand, she left the premises like a scalded dog as her mother urged George down the homestretch like the seasoned jockey she apparently was:

"Attaboy, attaboy, attaboy George!"

14

She was sitting in the Target parking lot after killing an hour looking at cute clothes she couldn't afford. She wasn't sure where to go next. All she knew was that further exposure to the geriatric Summer of Love was out. Her car was getting hot, so she rolled down the windows and drummed her fingers on the steering wheel for a bit. She had complete freedom of movement and seven dollars to her name. She looked at her purse, sitting lumpy as a dissatisfied Buddha across from her. Including all the contents and even the purse itself, the whole bundle was worth about twenty-one bucks. Then again, if you counted the overburdened credit cards the purse contained, it was worth approximately negative six thousand dollars. She reckoned this was the brokest she'd ever been, and that was no small statement.

A family arrived and started to enter the car next to her, all of them pausing to gawk at her a bit, as if they found it odd for someone to be hanging out in a Target parking lot on a beautiful Saturday afternoon. She smiled and gave a little wave, then started her engine back up to give the impression of places to go and people to see. As soon as the family pulled out, she turned the motor off again, feeling ridiculous but smiling at her self-consciousness. Was this the same devil-may-care woman reclined on the HHR's waterbed? She thought not.

Now she was thinking about that stupid photo again. What were the odds of Weasel working his lawyer persona and getting that thing removed? Could you have a less than zero chance of success?

Not knowing what else to do, she reached for her purse, hoping she still had a piece of gum left. She didn't. But in her scramble, which ultimately included dumping the whole purse on the car seat, a phone number came fluttering out. Oh yes, she'd forgotten, the mother reading the smutty book at baseball practice. She said to call sometime. Well, this was sometime.

Penelope picked up the phone and dialed.

Penelope sat at the bar at Applebee's with Missy, mother of the individualistic second basemen. Missy was again wearing jean shorts and a rock T-shirt. In fact, she and Penelope were wearing the exact same Nirvana shirt, the one with the screwy-looking smiley face. They'd both had a laugh about that when meeting up at the hostess stand. Now she nursed a beer, painfully aware of her finances and nervous about agreeing to Missy's proposal of a running tab. Penelope had ordered a water in addition to the beer, thinking her costly beverage might last longer if she alternated sips. She concentrated on not being hungry, but in her heart of hearts, she wouldn't have turned up her nose at a complimentary peanut basket.

"Oh yeah, your husband is definitely dating a teacher," Missy said, slurping audibly at her frozen mango margarita. "All the evidence points to it."

Penelope nodded. She'd just laid out the Facebook case against James and hadn't spared the details. It was as she figured.

"Whose homeroom is Theo in, anyway?" Missy said. "That's where I'd put my money."

"Ms. Dunleavy," Penelope said, though she felt weird saying it out loud.

"Oh, I know that little floozy. She's one of Damien's teachers."

Penelope took a sip of water before replying. She was still a little freaked out about Missy naming her son after the Devil in *The Omen*. Her new friend hadn't actually said that her son's namesake was the cloven-footed one, but surely she'd seen the movie. Why not just name him Satan or Beelzebub? It'd be the same difference.

"Is she really a floozy?" Penelope asked. "She seemed kind of shy and withdrawn when I met her for the parent conference first of the year."

"Don't let looks deceive you. I've seen her in here about fifty times in the last two years. She's on the make, trust me on that. She's definitely Suspect Number One. Those glasses of hers aren't fooling me for a second."

Penelope did recall the glasses, but not much else about Ms. Dunleavy. She and James had just filed for divorce when they had to go to the teacher conference together. It was just one of those perfunctory things, where the teacher meets with about twenty parents in two hours' time. They were told that Theo's work was fine, though he spent too much time drawing Pokémon figures on his math homework and seemed to relish attention any way he could get it. Ms. Dunleavy hadn't mentioned it, but Penelope now surmised that his gastric shows for an audience had started way back in September.

Frankly, Penelope hadn't paid much attention to Ms. Dunleavy after she said Theo's grades were fine. She'd been too distracted by James's cowboy boots and western-style jeans shirt. It was too hot for either, but James liked to seem down-home and capable when meeting authority figures in Hillsboro, which he considered rural and beneath him. He was a Tarheel, after all. He was talking deeper than normal, and kept saying, *yes, I understand,* or *yes, that sounds like our boy,* in a way that touched her last nerve. He seemed to be posing as a well-educated artisan, the type who'd recently decided to quit the rat race and raise free-range chickens. He often did this when talking to people who wore glasses. The end result was that she'd been so distracted by James and the eco-friendly chicken coop he was going to build that she'd paid scant attention to Ms. Dunleavy.

"I know where she lives," Missy said. "We should drive by to see if your husband is there."

"Oh, I don't think he's over there tonight. He's got Theo this weekend."

Missy shrugged. "Maybe all three of them are doing something together. Watching a movie or making Sloppy Joes. You know little boys always have crushes on their teachers."

Penelope didn't like the sound of that. It was too soon for Theo to witness parents on a date. Especially if the date was a teacher he liked. James's place was already too much competition without throwing in that *x* factor. First the zipline, now this. Theo would want to stay over there all summer long. Making this possibility even more irritating was the thought of James using his *person-with-glasses* voice as he patiently explained to Theo and Ms. Dunleavy: *Of course, Anna Karenina is an opus in every sense of the word.*

Oh, she was being ridiculous. Missy had no idea what she was talking about. They weren't all watching *To Sir, with Love* together. That was crazy talk. Who knew if Ms. Dunleavy was even the teacher James was seeing. There were tons of teachers at that school. It could be anyone.

Now Missy was motioning to the bartender for another round. Penelope hadn't finished her beer yet and could hear the credit card whimpering from her purse. The villagers had raised the wooden stake and were about to plunge it through the Visa's dark and wily heart once and for all. Well, it'd been a good run.

As the second round was put on the bar, Penelope ventured into the neutral territory of motherhood, outlining Theo's recent troubles on the bus with bullies without going into the specifics of the names he was being called. Missy had seen his Shakira dance on the baseball field: no need to explain more.

"What are their names?" Missy asked. "I bet I know the little shitheads."

"It's several kids apparently. But the main one is Alex, I think."

"Oh hell yes. Alex Greer. And I bet Ty Turner is with him too."

"I think the other kid's name was Ty, now that you mention it. How'd you know that?"

Before replying, Missy took a long, aggressive sip from her margarita and spent several seconds savoring the salty residue on her lips. Penelope had to admire the relish with which she enjoyed her cocktail, and wouldn't have minded a frozen concoction herself.

"Damn that's good," Missy said. "So anyway, this little Alex shithead and his assface friend, Ty. Everybody in our neighborhood knows them. Damien rides that same bus."

Penelope was shocked at nine-year-old boys being the subjects of such frank analysis, but was hard-pressed to defend them. They'd turned her son into a laughingstock, after all.

"I know where they live too, both of them," Missy said. "If you want to go by there right now and confront their parents, I'll go with you. But before you do, you should know that their parents are shitheads and assfaces too, all four of them. One dad's a lawyer, and the other's on the school board. And their mothers sit around the country club pool all day drinking mimosas and making up stories about other women. Usually divorced women. So that ought to tell you something right there."

Penelope wasn't sure how much of this was fact or opinion, but nodded anyway. Sometimes the apple truly didn't fall far from the tree.

"I'm from Hillsboro," Penelope said. "And I've never even heard of these women."

"Well I'm not from here, and neither are they. We met through a mom's club when we'd all just moved to town. What a crock. All the married mothers would segregate themselves from the single ones and the divorced ones. It was basically class warfare every other Tuesday at Fort Funigan."

Penelope laughed at this, unsure if Missy was joking or not.

"I'm dead serious," Missy said, though she was cracking a smile. "They were too good to eat corn dogs like the rest of us. So they'd bring this olive loaf and salami and make muffulettas. Just this one little group of married Stepford wives, Sarah Greer and Blake Turner and all them. Muffulettas! Can you believe it? Like that's the height of classy or something. Like that's way better than a corn dog. Oh, and get this, they wouldn't let their kids have slushies either. Something about the artificial coloring. And God forbid one of them should sneak into the ball pit. *Alex, Alex, come to Mother, come to Mother. You're crawling in the poor kids' germs. You'll get tapeworm, Alex. Their mothers are divorced, Alex. You'll get head lice.* And then the hand sanitizer would just fly. Literally. Like just pouring the whole bottle on his head. It's no wonder he's the way he is. Seriously. He probably has some kind of sanitizer toxicity condition that hasn't even been discovered yet, and that's what makes him so mean. I'm just telling you, if you met Sarah Greer, all your questions about shithead DNA would be answered. Her and her olive loaf. Give me a break."

Penelope was laughing at all of this, believing hyperbole was surely at play.

"So anyway," Missy said, "do you want to go by their houses right now and have it out? Just tell them where they can stick their mimosas once and for all. Trust me, it won't be my first rodeo with them. Those kids used to give Damien the business too until I raised absolute holy hell."

"I am definitely not going by their houses tonight," Penelope said.

"You could wait for those brats at their bus stop on Monday, then grab them by the scruff of the neck and just shake the hell out of them. *You listen to me, you little sons of bitches. Do you hear me? Do you hear me, assfaces?*"

The bartender came over now and looked at Missy as if accustomed to such behavior from her.

"Missy," he said, "you can't just be screaming profanity. There's a lot of kids in here. You're going to get me in trouble with the manager."

"Gotcha, Super Steve. My bad. My friend here just got divorced last week and I'm trying to cheer her up. Penelope, this is Steve. Steve, this is Penelope. And for the record, Super Steve, her boyfriend is a muscle-bound cop who's crazy jealous. So don't be getting any of your big ideas about a little of the you-know-what."

Penelope gave her a look.

"Steve's super horny," she said.

Penelope could feel herself blushing, but the bartender simply said *nice to meet you, Penelope* and walked off, smiling and shaking his head.

Missy was chittering that wrenlike laugh of hers now and waving off Penelope when she claimed embarrassment.

"Don't worry about it. Look at him in those khakis. He's about as horny as a tube sock. He knows I'm joking. I'm here all the time and I tip like a mother. Don't think a thing about it. This place would go out of business if I stopped coming in."

"Okay, I'm not worried about it," said Penelope. "But back to Damien and those kids on the bus. Were they just calling him names?"

"Lord no. Wedgies. Wet Willies. Indian burns. You name it. They had their hands all over him. That's what got me so pissed."

Theo hadn't mentioned anything other than name-calling, but that didn't mean it wasn't happening. That settled it. She would have to take the bull by the horns next week or this would be hanging over her head all summer.

As if reading Penelope's mind, Missy said, "What about this? Contact Ms. Dunleavy and set up a conference to talk about Theo's situation. She can alert the principal or the parents or however they're supposed to handle shitwad kids. And the whole time you're just checking her out. If she's really nervous and fidgety, you'll know she's the one who's banging the hell out of your husband."

"I didn't say they were banging."

"Oral then. Whatever. They're doing something, I guarantee that. She's a spicy little thing. Don't judge a book by its cover. I'd bet my last dollar she's banged a couple of dads right there under the multiplication tables."

Penelope was skeptical but didn't say so. Meanwhile, Missy had her phone out and was typing away. Then she was thrusting the screen at

Penelope and saying: "There's her email. Go ahead and contact that spicy little piece of ass and let's see what she's made of."

"I'm not contacting her right now."

"Hot for Teacher. *Mr. Holland's Opus.* You've got the clues. Now you just need hard evidence. Face-to-face proof. If she's doing what we think she's doing—blowjobs in the parking lot—she'll be jumpy as hell. Plus, don't forget, you're handling Theo's deal. You're being a good mom and also getting the dope on your sex-addict husband. It's a no-brainer."

Penelope weighed the e-mail address being wiggled inches from her face. She'd already decided to contact Ms. Dunleavy, but did she have to do it now?

"You're thinking about it, aren't you?" Missy said. "You know why? Because it makes perfect sense. Two birds. One stone. No more bullies and we solve the hot-for-teacher mystery. Or at least rule out one as a suspect. You've got nothing to lose."

Penelope thought any solution hatched by Missy was unlikely to make perfect sense, but why put off the inevitable? She took out her phone and composed a short, formal e-mail to Ms. Dunleavy requesting a conference at her earliest convenience to discuss a bullying situation on the bus. Beside her, Missy nodded aggressively and sucked on her mango margarita, murmuring, *Now you're talking. Now you are talking.*

15

"All right, I'm starving. What say we order some food?"

"I'm not really hungry," Penelope said.

"I don't believe you."

"Don't believe what?"

"That you're not hungry."

Missy pushed herself back from the bar and turned until she was facing Penelope. Penelope sat where she was, trying not to be unnerved by the wild woman's interrogating gaze.

"Let's see," said Missy. "You're living with your mom like a recently graduated philosophy major. Nursing two beers and looking at my margarita with lust in your eyes. Drinking about a gallon of water, likely trying to fill up. Yanking head toward kitchen every time the door opens. You're broke, honey, aren't you? Come on, you can tell me. Nothing to be ashamed of."

"I'm just not hungry."

"Liar liar pants on fire. You're broke and I'm buying dinner."

"I can't let you do that."

"The hell you can't. You've got no pot to piss in. Why don't you tell ole Missy all about it?"

Penelope shook her head, but she could feel the words welling up. Then they came tumbling out in a torrent.

When she finished the summary of her last day at Coonskins and the depths of her financial straits, Missy reached over the bar and grabbed a couple of menus. She passed one to Penelope.

"Honey," she said, "I can get you a job. In fact, you've got a job. I just hired you. You start Monday. Now what are we going to eat? It's my treat, and I won't hear another word about it. But first things first—Super Steve, get this gal a margarita. She's got some catching up to do."

Penelope was sipping on a fresh mango margarita, her head spinning from the recent turn of events. They'd spent the last few minutes surveying the menu and getting their orders in, so Penelope had not yet ascertained the exact nature of her job, other than it was some kind of office work.

"Are you sure I'm qualified?" she asked.

"Overqualified if anything," Missy replied.

"But you haven't seen me do anything but watch little kid baseball and drink beer."

"Exactly. You're perfect."

"Okay, but what kind of job is it?"

"Receptionist, mostly."

"Where?"

"At a trailer park."

Penelope's face must have shown surprise, for Missy sighed deeply and pushed her margarita away with no little drama.

"All right. I was gonna wait till Monday to give you the lowdown, but I can tell you're not going to let me drink in peace until you get every last scrap of information about your pending employment, so here goes. My dad owns or manages a string of trailer parks, or, as he prefers to call them, *mobile home communities*, though I've never seen any of these fuckers get up and hit the road. But whatever. Actually, I think I'm supposed to call them *manufactured homes* now. They change the name about every two weeks, but they're trailers. I'm vice president of the company, and I move around every few years when we start a new community to troubleshoot until it gets up and running. Anyway, my dad just wants me to prove that I can work before I inherit the company in a few years. He doesn't want me to be a spoiled little rich girl, which is unfortunate because I think I could really grow into that role. Just sitting around eating muffulettas and chatting with some friend named Bridgett about bronzer and tennis skirts all day."

"Wait. How many manufactured-home communities are we talking about?"

"Around eighty."

"And your dad owns or manages all of them?"

"Yep."

"And you're going to inherit all of it?"

"The whole enchilada, yep. I'm a trailer park heiress is what I am. I'm the hillbilly Paris Hilton. So yeah, honey, I'm richer than God. Now can I get back to my mango marg?"

"Last thing. What will I do in the job, and—"

"How much will you get paid?"

"Yes."

"I don't know. How much do you need? Pitch me."

"At least as much as I was making at Coonskins."

"That's your salary pitch? That's how you negotiate? Come on, sister. Show some sack."

"I don't know how much I need. Wait, yes, I do. I need to make enough so that I can move out of my mom's house before June 28th."

"Why that date?'

"That's when my aunt and uncle come, and if I'm not out of there by then, we're all roommates down in the basement and sharing the same bathroom. Can you imagine a seventy-year-old man using a Neti Pot in the shower? Cause that's what I'm looking at. I'd have to use galoshes in there for the rest of my life."

Missy sucked thoughtfully on her straw. She seemed to see where Penelope was coming from. "So," she said, "while your dear hubby is out nailing every teacher at Jackson Elementary, you're watching *Matlock* reruns and drinking warm buttermilk with the folks."

Penelope hated to interrupt but felt she had to. "It's much worse than that."

"Wow. That's all I can say. Worse than drinking buttermilk on a scratchy sofa while watching *Matlock* and it's about 150 degrees in the house? I'm imaging my grandparents now, but regardless, I see your situation loud and clear, and the heart bleeds."

Penelope was about to go into a few of the less graphic details about her mother, the randy square dance caller, but Missy cut her off.

"All right, I've heard enough," said Missy. "Actually, I haven't heard much, but I've imagined a lot, so same diff. I'll have to okay the salary with the old man, but I think I can safely say that you will make at least as much as you did at Foreskins. As for your job, I don't know yet. Probably taking checks from the tenants and logging them in and answering the phone so that I don't ever ever have to talk to another tenant with a drain problem for as long as I live. Oh, and you'll have to go to lunch with me. Now for the love of God, can we stop talking about work? It's Saturday night, for crying out loud, and we don't have our kids. We should be bopping half the bar by now."

Smiling, Penelope took another delicious sip of the margarita. Soon, food would be coming her way, both an appetizer and an entrée. She could hardly believe her luck. What a reversal of fortune after the day's rough start. And to think that Rachel and Sandy had been questioning her ability to find solid friends without their guiding hand. She considered sending them an in-your-face text, but they didn't deserve even that after abandoning her for their families over the weekend. They'd just have to wait to hear the good news. It would serve them right, the proud marrieds. And humming the tune "Proud Mary," but substituting "Proud Marrieds," she dove headlong into her icy-cool cocktail.

They'd just finished dinner and were contemplating whether to stay at Applebee's or try one of the other options a hopping little burg like Hillsboro had to offer middle-aged women out on the town. In other words, should they stay put or check out the hordes of interesting, available men across the interstate at Outback Steakhouse?

Missy excused herself to go to the bathroom and Penelope pulled out her phone. She planned to see if Fitzwilliam had replied to her message, but somehow, without meaning to, found herself on the Facebook page of her ex-husband.

Shaking her head at her obsessed and disobedient fingers, she began scrolling through James's timeline. She noted two new photographs. The first was a shot of her son's bat making actual contact with a thrown cowhide sphere. The fact that his eyes were closed and his mouth twisted in gargoylian recoil couldn't alter the fact. He'd hit the ball. She felt pride coursing through her, a lot more than she would have thought possible if you'd asked her about this only the day before.

And she'd missed it. Damn it to hell, she'd missed it.

Meanwhile back to her detective work. The second addition to James's timeline was a photograph of a black puppy running past the camera in profile, as if chasing a recently thrown object. The caption read: *Not sure who is more tuckered, me or my new buddy.*

Penelope stared long and hard, her instincts alive and twitchy. A puppy was better—a ton better—than a zipline as an inducement for Theo to spend more time at Dad's house.

But something was off. James's run-ins with Hillsborian canines were a matter of public record. You could ask anyone in their old neighborhood. This battle between man and dog was worthy of Jack London and stemmed from the fact that no one in the universe could find a dog's leavings and then step in them like her ex. The crux of his ire was that the leavings that he continually stepped in were in their yard, yet they owned no dog.

It became his obsession to find the culprit, the owner who allowed his charge to use James's beloved fescue as a public lavatory then refused to clean up afterwards. Penelope couldn't begin to count the hours he spent standing at the window at dusk, armed with flashlight and binoculars, hoping to catch the owner/dog in the act. He'd considered night-vision goggles, but found the cost prohibitive.

Penelope had laughed and laughed to herself about this obsession, as she could run across the yard all day long and never once soil her shoes. How James always managed to find the pile and she didn't was one of the delightful mysteries of their married life. When Theo was a toddler and making his first forays onto the lawn, James's obsession had turned truly mad. There simply weren't enough sticks for James to clean both his shoes and Theo's. Frantic, he decided to shame the negligent dog owner by chalking a poem in the road. The letters were three feet high and the completed lyric stretched from curb to curb.

DEAR LITTLE DOG,
IN YOUR YARD
THEO DOESN'T POO
SO WHY IN HIS YARD
DO YOU?

Penelope was smiling about the whole ridiculous affair when Missy returned. When her new friend was seated, Penelope displayed the photo of the mystery pooch.

"What do you make of this? James doesn't own a dog."

"That's the teacher's dog," Missy said, glancing at the photo for all of one second. "The BJ Queen. You can bet your bottom dollar on that. They're not just banging, though. They're a dog-at-the-park couple. They probably took a picnic basket too. I told you Ms. Dunleavy was a hot number. But what do you say? We staying here, or do you want to hit Outback?"

Penelope didn't like either choice. What she wanted was to lie in her bed in the guest room and stew about romantic dog-boy James and how much fun Theo had staying at his nice new house, then close out the day with a healthy dose of *The Stranger Within*. Unfortunately, she couldn't bail this early in the evening on the woman who'd just bought her supper and offered employment.

She was weighing the chain restaurant options when a tiny tinkling church bell sounded on her phone, the Divote app announcing that someone had just sent a virtual *box of chocolate*. In other words, she'd been candied for the second time.

Her suitor was none other than BrettCorinthians2:2. He still hadn't located a shirt, and he was still young, young, young. Penelope held the phone up to Missy.

"I have two questions for you," Missy said. "Who's the hottie, and where do we meet him?"

Penelope offered a brief overview of her new app, then explained how it was much better suited for Christians on the go than two divorcées in Nirvana shirts bellied up at the bar.

"I need a better look," said Missy. So saying, she snatched the phone out of Penelope's hand and put it as close to her face as she could.

"I just want to lick the screen right now. I want to rub anointing oil all over him. Look at that six pack. Praise Jesus and hallelujah, that is one hot Christian boy."

Penelope took back her phone and had another look. He *was* handsome, there was no disputing that. Athletic with broad shoulders and a good head of blondish-brown hair, though he kept it a bit shorter than she'd have liked. His grin was definitely cocky and Penelope thought of pride going before the fall.

"How old do you think he is?" Penelope asked.

"Old enough. Look at the grin. Tell me he's not begging to be corrupted. Send him some candy and let's see what happens."

"I don't think so. I haven't even been on a date since the divorce."

"What?" Missy said, her eyes practically bugging out of her head. "What are you waiting for? Time to get back on that horse and ride, ride, ride."

Penelope shook her head no.

"Do you have any other prospects right now, my picky, celibate pal?"

"Not really. Well, one guy did send me a message on LoveSynch. He seemed kind of interesting."

"Let's see him," Missy said, motioning for the phone. "Let's compare your suitors. I won't steer you wrong. You can trust old Missy when it comes to men."

Reluctantly, Penelope found the LoveSynch page, and then Fitzwilliam's **Portnal**, before handing the phone over with a sheepish smile.

Missy read over the totality of what Fitzwilliam had to say about himself in three seconds, then handed the phone back to her. In a faux British accent she said: "The old fart in the cardigan or the hot shirtless dude? Seriously, old chap, do give me a break."

Penelope smiled but didn't reply.

"Old chap. The night is young and Fitzwilliam is already in bed after his tea and jam and singing 'God Save the Queen' for an hour or so. Why not see what the young hottie is doing? What do you have to lose?"

Laughing and thinking *what the heck,* Penelope went back to Divote, swiped right to BrettCorinthians2:2's request to meet up, and sent a tiny *candy box* flying into virginal cyberspace.

16

The Divote app worked with the speed and efficiency it advertised, for twenty minutes after responding to BrettCorinthians2:2, Penelope and Missy found themselves at a lawn party with the young adult group from the largest church in town. They'd been quickly incorporated into the festivities, so much so that they were now sharing the same side of a beanbag toss game, waiting their turn to fling rosined cloth sacks filled with corn kernels in the hope of sliding one through a hole cut in the middle of a tilted board. *Cornhole,* as it was colloquially known, was the summer game of Hillsboro, and Penelope had thrown many a bag through a proud stag's antlers or the V and T of the Virginia Tech Hokies.

Despite her years of experience on the local circuit, the boards she was currently playing on were a first, decorated as they were with a polyurethaned graphic of Jesus wearing his crown of thorns. Penelope found the image more cartoony than was generally accepted for images of the son of God, his beard and mustache looking especially bushy and curlicued and his eyes too far apart and buggy. In short, Jesus looked like an alien deer with a beard perm.

The fact that his crown of thorns was the circle through which the beanbags were meant to plop added little gravity to his likeness.

"This is the worst decision I've ever made in my life," Missy said. "Like ever. You'd think they'd have hard cider or something at least.

How can anyone play this stupid game and not be drinking? I've never even seen it attempted before."

Penelope smiled. She wouldn't admit it to Missy, but she really enjoyed cornhole, drinking or sober, and had spent many a pleasurable hour playing. It didn't hurt that she and BrettCorinthians2:2 were routing Missy and her fellow across the way, another tall young dude with a body to kill for.

Both men wore backwards-turned baseball caps and long-sleeved pastel-colored dress shirts rolled up past the elbow. The shirts were tucked into Bermuda shorts. Penelope hadn't known that the preppy meathead look was even a possibility before now, but apparently it was all the rage, at least in young Christian circles, for nearly every fellow at the lawn party was similarly dressed. The young women primarily wore sundresses and flats. Everyone had been nice, despite the surprise entrance of the motorcycle mommas in matching Nirvana shirts, and Penelope found that she was having a good time.

"Can you see my pits?" Missy asked, raising her arms. "I'm sweating like a pig and it feels like I'm heading toward Frisbee Central down there."

"You're fine," Penelope said, picking up beanbags from the board and ground. It was the ladies' turn to throw. Last time out, Penelope had scored one through the thorny halo, and elicited a sprinting fist bump from BrettCorinthians2:2. He and his pal were a high-fiving, fist-bumping duo, and the crowd in general seemed poised at a moment's notice for a mass hand-jive celebration. She'd not known before how easily made jubilant was the young devoted crowd. They were a slap-happy bunch to be sure and the lemonade was going down by the jug.

But it was time to focus. Just one more bag through the crown that rested upon Cornhole Jesus's head, and her team would win. She handed the red bags to Missy and kept the blue for herself.

Missy said: "Do you think it's just a coincidence that I got the red bags? Or has the Osmond family here definitely marked me as one of the Devil's own?"

Penelope thought again of Missy naming her son Damien but didn't mention it. She was trying to concentrate. Her earlier peanut throwing session at Coonskins had warmed her up nicely and she felt zeroed in on the target. Missy, on the other hand, was wilting like a skinny brown flower under the humid night, the hearty fellowship, and the slow death of her margarita buzz. She'd yet to score a point for her team, and more often than not couldn't manage to fling the bag the full distance to the board. The fact that every song on the stereo belonged to the Christian rock genre wasn't helping her pep either.

"Do they have even one song that doesn't have *Jehovah* in it?" Missy asked. "It's a damn hard word to rhyme. *Noah. Leaf blowa. Tabula Rasa. Crimson and Clover.* That's Joan Jett. God, I love Joan Jett. I mean, *Jehovah*, I love Joan Jett."

She began to sing now, quietly, so no one but Penelope could hear.

> *O Jehovah, bring me a whiskey and soda*
> *Or maybe a mimosa*
> *I'll drink it in my Toyota*
> *And let that Christian boy turn me ova*

Finishing the verse, she flung a bag sidearm—like the heaviest of hand grenades—where it landed three feet shy and far to the left of the board.

"Cornhole Jesus, I'm bad," she said under her breath. "And how much longer does this last? I need to sit this cornhole of mine down before I pass out from crappy music. And do my ears deceive me, or is this song called 'Love Song for Jesus'? OMG. My bad. OMJ. I'm serious, it's not enough that even in his leisure time Jesus has to wear a pricker bush on his head, or that his face is getting pounded every three seconds by bags of corn. But he also has to listen to this music? As for me, I choose crucifixion."

"You're going to hell," Penelope said, smiling.

"Honey, I'm already there."

Across the way, their dates had put their heads together and were singing in a hammy sort of way to 'Love Song for Jesus,' which was about a field of blooming dandelions along a lonely country road and the impression the image made on the singer as he drove by on his motorcycle, namely that everyone was a flower and not a weed.

"Seriously," said Missy. "This is the worst thing I've ever heard. Now come on, let's get this game over with and skedaddle out of here with the Ken dolls back to my place. God, they're cute. What do they want with a couple of old broads like us? You don't think this is some kind of missionary work, do you? And before you answer, just know I passed up about a hundred puns just now. Seriously, look at all the cute young girls here, just ready to breed and watch *Duck Dynasty* till the cows come home. Something's fishy, but do I give a damn? No I do not. Mommy Barbie wants her baby Ken and doesn't care how she gets him."

Penelope was laughing at Missy's monologue and put too much mustard on her third throw, the bag skidding off the board, the thorny crown not slowing it down a bit.

For her fourth and final effort, Missy offered up a two-handed granny toss that went higher up than it did out before landing halfway between the boards in a sad cloud of talcum powder.

Missy's partner, the blond in the pink, not yellow Oxford shirt, said: "Use your legs and put your caboose in it a little bit more. You're just using your upper body."

Missy nodded and said under her breath: "I'm saving my caboose for later, you hot little missionary you."

Penelope vowed to concentrate on her last throw. It was dark now and she was getting a little tired. It was time to head home. Brett, her date, if that was what this could be called, wasn't her type. She wasn't sure what her type was, but knew it was a little less backwards-cap and young than this. A little less *Bro* and *Bru* and *Brah,* which Brett and Brandon felt the need to say every ten seconds or so. She was having flashbacks to *Dog, the Bounty Hunter,* one of James's favorite shows when he felt like slumming it and seeing how the other half lived.

Damn it to hell, she was back on James and sexpot Ms. Dunleavy and the mystery puppy on James's timeline that Theo would want to spend all his time with. Anyway, forget all that. She needed to throw this bag through a crown of thorns and get the hell out of Gethsemane before she was roped into prolonging the night at Missy's house.

So thinking, she swung her arm back and released with the smoothest of follow-throughs, the bag rising in the air with a graceful arc and landing—nothing but net—dead center in the middle of the board.

Brett let out a whoop, did the six-shooters motion at his bro, Brandon, then sprinted toward her.

"Praise Cornhole Jesus, it's over," Missy said.

Brett had hands raised for the double high five, which Penelope obliged. And then she was offered the double fist bump, which she also obliged.

"Seriously," Brett said, "that was totally sick. You're a cornhole queen."

Penelope could see Missy smirking beside her as Brandon walked over to join the group. The word *sick* as currently employed was a new one for her, but she assumed it must be the next *awesome* in dude lexicon.

"Hey," said Brandon, pointing toward the patio where people were starting to gather. "It looks like Sonshine Funk is about ready to jam. You gals will love this. It's kind of Jars of Clay meets Pearl Jam. They rock hard."

Penelope looked and saw several men in goatees and hip glasses setting up their amps and microphones. They smiled and bantered with the crowd in a familiar way, and as they did, Brett and Brandon sprinted off for more lemonade. They seemed eager for the show.

Penelope noticed Missy staring at the musicians and said: "You look confused."

"I am. What are they?"

"I think they're a praise band."

"A what band?"

"Praise. It's a rock band for church."

"Rocking Christians? Hipster church? It's oxymoronic."

"I guess, but it's kind of the wave of the future. They made a half-hearted attempt at my church but all the fogeys raised too much Cain."

"I mean, what the hell. Is nothing sacred? We're talking rock and roll, for the love of Jehovah. I don't think it should be tampered with and muddled up with a bunch of *hosannas* and *kumbayas*. That's what campfires and acoustic guitars are for. I say just leave the electric guitar out of it and dance with the one that brung you, pump organs and the Vienna Boys' Choir. Christian rock makes me sad."

Penelope basically agreed but didn't want to egg Missy on. They were guests, and she didn't want to appear disrespectful. To each his own, she felt, especially when it came to music. Hard as it was to believe, not everyone loved Van Halen.

"Listen," said Missy, "this band could be so bad I'm tempted to stay, but if I drink one more glass of lemonade, I'll be floating in my own Sea of Galilee. Seriously. My bladder is about to pop, but I'm too scared to go to the bathroom in that house. I bet that's where they store the brainwashing juice."

Missy was smiling and nodding in a spastic way to her own sentiments, and Penelope wondered if she might be suffering from a minor overdose. Lemonade was Christian moonshine, after all, and Missy was likely unaccustomed to its sugary power.

"Good," said Penelope. "I'm ready to go home too. Let's get out of here."

"Oh, we're not going home. We're going to invite Bryce and Brant or whatever their names are over to my house for a little dip in the pool."

"Brett and Brandon."

"Right. Got you. Which one's mine?"

"The one in the pink shirt. Or either, actually. Take your pick. I'm not interested and I've got to get home. I'm beat."

"Are you kidding me? You're not thinking about Fitzpatrick, are you? I can assure you that at the moment he is running a lint brush over his trusty cardigan. Then two cups of Earl Grey before lights out. Trust me. I know a boring old coot when I see one."

"It's Fitzwilliam," Penelope said.

"Of course it is. Now when are you ever going to have guys this cute, this fit, and this young interested in you again? It's like we're in a Christian sci-fi experiment. They've got some kind of machine in there, fueled by potato salad and lemonade, and they're spitting out hotties every fifteen minutes. It would be un-American not to at least try and take a couple home with us."

There was something to Missy's lemonade theory. Dale Mercer, the boy she'd led to the fallen state in high school, had chugged it by the gallon just before thumping away on the outside of her jeans. Perhaps, thought Penelope, it was the very fuel for his tireless jackhammering motion. But now Brett and Brandon returned with four fresh glasses. Penelope had worked up a thirst during her cornhole domination so she took her glass eagerly.

"Hey," said Missy, smiling at Brandon. "I know this band is going to be sick, and that they rock super hard, but Penelope and I are about to head back to my house for a swim. You guys should join us."

Brandon looked at Brett, who nodded back to him, as though agreeing that this was the proper time to pose some question or make some statement they'd agreed to while fetching the jackhammer juice. Brandon straightened his baseball cap until it was perfectly backwards. It had looked backwards to Penelope before, but he seemed fussy about it being just so. One of them had made a quick stop at the bathroom as well, because the tang of body spray wafted in the air like a goatish night flower. Penelope sneezed, and Brett took one subtle step back.

"Listen," said Brandon, looking at Missy with his liquid brown eyes, his perfectly backwards hat lending authority to the moment. "We're having a great time, but me and my amigo here were wondering if you two have a personal relationship with Jesus."

"So you're asking me about a personal relationship that I might be having with a man?" said Missy, smiling devilishly. "Listen, honey, the first thing you should know about me is that I never kiss and tell. And I mean never. Now do you want to go swimming or not? Because me and *my amigo* are hitting the road."

17

This seemed like the exact type of situation that Rachel and Sandy would lecture her about or had lectured her about or were dreaming of lecturing her about. She was driving a twenty-something bro to go swimming at the house of a woman she'd met while that woman was reading a nasty novel at a little-kid baseball practice. Up ahead, Missy was being driven to her home by Brandon. Penelope's protests about being tired and not having a bathing suit and really just wanting to go home had fallen on deaf ears. This was not her first go as a wingman for a lusty girlfriend, and she'd do her part for an hour or so, but that was it. You had to draw the line somewhere.

In the passenger seat, Brett was going on about a dream he'd had the night before. The dream started with him flying, and then he was dunking a basketball from half-court as hundreds of cheerleaders yelled their approval. Anyway, basketball soon morphed into surfing, and he was awesome at that too, even though he'd never tried it in real life. Unfortunately, right when he was really starting to hang ten, a massive white shark came up and tried to attack him. Luckily he woke up in the nick of time. One more second and dream Surfer Brett was done for.

In the middle of recounting this, he'd reached over and turned down the volume on the car stereo, which was playing Led Zeppelin's "Immigrant Song." Penelope found this off-putting but had listened to his dream patiently nonetheless. When she was married, James hated listening to recaps of her dreams, this despite the fact that she had really interesting ones and could recall them fully and in Technicolor. Of course, when it was *his* dream, he couldn't talk about it enough. Most of these involved a doomsday scenario and his archery coming into play. Dream James had slain all kinds of things that were menacing his family, and after one of these heroic nocturnal episodes, he could be found rosining his bow at the kitchen table. Penelope had seen him use the bow twice in all the years they were married. It cost twelve hundred dollars. And that didn't include the arrows, tips, targets, rosin, and subscription to *Modern Day Robin Hood* magazine.

And still he complained about the length of her showers.

The HHR, on the other hand, had loved to hear about her dreams and would often interpret them during his morning wake-and-bake sessions. Almost all of these interpretations came round to Penelope's subconscious feelings about sex and fishing.

She'd spaced out for a bit, distracted by the low volume of "The Immigrant Song." It didn't sound right so soft. Now she realized that Brett was waiting for a reaction to something he'd said, so she asked him to repeat it.

"I said that I took this dream interpretation class at Liberty, and I'm pretty sure that shark represents Satan."

"If the shark is Satan," said Penelope, "then what about the flying and the dunking and the cheerleaders? What do they represent? Awesome stuff in life that he's trying to distract you from?"

Brett nodded vigorously to this and shook his pointer finger in the classic *that's what I thought at first* motion as perfected by every high school science teacher Penelope ever had. Mr. Chaney had wagged that exact finger just before exploding a methane-filled soap bubble in her shocked hands during chemistry.

"No," said Brett, turning the stereo all the way off. "All that other stuff is Satan too, but I didn't realize because I was too tempted by it. The surfing is me trying to escape the corporeal world before it's too late."

Penelope was perplexed by how dunking a basketball could be associated with Beelzebub, but she wasn't prepared to travel very far down this conversational road. The young man beside her was, after all, en route to an empty house with a woman he'd just met, and no one who'd been to an American high school could fail to associate night swimming and sex. Or at least reasonably heavy petting.

Penelope sure made that association. She'd first hooked up with the HHR when Reggie Mason, the dentist's son, invited some people in the Burger King parking lot to his house while his parents were away. One thing had led to another, and she and the HHR ended up making out in Dr. Mason's study, under his diplomas, with Metallica and bug spray wafting through the open window. She was weighing whether to take off her wet bra, both because she liked the HHR and because it was starting to rub raw, when the cry of *Cops!* sent them scurrying out the back sliding door and over the fence. They'd all ended up back at Burger King, and from then on she and the HHR were a couple.

As for young Brett, swimming would be the beginning and the end of any encounter he might be hoping for. She was forty, after all, not some teenager at the dentist's house, but it was messing with her stereo during "Immigrant Song" that had absolutely, no question, proved his Waterloo in the make-out department. Having no taste in music was one thing; being rude was quite another.

He was currently smiling in a pleased way at something on his phone, and Penelope considered why a guy like him needed a dating service. Missy was right. There were a ton of cute, age-appropriate girls at the party they'd just left.

Then a thought struck her. Was this virile boy possibly gay? He and his bro Brandon had not been sparing in their chest-bumps during cornhole. Could the shark in his dream be the desire he refused to face?

Yes, of course it could. It was all beginning to make sense. She and Missy had been invited to the cookout so Brett and Brandon could be seen with single women at a social gathering. This would explain their reluctance to date—or already be married to and breeding feverishly with—the bevy of cute girls from the contemporary service. And now the rumors would fly about them leaving with two middle-aged women to go swimming. At night. Talk about salacious. They'd be the scandal of the young adult group. But a *heterosexual* scandal, and one where nothing actually happened. Dale Mercer and his fall from grace all over again! But without the fall!

She and Missy were beards.

This notion made her smile for reasons she couldn't fully fathom, though it likely had to do with getting credit for a fall from grace without having the blue rubbed completely off her jeans.

Brett said, "What?"

"Oh, nothing. You're probably right about that shark."

Brett nodded in a satisfied way, then told her more about his job at Verizon. He'd already told her plenty, but cell phones and their apps were his calling. She'd heard about his college, and his high school soccer days in Lynchburg, and also a fair amount regarding his mother and father. Almost all this information had come as a response to Penelope's queries. On the other hand, he'd yet to ask her anything about herself. Not about her job or whether she was from Hillsboro or whether she had kids. Penelope found this weird, but maybe he was still too young to know that conversation required questions and answers from both parties. Thinking of two-way discourse made her think of Fitzwilliam Darcy and whether he'd responded to her message or ever would. Maybe the poem had been a dumb idea. Oh well. She probably wasn't ready to date anyway.

In the car ahead, Brandon was turning into a nice neighborhood. Meanwhile Brett firmly recommended an app that counted your cardio exertion throughout the day. Now Brandon drove tentatively down a cul-de-sac, stopping, then starting again, as if the copilot had forgotten where she lived. Suddenly he slammed on the brakes, and Penelope had to lock up quickly as well. Brett was unperturbed, even with his head being yanked forward, and was no worse for wear after adjusting his cap to its proper backwardness. The cardio app, he confided, was solely responsible for his current body fat percentage of seven.

Now Missy was out of Brandon's car and tromping across the yard toward Penelope, motioning for her to roll down the window.

"Well," she said, sticking her head in and smiling, "here it is."

"Your house?"

"No. I live in Wooded Acres. This is you-know-who's house."

"Who? What?"

Missy backed out of the window to an angle where Penelope could see her but Brett couldn't. She then opened her mouth, stuck her tongue in her cheek, and made a rapid motion with her hand. Penelope had always found this gesture more graphic than necessary and was confused by it to boot.

"I don't get it," Penelope said.

"BJ Queen," Missy whispered.

Penelope gave her friend a quizzical look.

"Ms. Dunleavy's house," Missy said. "It's time to get to the bottom of this James situation once and for all."

So saying, she stomped toward the front door, leaving Penelope frozen in her seat. The only light in the house was a faint bluish glow from the TV in the den. Realizing things were on the verge of getting out of hand, Penelope popped out of the car, gently shutting the door behind her, and jogged toward Missy as quietly as she could. A dog had started to bark next door and Brett hung his head out the window and said, "Hey, what's going on?"

Penelope shushed him over her shoulder as a porchlight came on at the home of the barking dog. Penelope grabbed Missy by the arm and drew her to a stop.

"Are you ready for Freddy?" Missy said.

"No, I'm not. Now get back in the car before someone calls the cops."

"You mean your cop boyfriend? Now that would be a scene, wouldn't it?"

It took Penelope a moment to remember the joke with the bartender from Applebee's.

"What if your husband is in there right now getting a hummer?" Missy said, smiling and nodding at the door. "God, I'd love to see the look on his face when we come busting in."

"James isn't in there. And we're not busting in anywhere. If there's anything to find out, I'll find out at the teacher conference. Now get in the car before you get us in trouble."

"All right, all right. Don't get your panties in a wad. I'm leaving."

Penelope sighed and let go of Missy's arm.

At which point her new friend sprinted to the front door, rang the bell, then raced back to Brandon's waiting car.

"Book ass!" Missy yelled.

And Penelope did.

18

She was in a hot tub with Missy while the hot Christians frolicked boisterously in the pool. It had taken a while to calm down after fleeing Ms. Dunleavy's, but she felt okay now.

"Hey," said Penelope. "I told Brett that I didn't know whose house that was you rang and ran. I don't want to get into the whole James-and–Ms. Dunleavy thing with these guys."

"Too late," Missy said. "I already gave Bluffton the scoop on the way over here."

"No you didn't."

"Don't worry about it. My little hottie promised not to mention your ex—or his taste for backseat BJs—to your little hottie until they get home. It's all cool."

"You didn't actually talk about oral sex to that boy, did you?"

"Of course not," Missy said, fanning herself dramatically in the bubbly hot water. "I respect his biblical upbringing. So I simply referred to it as *parking lot sodomy.*"

"That's not what it is."

"It's both, my friend. Look it up."

"Those are two quite different things."

"Tell me about it, sister."

"There should be two different words then."

"I couldn't agree more. Maybe *sodomy* and *bobomy* or something."

Saying this, she'd bobbed her head downward in a rhythmic motion, smiling as she did so. *"And verily, Ms. Dunleavy committed bobomy on one whom she had not yet lain with in marriage and was thusly stoned."*

Penelope realized she was having a semantic discussion about sexual acts that likely weren't happening, at least not in the school parking lot, and let the matter drop. She also staunched an impulse to offer her Brett-and-Brandon-as-suppressed-lovers theory, and its corollary that they were beards. No need for that. Not when her friend had such high hopes for an erotic romp with a hunky boy.

Now she was sweating like a pig and feeling chafed under the suit Missy had loaned her, which was two sizes too small. She'd entered the water wearing her Nirvana shirt to be modest, but was now lamenting the drive home in wet garb. In the pool, the fellows were having a grand time, wrestling and roughhousing in a manner Penelope found potentially telling. They were laughing and talking, but Penelope couldn't hear what they had to say over the music that cranked from the outdoor speakers. Missy had chosen The Clash to cleanse her bruised ears after "Love Song for Jesus" and was definitely getting her money's worth from the volume knob.

"Aren't you worried about the neighbors?" Penelope asked.

"They're old and deaf on this side," Missy said. "And out of town, I think, on the other. Don't worry about it. My neighbors love me."

Penelope thought this a dubious claim, but didn't say so. The bros were now jostling each other about who would next use the diving board, their upper torsos glistening in the light from the pool as they pushed and pulled each other toward the water. Looking at their ultra-smooth chests, Penelope recalled the phrase her mother used when giving her a bath as a child—*clean as a whistle*—but immediately regretted this thought. The phrase had taken on a grave new meaning with her mother. Regardless, these boys were serious about their grooming. They were slick as seals.

She considered again what Sandy and Rachel would say if they could see her now. They were always so disapproving of her wilder friends, her *non-them* friends. But didn't they realize that she was *their* wild friend, supplying them, she was sure, with all kinds of vicarious thrills—and likely the occasional moment of catharsis too—that came with the inexplicable things that seemed to happen to her? Didn't they realize that? It was a double standard.

Regardless, it was time to get the show on the road, help Missy out long enough to make a move with Brandon, then head home. She was exhausted.

"Hey," Penelope said. "You guys should join us. It feels great in here."

After giving Brandon one last heave over his shoulder and receiving one more arm bar under the crotch and then a flip into the water in return, Brett hopped out of the pool and made his way toward them, his wrestling partner close behind.

Penelope and Missy were sitting opposite each other with the hairless hot Christians in between. Missy was drinking a vodka tonic from a Big Gulp cup while Penelope nursed a beer just to be a sport and not make her friend look like the lone booze-hound. The Jacuzzi was large enough that no one was squished up against one another, and the result was they were spread out like points on a compass. At least initially. Every few seconds Penelope noted Missy drifting toward Brandon like one of the HHR's fishing bobbers on a windy day. Brandon either didn't notice or didn't mind as he yakked away about the heat of the tub and how much he was sweating. Brett agreed with the sweating comment and every so often removed his cap to cool his scalp and lovingly run his hand through his close-cropped hair. What he needed was more ventilation. The cap was acting like the lid of a teapot, keeping the steam in. But back it would go, neatly backwards. He really liked that cap.

"So," said Brett, sitting on the edge of the tub to cool off, "Missy tells us you're recently divorced, Penelope."

Penelope narrowed her eyes at Missy, who then passed the look on to Brandon. She wasn't yet sitting in his lap, but if the breeze kept up, the little bobber might get there yet.

"Hey," said Brandon to his bro, "I told you not to say anything."

"Oh, who cares?" said Brett. "It's not a big deal."

"It's okay," said Penelope. "I don't mind."

"And now your husband is hooking up with your son's teacher? Wow. That's crazy."

As Brett talked, he scooted in her direction, the cocksure smile from his Divote page making its first appearance of the evening. Across the hot tub, Missy and her young hunk were just about shoulder to shoulder and Penelope began to reconsider her forbidden-love theory. By all appearances, they were acting like regular Joes on the make, and pretty experienced Joes at that. Brett's knee brushed her own, and then his foot slid down hers.

Feeling trapped, Penelope said: "I don't know that he's hooking up with my son's teacher. I think he's dating a teacher. I feel pretty sure about that. Everything else is just speculation."

"We think there's some bobomy going on at the very least," said Missy, smiling her mischievous smile.

The guys exchanged puzzled looks as Penelope declared: "No we don't. You do, but I don't."

"What's bobomy?" asked Brandon, teasingly splashing Missy in the process.

"Wouldn't you like to know?" said Missy, hopping onto him and trying to dunk him under the water.

After he'd struggled free of her grasp, she said, "You started it. And paybacks are hell."

At this point, Brett placed his hand on Penelope's thigh and said, "Don't you mean paybacks are heaven?"

19

Brandon laughed so much at his brah's *paybacks are heaven* line that he had to dive under the water so as not to make a spectacle of himself. Penelope could feel her already hot face getting hotter and removed Brett's hand with a very firm yank. It was clear now that he didn't want her for a beard. He wanted her for the tan lines and come-hither finger on the HHR's waterbed. Unbelievable. The Christian playboy was mining for MILF gold.

Damn the HHR and his nostalgic porn collection so easily stolen. Damn the random weirdo who'd posted it on the Internet. If these choirboys had seen it, who else had? Was the red hair fooling no one but herself?

"What?" said Missy. "I don't get it."

"Me either," said Penelope, moving away from Brett's roaming hands and feet.

Brett gave her a skeptical look and shared a raised eyebrow with his bro across the bubbly divide. They'd obviously spent a fair amount of time comparing her Divote photo with the nudie shot on Paybacks. Damn the Internet. Damn these lubricious Sherlock Holmeses.

Before the interrogation could continue, the reflection of swirling blue lights came across the pool area. Penelope knew those lights and thought WTH? But that wasn't strong enough medicine. If ever there was a true *WTF* moment, this was it. Seriously. What in the F?

Missy knew those lights as well, for she shook her head angrily and said, "I don't believe it. Not again."

Penelope had never been the *I-told-you-so* type, but this was about the blaring music, she felt sure. If she got arrested on top of everything else, Sandy and Rachel would have a field day. They'd been licking their chops for a nugget like this, and the advice would come fast and furious. And the crafting suggestions! They'd have her on a potter's wheel morning, noon, and night.

"I think that might be the cops," Brett said, wide-eyed.

"No shit," said Penelope.

Brett's smirk was gone now and she wondered if this was his first encounter with the fuzz. Despite her own concerns about heading downtown, she found that she enjoyed watching the smug little hypocrite squirm.

Missy was out of the tub and heading toward the backyard gate, which a flashlight beam was approaching, accompanied by the squelchy feedback of a shoulder radio and a disembodied voice talking about a wreck on Jefferson Street. Penelope stood dripping near the pool. If need be, she'd run, just like the time at Reggie Mason's. Flight had always been the HHR's preferred method of dealing with the police, and Penelope considered this a sound philosophy.

Brett and Brandon, meanwhile, sat like statues, their matching caps and baby-smooth chests making them seem very young and very scared in the blue lights that flickered round the pool and in the trees overhead.

The cop was huge and had angry eyes. That he wore a mustache went without saying. Penelope knew a few guys on the force from high school, but she'd never seen this guy before. From what she surmised, he was not the type to let noise ordinances go unenforced.

Penelope thought a guise of remorse and contrition was the only way to go in a situation such as this, but Missy had other ideas. Her plan, evidently, was to meet the firm hand of the law with a firmer one of her own. She started by walking briskly toward the stereo, the flashlight shadowing her as she went. When she got there, she very dramatically flipped off the cop, using both middle fingers. It had been a while since Penelope had seen someone employ the double bird, and she'd forgotten how effective it was in conveying contempt. Then, just as dramatically, Missy turned the volume as high as it would go.

"Can you hear it now, Gary?" she yelled. "Is this loud enough for you?"

The cop ignored her but rapped the flashlight once very hard on the fence, before rounding on the two young altar studs.

"You boys get out of that tub," he shouted. "Now. And don't bother putting your clothes back on."

"They're not naked, you imbecile, you jackass, you big buffoon," Missy yelled.

The HHR would have frowned on this tactic for dealing with the men in blue, and so did Penelope. The flashlight was now shining in her face and she wondered if her bathing suit was on straight. But the big man found her uninteresting and flashed it back on Brett and Brandon, who were now dripping in their Bermuda shorts and looking more than a little vulnerable and exposed.

"What's the problem, officer?" Brett said, making a tentative step toward the policeman.

"Nobody told you to move, Junior. Just hold on to your little pecker for a minute. I'll deal with you when the time comes."

Penelope smiled at this line, and at Brett's face. He looked like a surfer who'd just been dumped from a tasty wave he thought he'd mastered. And were those sharks in the water?

"You think that's funny?" said the cop, wheeling on Penelope and shining his light in her face.

"Yes, actually," said Penelope.

"You think this is some joke? Is that what you're telling me?"

"I thought that one line was funny. That's what I'm telling you."

"You're George's stepdaughter, aren't you?"

"Yes."

"I play poker with him every now and then. He's a good old guy."

"He is."

"All right, you can go. And Missy, just head in the house and I'll talk to you in a minute. I want a word with these little smart-asses here. *What's the problem, officer? What's the problem, officer?*"

The policeman said this last part in a falsetto whine that Penelope could tell he saved for college boys and other young hotshots used to talking their way out of things.

During all this Missy had kept up a steady string of insults, many of them personal in nature, and a few specific about the officer's own gifts below the gun belt. If the gibes could be trusted, it took one to know one in the little-pecker department.

The officer was now standing in front of the Christian bros, his light bouncing from one scared face to the next. They stood at attention like soldiers meeting their drill sergeant for the first time, a drill sergeant who seemed to find their backwards caps nonregulation, for he brusquely turned one and then the other around to the traditional forward manner.

"If you're going to mess around with a cop's girlfriend," he said, "at least try to look like a man."

Penelope looked at Missy and whispered, "You're dating the cop?"

"No. Of course not. I mean I used to. But he's way too possessive, so I gave him the boot about month ago. He's taking it kind of hard."

Missy glanced toward the hot tub area, where the policeman had sent the young guys scrambling through their things for identification. As he waited he lightly, leisurely, pounded flashlight to palm. He looked to be milking the moment.

"I guess you can go," said Missy, turning back to Penelope. "This party's over, unfortunately. And right when those boys were finally starting to loosen up."

"You sure? I hate to leave you holding the bag."

"Hey, it's my bag. You were just hanging out for my sake anyway. So get along home, little doggie. Gary will stomp around for about ten more minutes trying to get them to wet their pants and that will be the end of it. Then he'll probably start crying after everyone leaves and beg me to take him back. That's what he did last time."

There was one question Penelope needed to ask, but she felt a little weird posing it under the circumstances.

Missy must have read her face, for she said: "You're still my favorite new employee even if you didn't get me laid. I'll see you Monday at the trailer park."

Penelope smiled, then grabbed her purse and sandals from where she'd left them by the sliding glass door. She had a job and she wasn't going to get arrested. Maybe her luck was turning after all. So thinking, she walked barefoot through the gate in a borrowed swimming suit, her wet sandals squeaking as she went.

20

She'd driven home without stopping for gas though she badly needed it. She still had the seven bucks in her purse but didn't feel she could risk another stop before reaching her bedroom. Trouble had her scent tonight, and she knew that if she stopped at the 7-Eleven, it would be the exact night it got robbed. So though the gas light was gamely dueling the veteran oil light for asshole preeminence, she'd driven home on fumes—the fumes of fumes—all but coasting into the driveway. She'd have to get her mom or George to follow her to the gas station in the morning before church.

Now she was lying in bed, trying to unwind. What a day. Definitely one of the five or ten weirdest of her life. More bad than good, but she'd finished strong. Tomorrow was a new day, and maybe Theo would change his mind about staying at his father's. She'd make Sloppy Joes and Rice Krispies squares, his favorites, and they'd have their own celebration about his first foul ball.

Feeling a little hopeful, she picked up her phone from the bedside table and immediately knew that it was loaded with communication, the likes of which would please, disappoint, and/or enervate her. She would be hard pressed to describe, even to herself, the intimacy of her relationship with her phone, platonic though it was. In a word: telekinetic.

And at the moment it was, if she could borrow a line from Sonshine Funk, *humming like unleavened bread in the great Baker's hands.*

First she checked her texts. She had one, a response from Ms. Dunleavy regarding the parent/teacher meeting for this week.

Ms. Lemon, yes let's meet about Theo. How does Tuesday at
4:00 work for you? Arlene.

Arlene? James was engaged in backseat acrobatics with someone named Arlene? Okay, Missy had obviously brainwashed her. Back to Tuesday. Did it work for her or didn't it?

It would have to. New job or no new job, she wasn't prepared to go the whole summer with Theo identifying as Fart Boy and Weird Turd every time he came across someone from school. And if it didn't get fixed by Wednesday, the last day of school, it would all roll over to next year. That was just the way bullies were.

With this in mind, Penelope texted: I will see you Tuesday at 4:00. She was dreading the meeting with Ms. Dunleavy.

But whatever. Summer was coming, summer was coming. Soon she'd be dodging the babies in their swim diapers at the city pool. Plus she had a new job. If her car could just hold on, or perhaps need only a minor adjustment to the defibrillator or whatever the hell was wrong with it, then she could be in her own place before Uncle Doozy turned her bathtub into his personal Kleenex.

Thoughts of her own place led to speculation about her new salary, which she tried to guess but couldn't. Nevertheless, just having the words *salary* and *apartment* lolling around in her mind pepped her up considerably and she felt ready to hear the voicemail, which always contained the most volatile of her correspondences, save for her mother's notes about Uncle Doozy. Putting a brave but curious ear to the receiver, she pushed *play* to hear her lone message:

Hey Penelope. Just wanted you to know that Weasel has
agreed to take the case. He's not sure if he's going to go with
invasion of privacy or libel or just straight trafficking in stolen

goods. He was toying with an intellectual property angle, with your naked form being the property in question, but he thought that might be too sophisticated for the pissants who are likely running this website. That's more a Supreme Court kind of case.

(Here ensued a short coughing fit, a pause, and then the gurgle and swoosh of water whirling swiftly through what Penelope assumed was the new chillum.)

Anyway, he tried out a couple opening arguments on me and they were damn good. You're in excellent hands. He's going to the library to check out the first three seasons of *Law & Order* just to bone up a bit. Maybe some *Boston Legal* if he decides to go for more of a civil-action angle. According to Weasel, it's six one way, half a dozen the other when it comes to the civil-versus-criminal approach to a case like this.

(Another pause, then a shout at someone to *Stop piling more wood, dumbass!*)

Hey, listen, I need to run. I got a brush pile going out back that I need to keep an eye on. The wind's picked up here like a mother, and I don't need the fire department on my ass again. I'll keep you posted on your personal matter.

Lord, how the HHR loved a slow-roasting collection of limbs and twigs. The dearth of open-burning ordinances was the primary reason he'd always live in the county, that and his distrust of city water. Septic or bust was the HHR's ironclad mantra. Anyway, Weasel was on the Paybacks Are Heaven case. She had zero confidence in his success, but it was sweet of him to try, and with only six toes to boot. Yes, it seemed sure that for all eternity she'd be lying under that mounted fish, a testament to youth and raging hormones and homegrown red-haired sinsemilla.

But now it was time to move on to the next potentiality for human interaction, her LoveSynch account. She didn't know why, but she was simultaneously dreading to get a message from Fitzwilliam and not to. He was old, but he was charming, Missy's comments about his cardigan and his fogeydom notwithstanding. Plus he was smart. Then again, so was James. Regardless, he'd replied and it was time to dive in.

My Dearest Elizabeth (aka TheosMom75),

Where to start? With an apology for my unforgivable delay in responding to your perfectly rendered message? With a standing ovation (can you hear me clapping from the mezzanine?) for your fusing of W C Williams and *Star Trek* into a brilliant expression of *joie de vivre?*

Suffice to say the heart flutters, the mind gallops, to think that one such as you blooms like a desert flower in the miasma of 21st-century Americana in which it is our fate to dwell.

Oh, but now I sound morose. And I am not! Indeed, I want to write a billet-doux to Hopefulness and the eternal human spirit just knowing that one such as you exists—a sprite, a kindred spirit—in this bedrock of Applebee's and 7-Elevens and box stores that sell everything under the sun save nourishment for the delicate soul. Optimism, I am your champion!

Kneeling beside my white steed of Hope, would I seem too forward, dearest Elizabeth/TheosMom75, if I proposed forgoing further flirts, Eiffel towers, and computer-generated blends to consider an actual human encounter, a *tête-à-tête,* as it were? We could work

out the details later but I think fine wine, an assortment of artisanal cheeses, and a Swiss chocolate or two
would be general starting points around which to center
a casual meeting of the minds.

Ever kneeling, gloved hand extended in friendship,
awaiting your response—

Fitzwilliam

Penelope thought about reading through this a second time but it was getting late. She did glance again at his photo and still couldn't tell if he was more oldish or just flat old. Did she care? He seemed nice, and at least he was trying to give the impression that he was a gentleman. From what she could tell, those were in short supply these days.

She was about to put her phone away and tuck in for the night when she realized that her telekinetic friend was not quite finished relaying messages from the outside world. She looked at the screen, running through her options. She checked her Facebook page, but there was nothing of interest, and then James's, but it was unchanged since the last time she'd cyberstalked him. That cute little puppy was still happily chasing that stick.

Wait, she hadn't checked Divote.

She went there right away to find it bursting at the seams with correspondence. She'd received a whopping seven *boxes of chocolates*, four *cherubs*, and one *Ten Commandments tablet*, an icon she'd not seen before. For a moment she considered how many of those commandments she'd broken that day and whether someone had reported her to the Divote authorities. But that seemed unlikely, and she didn't care anyway.

Buzzing all around her page was a *tiny angel* with a scroll in its hand. It was her first Divote message, from none other than BrettCorinthians2:2. He must have escaped from Missy's cop boyfriend after all.

Really enjoyed the photo of you on Paybacks Are heaven and thought I'd repay the favor. Let's finish where we left off in the hot tub sometime soon.

Below this was a photo. Penelope looked closer. The angle was so close she couldn't really tell what she was supposed to be looking at. Toward the bottom corner she could make out half a sandal. Extending up from that, what looked like a baby-smooth man's leg. So that thing in the middle of the frame?

No way. Seriously?

It was a penis. An Anthony Weiner if she'd ever seen one.

She paused to consider if there were women anywhere in the world who liked photographs that consisted exclusively of male genitalia.

She didn't know. As for herself, she found Brett's *objet d'art* as interesting as a slab of salmon in the display case at Kroger's.

She turned off her phone. It was way past time to hit the sack. Come tomorrow, she hoped to be playing the role of a mom again.

21

Sunday before church, she spent the last seven dollars to her name on gas. For a moment, she'd considered the classic $5.50/1.50, gas/ Slurpee split, but this was no time to splurge. She had to be disciplined if she wanted to save the two thousand dollars—or fifteen hundred, or maybe even a thousand, depending on how nice the place was—that she needed for an apartment.

She pulled into the driveway past her mother's Impala and parked next to George's pickup, a yellow 1970 Chevy named Daisy. It was in this truck that she'd learned to drive. George had taught her at Judge Wyatt's farm one Saturday afternoon after they'd gone fishing. She was fourteen and worm-grubby, but that didn't stop George from letting her drive all the way home once she got the hang of it, with Buck Owens playing softly on the eight-track, *I got a tiger by the tail*.

Quickly debarking, she gave Daisy a friendly pat on the hood, then trotted toward the house. She glanced at the boxes stacked in the carport that contained nearly all her possessions, then flung herself into the kitchen as if entering a lush oasis after a hot and trying journey. She had the house to herself without the risk of stumbling upon her naked mother, for she and George were antiquing and wouldn't be back till late afternoon. She breathed a sigh of relief at the thought of a G-rated home for a change.

Her plan was to do a load of Theo's laundry, change his sheets, and throw together the Rice Krispies squares. Then she'd give Theo a call to see if he still wanted to spend an extra night at James's. She hoped not, but wasn't going to hassle him about it.

But before she started on her mom duties, she had to read the note she'd just spotted on the kitchen counter. As with the others, it was typed on Hillsboro Garden Club stationery, which meant it was both official and time sensitive in her mother's eyes.

Honey,

I knew I'd miss you after church, so I thought I'd let you know that June called this morning. As I was afraid, the hypnosis didn't take and Doozy had another sleepwalking episode. He must have been swatting his "spatula" everywhere because several of June's antique lamps took it on the chin. Today he is going to purchase a border collie to watch him while he sleeps. Apparently these dogs are bred to herd sheep, so if Doozy starts sleepwalking, the dog will head him off before he knocks into anything that might hurt him or the furniture (June has been worried sick about her pressed glass collection).

Doozy's had his eye on this dog for a while. A friend of his in Waco raises them. According to the owner, the dog can really bark but only does so if his herding doesn't do the trick. Lord, Doozy is such a heavy sleeper the collie will be barking all night long.

Anyway, I don't know if it's better or worse news

that they will be bringing a dog for their visit. You
will likely hear some barking, but at least the dog
(whose name is Yapper) will keep Doozy from trying to
get you up for reveille like that time in the camper.
At least that's the theory.

Xxxxoooo

Mom

P.S.: Do you agree that the children's sermon
thing has about run its course? I'm not sure I can
hear much more about Joseph and his colorful coat.
There's a reason they invented Sunday school, in my
opinion.

So it boiled down to this:

As Doozy chased her around the basement with his spatula—regardless of her high opinion of his succotash—an unfamiliar dog would be rounding the whole gang up, cattle-drive style, like something on the Western Channel that George used to watch before he started snorting exotic bark to satisfy the rapacious whims of her mother.

Her whole world felt upside down.

Thirty minutes later, she was on the phone with Theo, trying her best to sound natural and unbothered about the request for an extra day at James's. She didn't even bring it up, choosing instead to listen patiently to the plot summary of the movie he'd watched with his father the night before. The movie that followed the ice cream, which followed the Go-Karts, which followed the cheese pizza with extra cheese, a lot of extra cheese. Seriously, like two minutes on the cheese. Cheesiest pizza ever.

There was a pause as Theo regrouped after his dissertation on the pizza. Then he blurted out: "Dad says I need to come home tonight."

"Oh," said Penelope, pleasantly surprised. "Well, good. I've missed you."

"Yeah, Dad's got a date or something. So I have to come home. Okay. Bye."

Penelope stood motionless in the kitchen for quite a while after Theo hung up, brooding over the phrase, "*I have to come home.*"

Then she decided to make a batch of brownies too.

♥ ♥ ♥

Several hours later, Penelope and Theo were in the den, competing viciously in Mario Kart. Theo was playing as Toad and was just ahead of her in his Tiny Titan. She was Yoshi and driving her trusty Dolphin Dasher. She was not, repeat not, brooding about Yapper herding Doozy down in the basement as she tried to sleep, or wondering if this development was karmic payback for all the times she'd laughed about James and his ability to put shoe in doo. Nor was she brooding that Theo "had to come home." Or that her sex-machine ex had a date on Sunday night, which struck her more and more as a really playboy move.

She and Theo were on the third and final lap of the Mushroom Gorge maze and nearing the finish line. Penelope/Yoshi had been lagging behind, playing possum, for over a lap now, waiting for the exact right moment to lob the *bob-omb* she'd been saving for this occasion. Theo/Toad was defenseless, his last banana wasted when the Dolphin Dasher swerved nimbly around it. What did he take her for, an amateur? They were halfway through the cave. All she had to do was blow up Toad, dodge a few Goombas, and she'd be Mario Kart champion of the house yet again.

Yoshi lobbed the explosive, but the cave was narrower than she remembered—it had been ages since they'd raced the Mushroom Gorge—and the next thing she knew the Dolphin Dasher itself was blasted by the bob-omb and launched headlong into the never-ending void of the mushroom abyss.

Game over. Foiled by her own dastardly deed.

"SMH," Theo said, coasting past a few half-hearted Goombas in his path and across the finish line, the winner.

"What?" Penelope said, shaking her joystick. It seemed slow today. She should have been able to dodge that explosive.

"SMH. You threw a *bob-omb* in the cave? That's just asking for trouble."

He was right. There was too little room in the cavern to navigate around her own treachery. It was a rookie mistake. Doozy and the pending sheepdog festival had distracted her. Damn Doozy, and damn Yapper too. She had that game all but locked up.

"I know the move stunk, Theo. I'm asking what SMH means."

Theo smiled at her and shook his head in an irritating fashion. Smack talk was the norm in their games, but lately Penelope was starting to regret teaching him some of the jive talking moves she'd learned while playing Tetris against her friends at Starlight Arcade back in the day. He was getting better at the Wii games she used to dominate him in and turning into a real smart-ass in the bargain. She'd been spending too much time on stupid online dating sites and not enough time staying keen on the Wii. This was a wake-up call, though. No way she was passing her gaming crown to Theo without a fight.

"Just tell me. I see it online sometimes and have no idea."

Theo continued to shake his head and smile.

"Smeh?" Penelope asked. "Like bleh? Like if you saw something that was bland or boring, you would say, *this movie is just smeh?*"

Theo collapsed into his beanbag chair laughing. "That makes me want to LOL."

"Theo, what does SMH mean?"

"I am *shaking my head* that you don't know what SMH means."

"Shaking my head? Wow. Seriously? That might be the dumbest one yet."

Theo sat back up, still smiling. He reset the game and looked at Penelope for confirmation that she was up for a rematch.

"Wait, Theo, are you texting or something? How do you know all this stuff?

Theo looked sheepish for a moment, then pretended to be engrossed in the pregame selection of characters and vehicles, as if he'd ever be anything but Toad in the Tiny Titan.

"Answer me."

"Dad got me an iPod touch this weekend."

"Are you kidding me?"

"Just so we could Facetime when I'm over here. Plus I can Facetime with you when I'm at Dad's. It will be really practical."

Penelope got up from the beanbag and went to the kitchen for a drink of water, trying to collect her thoughts. On one hand, there were the countless sermons she'd had to endure from James about how technology was ruining childhood in general, and Theo in particular. These oratories usually happened during some epic mother/son Wii game. Usually there was some historical documentary on at the same time that James thought would be good for Theo. When Penelope reminded him—as she galloped around the den swatting imaginary tennis balls—that most people considered television to be technology, he went into a long monologue about not all television being equal. In short, *The Bachelorette* was television, the History Channel food for the mind.

So this was playing in her mind as she downed the water and poured a glass of milk for Theo. She also wondered how much an iPod touch cost and how James was so flush. Sandy and Rachel's insistence that James was squirreling money away before the divorce, likely well before it, was gaining credibility with her as she considered his new house, new window treatments, and new garden gnome.

She came back to the den, trying to keep herself from boiling over. She couldn't afford to take Theo out for Go-Karts or mini-golf or the cheesiest pizza in the history of cheese pizza. Okay, whatever. She had a job now. No need to get in a sour mood and spoil the good time she and Theo were having.

"I got you some milk, honey," Penelope said.

Theo took the glass and gulped down about half of it, chugging heartily and noisily. Then he looked at Penelope and said: "I mustache you a question." Smiling at this, he wiped the milky residue from above his lip with his arm and added: "but I'll shave it for later."

Penelope smiled and then laughed and then laughed hard. She dove at Theo on his beanbag and began to tickle. He squirmed, laughing himself, and gasping for breath, and bragging about how funny his joke was and how he couldn't believe she hadn't heard it because the kids at school did it every day.

She really had missed the little dude.

When they calmed down, Theo said: "You're not mad about the iPod touch, are you?"

"No, I'm not mad."

"Good. It's got all these games we can play. It's got a camera. It can do a million things. It really is sick. Let me show you."

The use of *sick* reminded her of the horny Christians from the night before, unfortunately. It had been nearly an hour since she'd obsessed about the naked photo of her making the rounds on the Internet or the likelihood of Theo somehow coming across it.

"Hey," Penelope hollered to Theo, who was back in his room retrieving his new gizmo. "Does your iPod touch have Internet access?"

"As long as you have wifi. Grandmom and George do. And so does Dad, so yeah, it's got Internet. I can look up anything you need. I can find all sorts of stuff. It's sick, I'm telling you."

He came dashing back into the den and took a flying leap onto the beanbag, his fingers never ceasing to punch at the device even as he ran and jumped. It had been a while since Penelope had seen him this excited. She was less so. She didn't know how to childproof a device, but she'd have to learn. And one way or another, she had to make that photo disappear. If Theo were to come across it, his head would explode like something in Gorzomo's dream.

He was now shoving the iPod in her face, blathering about games, apps, and all the assorted doohickeys that came with it in a way that would have been music to the ears of BrettCorinthians2:2.

"See, and look at all the pictures I took. I've got an Instagram account and everything. Pretty good, aren't they?"

"Instagram? You're like a teenager, Theo."

Penelope was imagining a pubescent Theo as she thumbed through the photos on his iPod with his milk breath hovering next to her. He'd scooted close in his excitement and now they were sharing one beanbag. The photos were all at James's house, mostly of Pokémon figures and her ex-husband smiling to beat the band. As Penelope ran through the seven hundred or so shots of Pikachu, she found her interest waning. Then from nowhere came a new subject of Theo's photographic eye.

"Theo, did your dad get a dog?"

"No, it belongs to some friend of his."

"Which friend?"

"I don't know. The puppy was at Dad's when I got there Friday. Dad dropped me off early at the baseball game for warm-ups, then took the puppy back to the owner on Saturday. Raisin's a really sweet dog. I thought I might get to see her again and that's why I wanted to stay an extra night at Dad's. She is so cute, Mom. You'd love her."

Penelope looked closer at the canine in question. Yes, yes, yes. It had to be the running pup as recently featured on James's Facebook page. Ms. Dunleavy's puppy, if James's Facebook clues pointed where she thought they did. She couldn't be absolutely sure though. Both photos showed a black puppy, but the one on Theo's Instagram had a prominent all-white ear. The running Facebook pup was in profile and only one ear was showing, and that ear was black.

"Isn't she cute, Mom?"

Penelope nodded, then forced a smile. She continued through Theo's photos, getting more steamed by the second. So James was buying their son expensive presents even when it wasn't Christmas or his birthday and now he had access to a puppy as well. His place sure sounded like a lot of fun.

"Theo, you're not unhappy living with George and Maw-Maw, are you?"

"No. It's fine."

"You know we're going to have our own place soon. And you'll have your own room that you can decorate however you want. I know it's weird sleeping in a guest room without all your stuff."

"It's fine, Mom. I don't mind."

She handed the iPod touch back to Theo and grabbed him in a bear hug.

"Honey," she said, "I hate to bring up a sore subject, but this has been on my mind all weekend. What do you think will happen tomorrow morning on the bus?"

Theo, who'd not resisted her hug, now squirmed to get free. She loosened her grip but wasn't ready to let him go just yet.

"I don't know," he said.

"Are you still ripping them to make people laugh?"

"No. I haven't done that in a long time."

"But those kids still mess with you?

"They mess with my hair sometimes. Maybe flick my nose."

Penelope felt her heart racing. She didn't want to overreact, but people were putting their hands on her boy.

"Honey, we're going to see those kids around town all summer. And you'll be on the bus with them again next year. We need to take care of this or it's going to keep hanging over your head. Do you agree with that?"

Theo shrugged, then wiggled free from her embrace. For a moment, she considered telling him about the meeting with Ms. Dunleavy, then thought better of it. She hated to add *tattletale* to the list of insults he could worry about in the future.

"Why don't you let me show you some moves?" Penelope said. "Then tomorrow when a kid says something, you can just take care of it yourself. Just the basics. Headlock, arm bar, Nelson. I used to wrestle all the time when I was a kid."

She realized she was smiling a little. The Coonskins episode would be a good story one of these days—maybe even this week—for Rachel and Sandy. She wasn't even that mad anymore, about the softball woman or about getting fired. It was surely for the best. And now she was in the proper spirit to show Theo how to handle a bully.

"Come on, Theo."

"I'm not wrestling with my mom."

"We used to all the time when you were little. You can learn a few moves and take care of those jerks on the bus. Who's the main one again?"

"Alex."

"Okay, just defend yourself one time. You stand up to the leader, and the rest will leave you alone. I guarantee it."

"I'm not fighting Alex."

"Is he a lot bigger than you or something?"

"No. But I'm still not going to wrestle him."

"Why not?"

"I'll get in trouble."

"No you won't. I'll back you up. And if you get in trouble, so what? They're not going to kick you out of school for defending yourself."

Theo shook his head.

"Okay," said Penelope. "If he just called you names and then you popped him, I could see you maybe getting in trouble. But if they muss up your hair or flick your nose or give you an Indian burn or anything else where they put their hands on you, then you can physically defend yourself, right?"

"How did you know about the Indian burns?"

"That's a classic bully move. One of my cousins from Manassas used to give them to me all the time. They hurt. So does getting your nose flicked. Wet Willies don't, but they're gross and irritating. You get Wet Willies too?"

"Yes."

"Okay, that's it. You're learning some stuff."

Theo again shook his head, but there was a glimmer of interest in his eyes. Deciding there was no time like the present, Penelope yanked the beanbag he was sitting on out from under him. She kicked it and the other one out of the way, then scooted the coffee table to the other side of the couch. The floor was clear.

Theo looked up and said: "Don't."

But Penelope had already pounced.

22

On Monday morning Penelope dropped Theo at the bus stop with reminders about leverage, reversals, and headlocks. When she shouted *Tower of power, too sweet to be sour* out the car window, the other kids looked strangely at Theo, as if they now understood that the Weird Turd didn't fall far from the weird turd tree. She didn't care. Theo had enjoyed their bout the night before and shown marked improvement, especially when she'd riled him up by threatening a Wet Willie. She wouldn't have, of course—Theo knew that—but he fought hard at the thought of a sticky finger in his ear. She told him that if he wrestled just like that he'd be fine.

Oh, it was just stupid boy stuff, as James called it—just minor, routine daily humiliation.

Now she was all fired up. She concentrated on ignoring the oil light on the dashboard, which taunted her in its yellow gaudiness. Asshole light. Now she was ignoring the oil light. It was time to calm down and imagine, in the most positive way possible, what her job would be like. Missy had given no idea about the dress code, and she'd chosen a nice skirt, blouse, and heels, thinking it better to be overdressed than too casual. She could always change outfits on the second day to better mesh with office ambience and style.

En route to the manufactured-home park, she passed Southside Speedway, where she and the HHR had spent more than a few Saturday nights watching the locals race and occasionally smash into each other in demolition derbies. Try as she might, she couldn't envision herself attending such an event in her current incarnation. The gal in the waterbed beneath the thrashing largemouth bass? Yes, she could imagine *her* there, but she was game for just about anything.

Obviously.

Penelope drove on, trying to reconcile the good student and college girl she had been with the co-owner of Jack and Jill Lawn Service, which she had also been. Maybe that was just life in a small town, a little of this and a little of that, but always some part of you Hillsborian, some part familiar with fishing and drag racing and country boy field parties no matter what college you attended or what profession you entered. She drove on absentmindedly, wondering where the years went and what essence remained and what was discarded as the complexities of life were navigated.

Pulling into Rolling Acres Estates, she was pleasantly surprised by how nice and neat everything was. It looked more like a neighborhood than she'd expected, or perhaps a retirement community. The homes were arranged like spokes off the wheel that was the office, each little road having four to six lots on it before ending in a cul-de-sac. The yards were small but well kept, and here and there an elderly lady was out front tending to a bird feeder or flowerbed. It was the kind of place Penelope envisioned in Florida.

She pulled up to the office, which was itself a mobile home. The lot was otherwise empty, and a CLOSED sign hung on the door. It was quarter to nine. She was early, she guessed. Missy hadn't told her what time work started. Deciding to get out and stretch her legs a bit, in case she'd be sitting most of the day, she popped out of the car, excited by a job that didn't involve Cobb salads.

She was thinking about her image of trailer parks versus the quaint little community before her and about how often life challenged preconceptions. You had to be careful about forming opinions built on stereotypes. She walked around the side of the office in a philosophical frame of mind, thinking that life would surprise you time and time again, and also that her heels were hurting her feet.

She was standing next to a vending machine, wishing it had Dr Pepper instead of Nehi Orange, which she'd never seen anyone over the age of six drink, when she noticed an unusual dwelling.

It sat atop the lone sharp rise within Rolling Acres and looked to have nothing in common with its neighbors other than its hypothetical mobility. It seemed to have grown out of the soil like a rusty weed decades before. If a dwelling could look like a troll, then this one did as it loomed over the tidy neighbors below. The only access was a gullied road of cracked red clay guarded on either side by grubby flags. One was the stars and bars of the Confederacy. The other showed a curled snake. Penelope couldn't read the words but knew what they said from history class: *Don't Tread on Me*. The flags had been fastened to green metal poles meant to hold bird feeders. The effect of this was that the banners were just barely airborne, and it would be a rare day when they could whip proudly in the breeze.

At the foot of the drive was a sign scrawled in Magic Marker that said *To Heck with the Dog, Beware of the Owner*.

She was wondering if she'd ever before come across crackery of this caliber and depth when Missy whipped into the driveway at interstate cruising speed, tires barking before the stop.

"That's Dewitt's place," she said, popping out of the car like a jack-in-the-box and pointing up the hill. "Or Dimwit if you prefer. And I think you will. Now come on in and let me show you the original Taj Mahal."

Penelope was glad she'd erred on the side of caution and worn business attire as Missy was dressed in similar fashion. Entering the neat little modular building, she felt the first signs of a blister developing on her big toe and cursed the inventor of high heels, a man obviously. She'd have to look for another pair of work shoes when she got home.

Once inside, Missy swung out her arm and said, "Behold, the nerve center of Rolling Acres Estates."

Penelope surveyed her new workplace: a small lobby area with a desk toward the back. Several leather chairs situated in waiting room fashion in front of a coffee table laden with magazines. An Ansel Adams print. A couple black-and-white photos of Hillsboro back in the 40s, and a high school football schedule. A bathroom was located just beyond the desk, and then another door that led, she assumed, to Missy's office.

"This is the Log Cabin model," said Missy, "which is the smallest trailer—excuse me, manufactured home—that we have. We also offer the Rancher and, swear to God, the Cape Cod model. That's for the fancy-pants, as you can guess."

She plopped down in one of the chairs.

"God, I think I'm still hung over from Saturday night. It took me forever to get rid of Gary. He was crying again. You'd think a cop would have a little pride, but he bawled like a baby lamb. Again. And then Damien's father, that asshole, dropped Damien back home at nine Sunday morning even though he was supposed to have him the whole day. Thank God Gary ran those hot little Scientologists out of there or Damien might have busted in on Mommy teaching Braxton a naughty lesson or two."

Missy cackled her strange, choking bird laugh at the thought.

"Oh, by the way," she continued, "did you know Theo hit the ball last game? I meant to mention it, but by the time you saw me I was knee-deep in margaritas. It was pretty cool though. He was smiling like crazy and everybody made a big deal about it, especially the coach. By the way, have we talked about how hot the coach is? All I can say is I'm definitely volunteering for team mother next year. Oh, and get this. I think I saw your ex-husband at the game. I didn't connect the dots until yesterday, but after we hung out, I think I put two and two together. Is he a tall, lanky dude with good hair? Kind of walks around with a constipated look on his face like he's about to solve the riddles of the universe? Frankly, if it's the guy I saw, it's hard to imagine him getting BJs in the school parking lot. But if he's with Ms. Dunleavy, that's what it is. I'd bet Dimwit's trailer on it."

Penelope had been smiling at the thought of Theo's hit, then had gotten irritated again that she'd missed it while wrestling in Coonskins, then got even more irritated about the sexual gymnastics that Missy described, fabricated though they might be.

"Yeah, that's him," Penelope said. "Did he happen to have a dog with him?"

"You know, I think he did. We had to get there early as hell to *warm up*, you know, since it's Major League Baseball, and I think I saw Theo messing around with a dog before he went out on the field. But this was a puppy. Wait. Are you talking about that dog you showed me at Applebee's?"

"Yep."

"That's Ms. Dunleavy's dog. I'd bet Baxter's chastity belt on it. Get me to your ex's Facebook page lickety-split, and we'll wrap this little caper up once and for all."

At this, Missy sprinted to the computer, turned it on, sat for half a second in the swivel desk chair, then raced to the waiting area and yanked over one of the leather chairs. She'd definitely received her full dose of morning coffee. She was foaming at the mouth with energy and swirling round and round in the swivel chair.

"Come on," she said, patting the chair arm beside her. "Let's look at the little lovemaker's page. I want to know this fucker inside and out. Wow, and what about that Ms. Dunleavy? Blowjobs and puppies? Talk about the whole package."

Penelope would have preferred to find out more about the job she was expected to do—hours, responsibilities, etcetera—before reopening the investigation of James and his *Very Special Lady*. She was also quite interested in the specifics of her salary and how often a paycheck would come: weekly, biweekly, or—heaven forbid—monthly, which would not work at all if she was to beat Doozy and his sheepdog out the door.

But now her new boss was scrunched against her as Facebook came up on the screen. Missy was breathing hard in her ear, a light wheeze that spoke of allergies or a too-rapid heartbeat. Penelope was beginning to wonder about the general health and heartiness of the woman next to her. She seemed hastily glued together, as if a hard wind might send her flying in multiple directions.

"Oh, look at this freak," she said, gawking at the screen. "Be uncooler if you can. Myers-Briggs results? Who in America gives a rat's ass that you're a ISTJ?"

"James loves all those Internet quizzes," Penelope said. "You should have seen him when he took one to see which *Harry Potter* character he'd be. He got Dumbledore! Seriously, Dumbledore! He was unbearable for a whole week, pacing around and stroking his chin, like he was figuring out how to defeat Voldemort. The only good thing was that he finally decided not to get a toddler leash for Theo. He said, direct quote: *Albus Dumbledore would never leash Harry.*"

Missy leaned back to consider this. The Myers-Briggs test posting had thrown her, but not like the bombshell about Dumbledore and the toddler leash. She recovered after a moment and was soon hungrily perusing all that James had revealed about himself on Facebook.

"I see it now," she said. "He's like a ten-year-old with all these clues. *Will you go with me? Yes or no, circle one.* Except now he's moved on to, *Will you chalk my Willie, Ms. Dunleavy, yes or no?*"

Penelope said nothing, letting Missy gasp and moan at all of James's postings until she came to the photo of the mystery dog running happily past the camera.

"I don't know if that's the dog or not," said Missy, squinting intensely at the screen. "It's hard to tell with this shot."

Penelope pulled out her phone and went to Theo's Instagram account. It took about three hours to get through all his Pokémon figurines, but eventually she came to the photos he'd taken of the puppy at James's house.

"Was this the dog you saw at the game?" she said, sticking the phone in Missy's face.

"Yep, that's definitely the same one I saw Theo petting on Saturday. I remember that white ear. Anyway, what a little cutie. Hey, listen, you can't hold it against the dog. It's not his fault he was adopted by the BJ Queen. But if that pooch could talk, imagine what he's seen from the backseat. Talk about gnawing on a bone. Poor little pup. He's an innocent bystander to this whole tawdry affair."

"Do you know if Ms. Dunleavy has a dog?"

"I do not," said Missy. "But if you find the puppy with the white ear, you find who Dumbledore is bopping. That's 100 percent certain. But back to this Myers-Briggs thing. What's an ISTJ? Never mind. I don't care. Let's just say that no matter how drunk I was, or how hard up, you can trust me around your ex-husband. I'm not sure I've ever seen a bigger tool. Now let's talk about those hot Jehovah's Witnesses from the other night. Namely, can you hook me back up with Bristol? I've got some spiked lemonade with his name on it."

"Don't we need to get to work?"

"Work, smerk. Let's check and see if our hotties are back in touch."

"Let's not."

"What? Why?"

"Brett's not my type. Let's just leave it at that."

"Okay, fine. But I wouldn't mind another shot at Beauregard's abs. When am I going to come across another Chippendale in Hillsboro? Help a sister out."

"I don't think so," Penelope said. "Brett sent me an inappropriate message afterward. I think he got the wrong idea about me for some reason."

"What did he send?" Missy said, a smile creasing her face. "Was it just dirty as hell?"

"It wasn't so much the message as the photo that came with it."

"No! He didn't. A dong shot? Really? Wow. I didn't think he had it in him."

Penelope nodded. *Dong* wasn't a word she typically used, but if ever there was a dong, that was it.

"So let's see that bad boy," Missy said. "Let's see what young Billy Graham is swinging."

"No way."

"I can tell you're a little traumatized. But just go to the page, turn your head, and let old Missy have a good look. Your virgin eyes won't have to see a thing."

"No," said Penelope, smiling.

"Was it bigger than a breadbox?"

Missy hopped off the chair as she said this and now held her hands about three feet apart from one another.

Penelope smiled but didn't reply.

"Listen," said Missy. "I'd take a dong shot over Fitzgerald's cardigan every day of the week. I guarantee all that old coot does, night and day, is eat crumpets and whey and watch *Downton Abbey* reruns. You know I'm right. So trust me on this one. Go with the young guy. That's just good common sense."

"I'm definitely not going with Brett. He's either super-immature or a straight-up perv, and I'm not interested in either. I probably won't do anything with Fitzwilliam either. I may be done with men."

"Yeah, right. Anyway, I've got to jet."

Saying this, Missy lunged out of her chair and stalked to her office. She returned with a handful of unopened bills, which she plopped on the desk beside Penelope. Motioning for Penelope to stand, she sat down at the computer and went to the website for the Hillsboro Savings and Loan.

"Okay," she said. "I've got you set up here to pay all these bills that I've been putting off. You know how to do online banking, right?"

Penelope nodded.

"Well, knock this out for me if you don't mind. Answer the phone if anybody calls. I usually get a few deliveries, so you can sign for those. I'll have some more stuff for you to do when I get back, but that's all I can think of for now. I really do have to motor. Have to meet with the mayor about this zoning thing. We're looking for a new location."

"Why's that?"

"I'll tell you later. But listen—if you need to go to the bathroom, use mine. It's right through that door and on the left."

"That's okay. I can just use the one here in the lobby."

"No. Don't ever go in that bathroom. Ever. You're fired if you ever go in that bathroom. Not really, but just don't. I'll explain when I get back."

With that, she was out the door, leaving Penelope alone in the solitude of the modular Log Cabin.

23

Penelope knocked out the banking quickly. The phone rang once, some elderly man calling to say the lawn service had run over two of his irises and asking what Missy planned to do about it. Penelope took down his number and promised to have Missy call. Another tenant, a woman around sixty who walked with a limp, dropped in to introduce herself, saying that she'd seen Penelope driving earlier and figured she just had to be the *new office gal.* They had a nice discussion about the weather, and life in Hillsboro, and how you just can't find a decent caramel cake anymore. The woman, Estelle, promised to return tomorrow to finish up where they left off, but right then she had to give Pepper her medicine. She was having a bad run with hairballs and Estelle was tired of the hacking.

Other than that, Penelope was left to her own devices. The office was cool, the air conditioner humming soothingly along, and she luxuriated with her feet up on the desk, thinking that when she got her own place she'd run the AC day and night after living these past months with people whose blood ran thin as prison gruel.

She was eating the peanut-butter-and-jelly sandwich she'd packed for lunch and thinking—as always—just how underrated the PB&J was as a food source. If she'd only had a cold glass of milk to go with it, her lunch would be perfect. As she ate, she studied, once again, the Myers-Briggs results that James had posted on Facebook.

According to James, despite only taking fifteen minutes to complete on the Internet, the Myers-Briggs quiz could accurately determine the very essence of personality. The results came back in four handy initials. James's were ISTJ. In a quarter hour, a computer had decided the following adjectives summarized him accurately and to the core: Introverted/Sensing/Thinking/Judging.

The test also came with a narrative summary, but Penelope couldn't remember much, other than the ISTJ was noted for his punctuality. When James insisted she take the test as well, she'd come back as an Extrovert-something. James shook his head knowingly at this result and went on about how much she, as an extrovert, liked to socialize, whereas he preferred the company of a *challenging book*.

She knew what he was implying and said she'd bet a thousand dollars that Teddy Roosevelt was an extrovert. Then she said that she'd bet ten thousand dollars that the old Rough Rider would rather hang out with her than him. You know, since they both *liked* people.

They'd not spoken for nearly twenty-four hours afterwards.

And now here he was again bragging about the ISTJ. He was such a proud man. Proud Tarheel. Proud Scot. Proud Introvert. Proud Albus Dumbledore.

Penelope sat steaming at the computer, the thought occurring to her that maybe his joy at the Dumbledore ruling was that it confirmed his robe fetish. Of course Dumbledore's came to the ground, and James's not quite to his knees.

She was back on that stupid kimono.

Feeling she would soon need a psychologist who specialized in poly-blended obsession syndrome, she bounced over to LoveSynch, badly in need of distraction.

She glanced through the *flirts, blends,* and *Eiffel Towers* she'd received, hoping that the most awesome man in the world had moved just yesterday to Hillsboro and wanted to meet her pronto. But it was the same old same old. Somewhat reluctantly she reread Fitzwilliam's message. She should reply soon. It was rude not to. She read the note a third time. What was a *billet-doux*? She Googled the phrase. He wanted to write a love letter to Hopefulness, capital *H*. Well, that had a nice ring to it. ISTJ James would likely prefer a billet-doux to Moping, capital *M*.

For a moment she considered dashing off a response to Fitzwilliam. She wouldn't accept his date, but would like to keep the pen pal thing going, at least until she had more time to consider his lunch proposal. But that moment was gone with the Myers-Briggs wind. Weren't extroverts supposed to spend their days happily planning family reunions and talking to any stranger who happened by? Then why couldn't she get out of her own head about everything that had to do with her ex-husband and his happy new life?

Since she was already annoyed, she might as well check Divote. She needed to erase the photo of BrettCorinthian2:2's penis selfie before Missy came back and asked to see it again. One look at that pale lump had been plenty for her.

To say that her Divote account had blown up was like saying Sonshine Funk rocked Christian hard. She'd received twenty *tiny angels* and fifteen *boxes of chocolate*. Good thing she'd had her ringer off overnight, or those church bells would have chimed right out of the belfry. Perplexed by the sudden bounty, she raced through the photos, almost all of which were of young clean-cut guys, some from as far away as Richmond.

She reached into her purse for the Starburst she'd bought last week when still employed and feeling flush, and unwrapped the first one. She was enjoying her sugar reverie when the epiphany came. Yes, there could be no other explanation for all those virtual Russell Stovers. Word was out on the Christian street and in every sanctified chatroom that those looking to stray from the path with an experienced MILF, if only briefly, could find just what they were looking for in PenelopeGenesis2:1.

Damn it to hell. If the straitlaced guys in the area knew about Paybacks Are Heaven, then who didn't? Thinking it much too long since she'd given the HHR a thorough cursing, she reached for her cell phone. Just as she did, the door to the office opened and a man walked in.

The man was small, gray, and stained. He wore coveralls begrimed and only halfway zipped between his shoulders and navel. His intent, it seemed, was to give plenty of fresh air to the bountiful, curly gray chest hair that sprang from his chest like hungry vines searching for good soil. Looking at his dirt-colored baseball cap, Penelope felt that the chest vines might find good purchase and a pleasant home atop of it. She was transfixed.

"Hello there," she said. "May I help you?"

The man seemed stunned by the question. He'd been in midstride when she'd asked it, en route to somewhere else in the office. He creased the bill of his cap with one hand, though the cap looked incapable of further malleability. When he moved his hand, Penelope could just make out the words crudely stitched on the cap, which were *Why Don't You Make Me?* Beneath the slogan stood a poorly rendered image of Yosemite Sam. This Yosemite Sam only had one of his legendary six-shooters blasting into the air, not the two Penelope was accustomed to seeing; his other hand was occupied with flipping a bird to one and all.

The stranger was standing just past her desk, still with the appearance of arrested motion. He'd not spoken, but Penelope could tell he had places to go. He was looking her up and down, then took a few steps to get a side view, lingering longer than was socially acceptable on her stockinged legs.

"Were you looking for Missy?" she asked.

"Who are you?" the man said, not taking his eyes from her legs, which she now tried to stuff farther under the desk.

"I'm the new receptionist, I guess," Penelope said. "I'm not sure what my official title is, but this is my first day on the job."

"Where's Doris?"

"I don't know Doris. Did she used to work at this desk?"

"What's your name?"

"Penelope."

"I like your shoes."

Penelope realized she should be fearing for her safety, but for some reason she didn't. Perhaps it was all the wrestling practice she'd had lately. If it came to an office throwdown, she liked her chances.

Any self-defense moves she might have been contemplating were rendered moot, for after memorizing her legs, and especially her shoes, the man continued in his original direction. Which, it turned out, was the bathroom Missy had forbidden her to use. He shut the door behind him with a gentlemanly click.

Then there was silence.

24

Penelope had been sitting for thirty minutes or so, hoping that the phone would ring or that someone would come in, anything to distract her from the fact that only ten feet away a man was doing something behind a closed bathroom door for a really long time. She was thinking about medical emergencies the man might be experiencing when Missy launched herself up the steps and through the door as if just hurled by an unseen giant down in the parking lot.

"Well, the mayor's an idiot, I can vouch for that," she said.

Penelope didn't reply and must have had an odd look on her face because Missy said, "What? Why are you looking like you ate a sour pickle?"

Penelope motioned to the bathroom door via a quick jerk of the head. Then she pointed with her thumb, hitchhiker fashion, and mouthed: *Someone's in there.*

Missy nodded, then mouthed something back that Penelope couldn't understand.

"What?" she said silently, raising her palms.

Missy frowned as if Penelope was slow, then crashed around the desk and jerked open several drawers at once till she located pen and paper, which she could have found in the top drawer if she'd just bothered to look before opening the drawers below. Penelope was beginning to realize that her new employer was a trifle impatient.

She was now standing over the desk, scribbling in a jabbing, aggressive motion. Then she violently pushed the notepad over to Penelope before needlessly gesturing for her to begin reading.

The note said: That's Dimwit.

Penelope took the pen from Missy and wrote: Dewitt? The guy who lives on the hill?

Missy snatched the pen back and wrote: I said Dimwit and I meant Dimwit. Yes, he's the troll on the hill.

Penelope responded: Okay, but why is he using the bathroom here?

Missy: Long story. He owns the land the trailer park is on. We rent it from him, then rent out spots to the tenants. His one condition is that he gets to use our bathroom whenever he wants.

Missy filled four entire pages to get the above message down, as she was not just writing swiftly, but also using huge letters. At her current rate of seven words per page, they would soon need another legal pad. Penelope found this wasteful but let it slide. She'd not yet been put in charge of office supplies.

She responded: Doesn't his trailer have a bathroom?

Yes.

Does it work?

Far as I know.

Then why does he want to use this one?

That's the question neither of us should think too much about.

Throughout this exchange Missy had been scowling, so much so that Penelope began to smile. Intense people fascinated her. She took the pen and wrote: He asked about Doris.

I'm sure he did.

Mr. Burke called to complain about the grass guy lopping off his irises.

Do I look like I give a good goddam about that old fart's irises?

Penelope laughed and then the toilet flushed and then Dewitt was standing in the office with them, glancing at the notepad which lay in no-man's-land between the two women, Missy's huge letters legible from where he stood if he noticed and could read. Penelope grabbed the notebook and placed it in the top drawer as gently and smoothly as she could while still moving at rapid speed. Dewitt was just standing there, the bathroom door ajar behind him. His cap was now quite askew, so much so that the scrawny Yosemite Sam was not shooting a bird directly at Penelope but out the window, in the direction of Dewitt's own place.

He nodded to Missy, tipped his grimy cap toward Penelope, then walked out. They both watched out the window as he marched up the dirt road to his trailer. Penelope couldn't be sure, but he looked to be whistling a merry tune. Likely "Jimmy Crack Corn."

"So now you've met Dimwit," Missy said after they'd taken a moment to reflect. "Welcome to Rolling Acres Estates."

"I don't understand," Penelope said. "What's he doing in there if he has his own bathroom?"

"I've given this some thought," said Missy, frowning in a contemplative manner. "A lot of thought, actually. And it seems to me there are two options. He's either doing what every man takes half an hour to do, even though every woman can do it in like three minutes. Or he's spanking that greasy little monkey of his like there's no tomorrow."

"Surely not."

"You'll note," said Missy, "that the office smells exactly as it did before Dimwit's arrival. And I have it on good authority from my maintenance man that he eats virtually nothing but Vienna sausages and Beanie-Weenies. So that rules out the *nature's call* option in my professional opinion. Which leaves us with the other sad and scary possibility. But let me know if you need me to draw you a picture."

"No way. Seriously?"

"Afraid so. Grubby self-abuse on the premises."

"Why do it here and not in his own place?"

Missy gave her a sad smile now, as if breaking the news about Santa to a small child. "There are no women up at Dewitt's place."

"OMG!"

"Tell me about it."

"How often?"

"Every day. But just once a day. We have our standards here at Rolling Acres. I thought I'd be back in time to warn you. He usually comes later in the day for his afternoon delight."

Penelope smiled at the song reference, gross as it was, but still couldn't get her head around this development.

"You're not going to quit, are you?" Missy asked.

"No. I need the job."

"Thank God. Because he ran Doris off after like two months. The gal before him didn't even last that long."

"He's not dangerous?"

"I don't think so. I think he's just a trailer-park whacker. You don't want to think too much about it when you're in the office with him. And you definitely—I mean never—want to think about what he might be imagining while he's in there beating it like a redheaded stepchild."

Penelope laughed, though Missy had yet to crack a smile.

"Hopefully, we won't be here too much longer," Missy said. "If I can get the zoning thing done with our idiot mayor, we'll be out within the year. We're tired of paying Dimwit. Plus my dad is pissed that his sweet little girl is being exposed to such debauchery."

Missy flashed her wicked smile at this. Penelope hoped someday to meet the father. It would be interesting to see the two of them together. But now it was time to get down to brass tacks. "I'm not quitting," Penelope said, "but I would like to know what my salary is or how much I get paid per hour. And especially when I'm going to get my first paycheck. I don't know if you remember our discussion at Applebee's, but I've got this sleepwalking uncle with a Neti Pot he uses in the shower, who is coming to stay with us for a month. A month! And now he's got this sheepdog that barks all night if he starts sleepwalking. If you can't guarantee me that I'll make enough to get my own place by June 28th, then I may have to look for other work. I'm sorry to be that blunt but I'm desperate. I absolutely have to have my own place."

"I hear you," Missy said when she'd finished her detailed summary of life in the rancher basement. "I'd forgotten about the sleepwalking Neti Pot uncle. And now he has a herding dog? Wow. That's a new one. Okay, I think I can handle my end of the bargain. I still have to clear the salary with my dad, but that won't be a problem. I'm thinking seven hundred a week to start out with. And then we'll see how it goes. You'd have to be here six months to get health care and all that. Paydays are first and the middle of the month, so that would be about a paycheck and a half before you have to start showering with your uncle. If you can sock away a good portion, that should be enough for a down payment, right?"

"I think so," said Penelope, relief washing over her. "And I'd be getting another July 1, so I can factor that check in too. Thanks a lot. That will work."

Missy asked three more times if she was really not going to quit. Finally assuaged, she gave Penelope a few other minor chores and her own key to the office, then showed her how to lock up. She was at the door when she said: "I can't wait for tomorrow, can you? You and the BJ Queen face to face under the chalkboard for the first time. It'll be like Shootout at the Blowjob Corral with erasers and staplers and those laminated hall passes flying every which way! And you just laying the wood to her!"

25

On the drive home, Penelope decided that her new job was weird, but that she could do anything for six months if it meant getting her own place, including surviving daily visits from the trailer-park whacker. He sure had liked her shoes. Those same shoes had been viciously flung into the backseat as soon as she entered the car, a just punishment for the number they'd done on her feet the previous nine hours. She drove barefoot, which was one of the secret loves of her life. The first thing she'd do when she got home was rummage through the mountains of boxes in the carport to find that pair of wedges. No one wore them anymore, but they were comfortable.

She hadn't relished Missy's comment about the showdown with Ms. Dunleavy, but like it or not, tomorrow was the parent/teacher meeting. She might not get to the bottom of the bus-bully stuff, but it was worth a try. And if Theo also was getting picked on at school, that would be worth mentioning if Penelope had to call the boys' parents.

That she might also discover, once and for all, if Theo's teacher was also his potential stepmother, well, that would be a bonus. All she needed was one picture in Ms. Dunleavy's room, just one, of that cute little pup with the white ear, and she'd have ironclad proof.

But all that was aggravating to think about after successfully completing the first day of a job that didn't involve peanut baskets or wearing a denim skirt. She'd be getting her own place soon, maybe as early as mid-June after she got that second check. And when she did, she had to do something special for Theo. Maybe she could put a mural in his room, one of Pokémon or Mario Kart or something of that sort.

Or what if the apartment had a pool? A pool would be competitive with a puppy, wouldn't it? Anyway, she wasn't just going to throw in the towel in the fun-place-to-live department. She and Theo would have a new life, a new adventure, and she couldn't wait to get started.

She smiled as she pictured herself lounging in a bathing suit without one million babies in steadily ballooning swim diapers like at the city pool.

Then her car made a noise. A loud screeching noise.

It sounded like a whole lot of metal things rubbing against one another without the luxury of lubrication. Her heart jumped. It was an awful clatter. And then came a hiss like R2D2 taking an ax to his titanium tummy—and smoke billowing from the hood. Panicked, she glanced toward the oil light, which was the same steady yellow it had been for the last week when by all rights it should have been a scalding hot red.

Engulfed in smoke, she eased two wheels onto the narrow shoulder, then into some people's yard. She was trying to make it another hundred yards to the front of a subdivision, where there'd be more room, when the car just died. Like it had given up all hope. She'd seen horses do this in the desert while watching the Western Channel with George. She looked to see if she was still in Drive, then put the car in Park. She got out, still barefoot. Oil refinery schmutz continued to leak from under the hood. Her car was dead.

26

She'd walked the mile home barefoot, and what damage the heels hadn't done, the rocky pavement had. Her dogs were barking something fierce. She could have called someone for a ride but was too mad to do it. She needed to blow off some steam and had a masochistic urge to punish herself for counting apartment chickens before they were hatched. For most of the day she'd felt like Schrödinger's cat, both living with her mother and already in her own apartment, but now the top had been lifted and the cat revealed dead. She should have known better.

In the carport now, furiously throwing boxes around, looking for the one containing shoes that didn't treat her feet like a mouthy POW, she didn't hear her mother walk up until she spoke.

"Well, George called Skeeter down at Hillsboro Auto. They'll get a tow truck out there right away, and he hopes to have a look at it sometime tomorrow."

Penelope nodded but didn't turn around. She continued pushing boxes here and there, boxes that were beginning to look more and more at home in the carport. Soon birds would be nesting among them, and when it got cold they'd be a handy spot for small mammals looking to hibernate. Perhaps she should build a few little alleyways to make their routes less cumbersome as they prepared their dens for Father Winter.

"George said once they get the car up on the rack he'll go down there himself and see what Skeeter has to say," her mother continued. "He's afraid it might be a blown head gasket, honey. And that's an expensive one. How many miles does that car have on it?"

"A lot," Penelope said, roughhousing boxes, the harsh sliding sound pleasingly hard on her ears. She hoped her mother would leave, but she stayed glued to the spot.

"You know," she said, "you might be better off getting a new car instead of sinking a lot more money into one that will just keep breaking down on you."

Penelope turned and looked at her mother in a way that said more effectively than words: *no shit.*

"I know, honey, I know. You've had a little setback. But you'll be back on your feet before you know it. Tough times don't last, but tough people do."

Penelope went back to bullying boxes. She wasn't even paying much attention to what was marked. At this point, she just liked knocking them around.

"You can stay here as long as you need. And listen, no argument about it, I'm calling June right after supper and telling her that we'll have to postpone their visit. It's not a big deal."

Penelope stopped with the boxes.

"No," she said, "you're not going to do that. You've talked about this trip forever. And you've already got tickets to the beer festival for Doozy. And the country jamboree down in Lynchburg. George has been looking forward to that for nine months. The Oak Ridge Boys, Alabama, it's all his favorites. Don't call Aunt June. I'll be fine. I'll get earplugs and shower shoes. It's not a big deal. Mom, seriously. I'm going to be really mad if you call."

Her mother wanted to argue but didn't. She was looking forward to Aunt June's visit even more than George.

"Okay, if you insist, but I don't see how you can manage Doozy and Yapper both down in that basement."

"Mom, I can do anything for a month. It's all right."

"Can I just tell you how it burns me up that James already has a new place? And after crying like the Sisters of the Poor in your arbitration. George is beside himself, he's so angry. He never did cotton to James, you know. Not in the least."

"I know, Mom. And I appreciate the support you guys have given me. I'll be fine. Seriously. Stop worrying."

"George said you could drive Daisy for as long as you need. It'll get you to and from work, so that won't be a problem."

"Thanks Mom. Y'all have been too kind."

Her mother waved this off, then went back in, letting the screen door slam in her wake.

Then Penelope dove back into the boxes. She was still barefoot, and every now and then she smashed a big toe in the tumult, but she didn't care. Eventually, she came to a box marked STUFF. She would have smiled at this normally, noting her tendency to get less and less particular about order and organization the longer she was forced to do a boring task, but didn't today. She should have gone into the house for scissors but punched a fist through the layers of duct tape instead, before ripping the top off with one violent pull.

Riffling through, she came across a pair of tennis shoes and sandals and a Jim Morrison T-shirt she'd forgotten she had. These she tossed onto the cement floor as things that she could wear over the summer.

And now she'd found those wedges, or at least one of them. She yanked it out and flung it over her shoulder with the pile. She was scraping the bottom of the box, rummaging through clothes and the occasional necklace or alarm clock, crap she should have thrown away a long time ago. There it was, the other wedge. It was entangled in something, something silky and smooth. What? Hadn't she gotten all of her underwear out? Surely she had, or she wouldn't be stuck wearing that old pair that was always on the roam beneath her denim skirt.

No, the silky thing in her hand was too big for panties. Maybe it was a lightweight nightgown. She could use one of those when she was sweating away down in her basement inferno.

Feeling that finally something had gone her way, she gave the remaining shoe and the missing delicate a good tug, and out they came. She stood up now, flinging the shoe on the pile as she did. What she held in her hand was indeed silky as a nightgown, but the garment was not one that had ever draped her body. It had, on the other hand, hovered over her and occasionally beneath her.

It was not a nightgown. And it was not a proper robe as worn by Albus Dumbledore. It was a kimono, a silky bit of nothing, meant, in some Eastern corners of the world, for a man.

The robe in question was yellow.

Theo chose this exact moment to take a break from his three-hour Pokémon battle and join his mother in the carport. He approached Penelope looking dazed of eye. And then his nose began to twitch and his whole face grew alert. He'd had many a story read to him in the yellow shorty. Likely it conjured pleasant memories of *Thomas the Train* and the comforting warmth of bedwetting.

Panicked, Penelope scooped up all the things on the floor and piled them atop the object of Theo's eye in a fairly obvious attempt at subterfuge.

"What's that?" Theo said.

"Just some of my things," Penelope answered, scooting past Theo and into the kitchen, *la di dah, la di dah.*

"Yeah, but what's that yellow thing? It looks familiar."

"I have a bunch of my things here, Theo. I'm sure most of it looks familiar."

Theo seemed to remember that his mother had recently walked home from an abandoned car and decided now was not the time to push her, though Penelope could tell he wanted to. The yellow kimono had totemic powers. Of this, she was now certain. Theo had inherited an olfactory system from his father, likely birthed eons ago in a Scottish bog, that was stimulated by women named Penelope when in the presence of poly-blended male nighties.

She walked to the sink, grabbed a trash bag, and jammed everything in, away from prying eyes. She never could tell what Theo knew or didn't know about adult matters between her and James. Would he remember, for instance, any details from the week the robe had mysteriously disappeared and associate that week with parental discord?

James had definitely moped with a special intensity afterwards—like a triple mope. Maybe quadruple. But was he so bereft he'd say something to Theo? Something like: *Yes, son, I'm just a little down today. You see, my yellow robe has gone missing and that robe means a lot to your old man.*

Yes, of course he would. He was always telling Theo things he didn't need to. It was the whole *adults have urges/spermatozoa/Origin of Species* talk all over again.

Maybe she should tell Theo—right now—something like: *You see honey, women have urges too, and those urges can be stymied quite harshly if their husband is wearing a robe better suited for a Japanese grandmother.*

Theo, with that sweet little nine-year-old-boy attention span of his, let it drop. Perhaps the plastic trash bag interfered with his olfactory sense or blocked his subconscious powers of association. Perhaps, through some intuitive osmosis, he'd heard her interior monologue about women's urges and taken the hint.

Whichever the case, Penelope breathed a sigh of relief when he said:

"So, do you want to wrestle a little bit before supper?"

"I don't think so, Theo. I've had a long day."

"Oh, come on. That was fun."

"Theo, my car just died. I am not in the mood to wrestle right now."

"Maw-Maw says it's probably going to be really expensive to fix the car."

"Probably."

"Does that mean we can't get our own place soon?"

"I don't know. I'm trying not to think about it."

Penelope tied the garbage bag tightly, then placed it at the top of the steps leading to the basement. She went over and squeezed Theo in a hug, steering him backwards toward the couch in the den, away from the contraband. She sat down and motioned for Theo to join her.

"Did those kids bother you again today?"

"Lately it's not all of them. It's just the one kid, Alex."

"What did he do today?"

"You know. Same stuff."

"Did he flick your nose?"

"Yes."

"Wet Willie?"

"Yes."

"Did you do anything back?"

"No."

Penelope found that her blood was boiling. Mostly at that Alex kid, but also a little at Theo for not taking up for himself.

"Why not? You know at least three good wrestling moves that you could throw at him right now. He'd never know what hit him."

Theo shook his head.

"And if you popped him one, or put him in a headlock or something, his friends wouldn't jump in and gang up, would they?"

"I don't think so."

Penelope nodded but said nothing further. Normally she would have given him a pep talk, but at the moment she didn't have the energy. Theo must have sensed her disappointment, for he didn't mention anything more about wrestling.

"Are you going to my game on Saturday?" he asked.

Penelope turned on the TV and scooted closer to her son. She put her arm around his shoulder and flipped channels without paying attention. She felt very tired.

"I definitely am," she said. "With my new job I don't have to work weekends."

"I'm going to swing at the ball again."

"That's great, honey."

"I'm going to swing every time from now on."

"Well, you don't have to swing if it's over your head or in the dirt or something."

Theo frowned, deep in thought, looking so much like his father that Penelope smiled despite herself.

"No," she said. "It's okay. Swing every time. Baseball is more fun if you're just letting it rip. Everything's more fun if you let it rip. Remember that."

Theo nodded, then snuggled his head into her armpit like he used to when he was little. Penelope continued to flip channels, looking for something they'd both like to watch.

27

Penelope sat in the yellow pickup named Daisy. On her blistered, cut, and swollen feet were the wedges she'd found the night before, a marked improvement. Theo was running behind, as he often was, though he seemed in a good mood over cereal, singing the Pokémon theme with unusual gusto. The song was bad but catchy, and it was stuck in Penelope's head. She couldn't not sing it and this always drove her crazy: *I want to be the very best.*

On the passenger seat floorboard was the plastic trash bag containing James's anti-erotic lingerie. She wasn't sure what she was going to do with it, only that the town wasn't big enough for the both of them. She felt weird throwing a perfectly good clothing item away, but also feared that if she dropped the robe at Goodwill, some other local man interesting in covering himself only so much might discover it. She thought of the man's poor wife and the effect the shorty would have on their relationship. She didn't want that on her conscience.

She also wondered how good a look Theo had gotten the night before and whether he might accidentally rat her out. Truthfully, until its discovery yesterday, she wouldn't have been able to say, under oath, if she'd hidden it, thrown it away, or buried it in the backyard. That whole incident was a blur, spurred one morning when James was singing "Sweet Melissa" by the Allman Brothers in front of the mirror while blow-drying his hair, his pasty legs swaying gently under the yellow silk. Coming out of the bathroom, microphone hair dryer in hand, legs pale as a Highlands sheep, James proposed that they had time to mess around before he went to work.

Penelope could oblige, but she'd crossed her Rubicon. She could be frisky in the morning, or he could wear the kimono, but never again would both occur simultaneously.

She sighed now and gave the steering wheel a little pat. Daisy understood what it was like. Then she honked the horn again for Theo, irritated that he was probably playing some game instead of finding his shoes like she asked.

She'd slept poorly the night before, thinking of bullies and teacher meetings and six months of Dimwit pleasuring himself in a Yosemite Sam cap ten feet away. She was also thinking of naked photos of herself that looked to be on the Internet forever and evangelical dudes who sent photos of their privates and how she never had responded to Fitzwilliam Darcy about that lunch date. Despite her best efforts, she also thought about her ex-husband and how he'd moved on so seamlessly since the divorce and was carrying on with a teacher who had a cute-as-hell puppy with a white ear. But most of all, she thought of the death of her car and how it meant the death of her independence. It might be a year before she could get her own place now. How much the repair would cost, if it even could be repaired, was anyone's guess:

Ma'am, your supercalifragilisticexpialidocious was shot all to hell. It's going to cost nine thousand dollars to fix. And that's before we lube the galinky valves. So you're looking at a quarter million dollars. Now that's not including labor.

She honked again and Theo came racing out in his funny kneeless gait, smiling and looking perkier than usual in the morning. Bully or no bully, it was the next-to-last day of school.

"Hey," said Theo, opening the passenger door, "what's in the bag?"

"A whole lot of none-ya."

"What?"

"A heaping helping of none-ya-business. Now let's roll. Do you want me to just drop you off at school today? You'd skip those guys on the bus."

"No, that's okay. But can I ride in the back to the bus stop?"

"No, just ride up front."

"Come on. You usually say I'm too much of a suburban kid and the kids in Hillsboro always used to do it. You did."

"It's against the law, Theo."

"That's what *I* always say. Then you say, *Who cares, it's fun. No one in the history of Hillsboro has ever been arrested for riding in the back of a truck.*"

This point about arrestability was basically true, the HHR being the lone exception. Of course he was naked at the time, save for fishing waders, and sitting on a bale of hay while Weasel ordered a Whopper at the Burger King drive-through. Some dare or another, the details of which escaped Penelope now.

"Okay, Theo," she said. "Hop in the back like the Pokémon farmboy you are."

"Yee-hi," he said, throwing his backpack in the bed, then clambering over the tailgate.

Daisy was properly warmed up now and Penelope put her into drive as smoothly as George had taught her. She backed out of the driveway, wondering who this kid was. She could hear him singing the Pokémon theme against the rush of the wind. Otherwise, she felt like she was carting around an unknown kneeless boy. End-of-school goofiness, she reckoned.

She dropped him off with the gaggle of kids already waiting. Theo's arrival didn't go without notice and the thought struck Penelope that what had been commonplace back in her day was pretty rare now.

Theo put a hand on the side rail and leaped over, stuntman-style. He nearly wiped out on landing but gathered himself quickly, his knees, if he had them, only buckling for a moment. He grabbed his backpack, then came around to the driver's side window. Penelope could see all the kids looking at him. He'd made quite an appearance.

She couldn't tell if this was Weird Turd/Fart Boy territory, the showy arrival, or if his peers were just a tiny bit impressed. He'd looked pretty cool hopping out. Or at least daring.

"All right, Mom," he said. *"Tower of Power, too sweet to be sour. Ohhh Yeahhhh!"*

And with that, he bade his mother good-bye.

28

It'd been a routine day at the office, if every office included a daily visit by Dimwit. Now Penelope was cutting out for her meeting with Ms. Dunleavy.

"So you'll definitely be back tomorrow, right?" Missy said, pacing in front of Penelope's desk and chawing at a hangnail that had bedeviled her all day.

"Yes, I'll be back."

"Because Doris said she'd come back, and I never heard from her again. Not even to pick up her last check."

"I assure you I won't be leaving any paychecks behind," Penelope said, scooping the last of the Starbursts into her purse. Nervous about the teacher conference, she'd pounded the pack all day. She'd have to be judicious tomorrow, or Friday would be snack-free.

"Doris said that too. But Dimwit wore her down. She said it was the silence that was the worst. The not-knowing. I think she had a very strong imagination and the picture in her head just got more vivid each day. She ended up thinking he was in there with axle grease and a mute chicken. I think that was because of this one day when he came out with a random feather on his coveralls. You swear he's not going to run you off?"

"Listen," said Penelope. "Dimwit could use my bathroom at home, with the door open and all lotion included, if it meant me paying off my car and getting an apartment sometime in the next decade. I'm not letting some little peckerwood run me off."

"Can you just promise me six months?"

"Yes. You have my word that I will stay six months. After that I'll probably be a hedge fund manager or brain surgeon or something, but I can give you half a year."

Missy looked relieved. "Okay, so let's go over it again. What are you going to do if you see evidence of that dog in the BJ Queen's room?

"I need to go," Penelope said. "I don't want to be late."

"Your husband and your son's teacher are doing it. In the parking lot. And then they go on picnics with a cute little puppy. You're about to shower with your uncle for a month. And share his Neti Pot. Have you bought those galoshes yet? You know, I think they call them Wellies in England. Ask Fitzbodkin about that."

Penelope gave her a look.

"I just want to make sure you're properly focused for the showdown," Missy said. "Find the white-eared puppy, and game/set/match. And then you just raise all kinds of hell. Maybe get the principal in there and everything. I mean just absolutely go to town."

"I'll see you tomorrow," Penelope said.

Penelope approached the school while checking her phone every ten seconds for an update from the mechanic, but none came. Maybe it was worse than she feared. She'd passed at least five of those payday loan places on the way and wondered if that was an option. Sure, they charged about 50 percent interest, but it was cash on the barrel, virtually no questions asked. From what she'd heard, as long as you could sign your name with an X and weren't literally dashing into the store with cops firing guns behind you, you could get a loan.

She pulled into Stonewall Jackson Elementary in a financial panic. Two words kept appearing over and over in her brain: *car, money, money, car.*

There was also the phrase *BJ Queen* bouncing around in her gourd, courtesy of the one thousand times Missy had used it that day, so she was in an unusual state of mind. She parked and got out with her heart racing. Several adults—teachers or parents, she couldn't tell—were looking at her strangely. Had they never seen a woman in a skirt and blouse get out of a yellow 1970 Chevy truck before?

She was a little worked up. She slammed her door, opened the passenger side, and grabbed the trash bag. She couldn't have said why. Her subconscious probably had its reasons, but she was too distracted to consider them.

Parcel in hand, she marched into the school, checked in with the secretary, and was pointed to the BJ Queen's room. Thoughts of bullies and ex-husbands and cars and money jangled around in her brain as she walked down the sterile halls. She knocked once on the open door of 11B and was told by the woman tallying a gradebook at the desk to come in.

Ms. Dunleavy gave Penelope an apprehensive smile as she approached, and then got up to pull two of the hard plastic chairs together so they could sit face to face. The chairs were sized for the average third-grader, and when Penelope took hers, she banged her knee smartly.

"Sorry," Ms. Dunleavy said. "I've said for years that we should keep a few grown-up chairs in here for conferences."

Penelope smiled. It wasn't her nature to be impolite. Then she checked the smile. She was still agitated on a number of fronts and wouldn't be swayed by niceties.

"It's fine," she said. "So you got my email about the bus situation with Theo?"

"Yes. And I wish I'd known about it sooner. Maybe I could have done something. Theo is such a sweet, sweet boy."

This bragging on her son threw Penelope off guard for a moment, but she recovered soon enough.

"Well, my ex-husband James doesn't think it's a big deal. My ex-husband thinks it's just typical boy stuff, but I know it's affected Theo.

They're not just calling him names, which is bad enough, but actually putting their hands on him. James thinks it will just pass. Or that Theo could just put on a Dumbledore robe and cast a spell and that would be the end of it. But I'm not so sure. Things aren't usually quite that silky smooth. Anyway, he and I seem to have very different ideas about what is and isn't appropriate in a school setting. Or even outside a school setting."

After this peroration, Penelope sat back, not wincing in the least when her knee banged the tiny chair a second painful time. The bag with the shorty robe was twitching to be opened, she could feel it. She knew now exactly why'd she'd brought it.

As Ms. Dunleavy rose from her own tiny chair and went back to her desk, Penelope thought of other ways she might work in the word *robe* or *appropriate* or *ex-husband*. The teacher had definitely blanched during her spiel and seemed now to be stalling. All she needed was solid puppy evidence, and then the mystery bag would be opened, the male delicate revealed.

"I'm sorry," the teacher said. "I'm looking for something. Just give me a minute."

Ms. Dunleavy was definitely rattled, temporizing, and trying to regain her composure. How many times had a teacher—Mrs. Sketchin especially—discomfited Penelope in just such a setting? It felt nice for the shoe to be on the other foot after all these years.

As she waited, she took in Ms. Dunleavy, studying her unabashedly, hoping the teacher could feel her staring. She was younger than Penelope by a few years, but was no spring chicken herself. She was around Penelope's height and build, and her hair was similarly wavy but not dark. Penelope wondered if perhaps James had a type. Ms. Dunleavy had the same soccer player look that she did. She even moved the same when nervous, her hands flitting busily, trying to feign obliviousness to the person intently watching. Penelope found the similarities off-putting and decided she'd had enough of looking at her bespectacled academic doppelganger.

Around the room, she saw the typical third-grade stuff: maps, motivational posters, a bulletin board. Nothing of note and nothing personal. She looked back to Ms. Dunleavy's desk. Again, typical teacher bric-a-brac: stapler, porcelain paperweight, penholder. This was the most boring room ever.

Hold on. That porcelain paperweight. Penelope squinted. Yes, it was a dog. A small, black cute one. Ms. Dunleavy had a small cute porcelain dog on her desk.

Her eyes cut back to the bulletin board. Aha! Yes, indeed, yes, indeed. There among the crude maps of Virginia drawn by her students, and the week's lunch menu, and a reminder that *Manners Matter,* was a very small photo of what looked like a very small animal. Penelope got out of her chair and ventured over for a closer look.

It was a black puppy like the one running on James's Facebook. And it had one all-white ear like the puppy on Theo's Instagram.

Here, staring her in the face from the Blowjob Queen's bulletin board, was the proof, once and for all, of what she'd intuited from the instant she saw Van Halen on her ex-husband's Facebook page: James and Ms. Dunleavy were a couple.

"I like your puppy," Penelope said, thinking how much Theo would enjoy playing with it all summer long. "That white ear is so unusual. So distinct. Once you see it, you're never going to forget it."

"Oh, thank you," Ms. Dunleavy said, again sounding nervous, not meeting Penelope's eye. "I loved her the first time I saw her."

The bag in Penelope's hand was beginning to feel sweaty. She could say something like: *"And do you love this the first time you see it? Because it's yours now!"* before flinging the robe onto the desk next to the porcelain puppy.

Penelope had her hand inside the trash bag, gripping the satin silky, in front of the bulletin board with the evidence that proved beyond all doubt that Theo's teacher was carrying on with Theo's father. Her heart was pounding as hard as it ever had in her life.

Then Ms. Dunleavy said: "Okay, I found it. Sorry it took so long.

It's a report Theo wrote yesterday. I asked the class to write about their proudest moment of the year. All the other kids took their essays home with them after school, but I asked Theo if I could make a copy of his and send it in to the newspaper. After I asked your permission, of course."

The piece was entitled "My Big Hit" and detailed, with considerable pathos, Theo's foray into baseball. Penelope felt confused and distracted and suddenly very tired. It had been a long day, a long week, a long year. And now this woman was reading an essay, aloud, with feeling and an effective quaver in her voice, that her son had written. It concluded as follows:

My mom had been telling me just to swing the bat. She said it didn't matter if I hit it or not. But I should try. I was still scared. But I kept telling myself that over and over as I walked that time to the plate. And then I did. I swung the bat. And believe it or not! I hit it! It was only a foul but I was very excited. The whole team and even my coach was jumping up and down and cheering. For me! I felt proud. The only thing that made me sad was that my mom was not there to see me. She had to work. She works at Coonskins. But I learned a valuable lesson. That it is always important to try. I hope I get a hit next time my mom comes to the game. The End.

Penelope's eyes were watering halfway through, and by the end she was crying freely. Having nothing else to use, she pulled a corner of the shorty robe from the trash bag and used it to dry her eyes, the poly-blend mixing with the plastic of the bag as she roughly daubed her face. She knew it was a messy show but couldn't help herself. Ms. Dunleavy now came over to the bulletin board and put her arm around Penelope's shoulder. It was an awkward gesture but strangely reassuring.

"Theo," Ms. Dunleavy said, "is one of the sweetest boys I've ever taught. He's nice to every kid in the class, and other than a few bad apples, all the kids really like him."

Penelope had just about gathered herself after the essay, but this line started a new flood. Now her nose was running like a faucet. She pulled the robe completely from the bag and used it to clear her nasal passages in a way that would have made Uncle Doozy in the shower proud.

When she'd stemmed the tide of tears a bit, she pulled the robe from her face and held it out in front of her, where both she and Ms. Dunleavy gawked at it. She'd always been a woman who got along with other women. The person beside her was not so different from herself, just another middle-aged, single working gal living in a small town. Yes, it wasn't the most appropriate thing to be dating the father of a student, but Penelope and James were divorced, had been since January. And no one knew better than she about the slim pickings for single women in Hillsboro.

The thought hit her like a forcibly thrown peanut that the only beef she had was with her ex-husband. Confronting this woman would be akin to sister-on-sister crime.

"This is a shorty robe," Penelope said.

Ms. Dunleavy loosened the grip on her shoulder and took a step back, looking perplexed.

"I found it last night, and then it was in the truck. I meant to get rid of it," Penelope said.

Ms. Dunleavy nodded to this nonsense but said nothing.

"I've got to give it to someone," Penelope said, still sniffling but about to regain her composure.

Ms. Dunleavy said: "I have a good idea who's been picking on Theo."

Penelope nodded, the thought striking her that Ms. Dunleavy likely hadn't seen James starring as Mopey Boy, or proud Introvert, or even heard him recite Robert Burns ballads for a really long time when there was a pretty decent TV show that they could be watching instead.

"I have a very good idea about who the main boy bullying Theo is," Ms. Dunleavy said. "And I can tell you that he's been a problem all year long. For students and teachers. I do wish I'd known about the bus issues, though. That's something the school will come down on if they know about it."

Penelope nodded again. There was a good chance Ms. Dunleavy had never seen James trying unsuccessfully to get dog doo off his shoe with a stick on the front porch or seen him rosin his bow before returning it to the garage for six more months or even had him time one of her showers.

She felt as if she should be the one comforting Ms. Dunleavy. The poor gal had no idea what lay before her. Penelope now gave Ms. Dunleavy a hug, a big one, nearly cheek to cheek, averting her head at the last second so as not to smear tears on the teacher's mascara.

"It's okay," Penelope said. "It's fine."

"It's not fine with me."

Penelope realized they were talking about two different things.

"I know who the main boy is," Penelope said. "And I think I'll call his parents this week. I don't want this hanging over Theo's head, especially since we'll likely see this kid around town this summer. And if his parents won't handle it, I'll get the school involved next fall."

"Let me know if there's ever anything I can do."

"I will. But listen, I have to run. I just wanted to get a better idea about the ringleader boy and how Theo has gotten along at school. Now I feel like I know all I need to."

"Okay," said Ms. Dunleavy. "I don't feel like I did much, but I'm glad I could help. Theo is one of my favorites."

Penelope smiled and said: "Thanks. And that really is a darling puppy you have."

29

She stood on the porch, being undressed by a garden gnome's eyes, waiting for James to answer the door. She had a few things to get off her mind, one of which concerned the plastic bag she held in her hand. She rang the bell again. What was he doing? Painting a portrait of Thomas Wolfe? Shortening the hem of a kilt for summer wear? Taking an IQ quiz? The possibilities were endless.

She rang again, waited, thought she heard furtive movement inside, then just laid on the bell. This did the trick, for James answered, or at least cracked the door. He peeked at her from a slit approximately three inches wide.

"I'm not armed, James," Penelope said.

He opened the door perhaps an inch more. "I'm kind of in the middle of something."

"I won't keep you long. Now are you going to let me in or not?"

Slowly the door opened.

James was not wearing an artist's smock. Neither did he have a tailor's needle in hand. Nor was he testing his intellectual quotient.

He was, however, wearing a robe. A karate *gi* to be specific. It was black and tightly cinched with a white sash. Most of his legs were covered. His feet were beslippered.

"Come on in," James said, motioning her toward the living room.

Penelope entered, trying—but failing—to suppress a smile. This seemed too good to be true. Sure, it had been a terrible week, and she was broke and living with sex-addicted seniors. But somehow seeing her ex-husband dolled up for what she assumed was another foray into the martial arts made things just a tiny bit better. The universe felt more harmonious. James was brooding as well.

"I've signed up for karate again," James said as Penelope took a seat on one end of the sofa and he on the other.

"Is that right?"

"Yeah, a new dojo just opened, and I think it will be a much better fit. It's more of a mind/body focus instead of just straight karate. You know, tai chi, that sort of thing."

Penelope didn't know about tai chi, other than the sound of it kind of made her hungry, but she nodded anyway. She had other business to conduct.

"Well, I won't keep you long if you're running late for your class," she said. "Just a quick word about those bullies on the bus."

"Actually," James said, interrupting as was his custom, "that's something I wanted to talk to you about. How would you feel about Theo taking karate with me? It would do a world of good for his confidence. And who knows? Maybe he could learn enough to take care of those bullies by next year if they're still messing with him."

Penelope found it a bit rich, this equating of karate and confidence-building, since it had taken her about forty handjobs and all sorts of cowgirl outfits to get him over his initial go at the Eastern arts. But she let it slide.

"I've already taught him to wrestle," Penelope said. "He knows plenty to handle those bullies."

James smiled his indulgent smile at this, showing just how much respect he had for southeastern-style wrestling and Penelope's ability to teach it. More than ever she regretted going half speed in their bed bouts. There weren't enough handjobs in the world to restore his confidence after the ass-whipping she could have put on him.

"We're talking karate, Penelope. Self-defense."

"I've just come from a meeting with Ms. Dunleavy."

The indulgent smile, always so slow and leisurely when making its approach, vanished at this. And the sash of his *gi* must have suddenly felt constricting, because James started fiddling with it in a herky-jerky manner.

"Oh yeah?" said James.

"I know you're dating her. It's kind of gross and definitely inappropriate, but whatever."

"Just since last month," James said, standing now and pacing across the room. He roamed aimlessly for several seconds before stopping under the framed copy of the family coat of arms, under the swords and the apples and the Scottish lions that shouldn't be stroked or petted. Penelope noted that her ex-husband didn't look quite so leonine as just moments before. In fact, he was downright kittenish.

"You could have waited till the end of school, when she wasn't his teacher. It's just tacky. But listen, I don't care, I seriously don't."

"I was going to tell you."

"It's fine, forget it. But while we're on the subject of slightly irritating things you've done. How about from now on you check with me before buying something like an iPod touch for Theo? You're the one who's always complaining about how much time he spends on screens."

"I wasn't trying to bribe him or anything."

Penelope found it interesting that he went there right away, but maybe he'd just anticipated her reaction. They had been married for more than a decade, after all, so he knew how she'd respond to most things.

"I believe you," Penelope said. "But I still think big purchases should be discussed. I wouldn't buy him a phone or something like that without consulting you first."

"I just thought it would be handy for Facetiming with whichever parent he wasn't with before he went to bed. But you're right. I should have asked you. I'm sorry about that."

Penelope nodded. James wouldn't have admitted fault so readily without the Ms. Dunleavy thing, but she didn't care. She'd hold him to this. They were no longer a couple, but their interests and lives would always be intertwined because of Theo. They would keep seeing each other, presumably, for the next thirty or forty years. She could handle that without being ugly, but she'd stay firm on issues that mattered.

"If Theo wants to take karate," Penelope said, "that's fine. I'm calling the bully's parents this weekend. But if that doesn't work, maybe self-defense classes will. I'm fine with it."

"Great," said James. "Fantastic. It will be nice to have someone to ride to the dojo with me."

Penelope knew he was surprised to be let off the hook so easily about Ms. Dunleavy, but she no longer cared what he did or whom he dated. Let someone else hear the word *dojo* about forty times a day and run point on a Manhood Reclamation Project. Let someone else wake up to an aroused man in a shorty robe.

Speaking of which.

"James, this is yours. I found it in among my stuff. I thought you might want it back."

So saying, she pulled the yellow kimono from the plastic bag.

"You might want to wash it first," she said.

James took the proffered silky with a misty look in his eye, as one sees at forty-year reunions or in movies when couples displaced by warfare reconnect. In the soundtrack of Penelope's mind, the violins were swelling. Or maybe it was something by Peaches and Herb. Needless to say, emotions were running high.

"I thought it was lost," James said.

"Apparently not."

"I bought a replacement just a few weeks back."

Penelope almost said: *I bet you did. Right around the time you took up with Theo's teacher.* But somehow managed to refrain. Other than that one pair of running shorts he sometimes wore in public, James's milky thighs would never again be seen by her eyes while his upper torso was covered. That was enough to stem the snarky comments piling up in her brain.

James gave a wry smile now, the one that had attracted her in the first place. "You never did care much for Old Yeller, did you?"

"I'll reserve comment," Penelope said, returning his smile.

"Well, thanks for returning it, anyway. My new one's okay, but it's too long. I don't like long robes. They get all tangled up in your legs, especially when you sit down."

He said this without irony, and Penelope did what she could not to smile.

"I'll let you know what I find out from that boy's parents," she said, turning to leave.

"Okay, thanks. And thanks for being so cool about the teacher thing. It wasn't ideal timing, I know."

Penelope waved a dismissive hand over her shoulder, then walked down the porch steps, past the garden gnome and the pansies and the shiny new garden hose, toward the old pickup that waited for her in the driveway.

30

She was nearly to her mom's, thinking the first thing she'd do when she got home was cancel her Divote subscription. The odds of meeting a cool guy had gotten a lot longer since word of the Coonskins Jezebel began making the rounds among the single and devout in the area. BrettCorinthians2:2 was really quite the tool. While she was at it, maybe she'd cancel LoveSynch too and just go cold turkey in the man department for a while as Rachel and Sandy suggested. Dating while living with her mom would be like high school without the sneaking out. She'd be sorry to leave Fitzwilliam hanging—she'd enjoyed his quirky notes—but likely it was for the best. Maybe he was too old for her anyway, as Missy kept saying. And what were a few more months, or even a year, without dating? It wasn't like she was competing with James about who had most successfully moved on, right?

Anyway, right after supper Divote would get the boot and her days of being candied by young Christians on the go would be over for good. She could decide about LoveSynch later on.

Pulling into the driveway, she detected three cars already parked there, though Daisy's traditional spot—nearest the house and George's heart—was still vacant. For a moment she wondered who was visiting, but then realized she recognized the car. She should have. It was her own.

She parked and sprinted into the house. Her mother was at the stove, stirring mashed potatoes in a pan.

"Hey, what's my car doing in the driveway? I never did hear anything." Her mother turned and smiled. "It's all fixed and ready to go. You're back in business."

"Is Skeeter just going to bill me?"

"Nope."

"How am I supposed to pay him then?"

"George took care of it. You know that poker game over at Judge Wyatt's? Well, a few months back George *pushed all in,* and Skeeter wanted to call but he'd spent all his money. Betty only lets him take a hundred dollars out the door. So Skeeter said if he lost the hand, George could just take out the difference next time he needed a car worked on. That's the way Skeeter's been doing it for years, to get around that hundred-dollar limit. That way Betty never knows. She pays all the bills, you know."

"That was super nice of George. And I appreciate it, I really do. But I'm not sure I'm okay with George taking care of the car. I've always paid my own way."

"I know you have, and so does George. He wants to do this for you, so why don't you let him? You know how he feels about you."

Penelope did. Good ole George. He was the best.

"Wow. I don't know what to say. This is crazy." She felt flummoxed in the best possible way. And then the magnitude of it struck her. "I can still use my first two paychecks on a new place."

"I know you can, honey. That's the best part."

"No. The best part is not having to share a bathroom with Uncle Doozy for a month."

"If that dog can't corral him," her mother said, frowning over her potatoes, "we're going to have to lock the door to the basement at night. I can't have him crashing into my ceramic ballerinas."

Penelope felt giddy and jittery and discombobulated. She'd come visit when Aunt June and Doozy were in town, they were nice folks. And Theo would like having a dog in the house for a month. But they would not, repeat not, all be roommates down in the basement.

203

"Wow, that must have been a big pot," Penelope said, feeling at a loss for words to sum up the emotions coursing through her.

"Big enough to pay for a new head gasket, that's for sure."

"I never would have guessed they played for such high stakes. George is a secret agent man."

"He will surprise you," her mother said, eyes twinkling.

Penelope laughed at this as if they were in on the same joke and apparently they were for her mother now offered a rakish wink, the saucy senior.

"Where's Theo?" Penelope asked.

"I think he's playing the Wii."

Penelope had long admired her mother's phrasing of *playing the Wii* and was glad she'd never corrected. She'd even warned Theo about it. Some traditions were worth maintaining.

"Frankly," her mother said, "I'm surprised he's not already in here. He's been asking me where you were every ten minutes since he got home from school."

Penelope gave her mother a look, or her back a look, but her mother didn't turn. "What's going on?"

"Just go in the den. He's waiting for you."

"Tell me if it's good or bad."

"You're being ridiculous. Go see for yourself. Supper's almost ready."

Penelope walked into the den to find Theo jerking this way and that with his joystick, so engaged in Mario Kart he didn't notice her.

"Theo, what did you do to your face? Why's it all scratched up?"

For the first time in recorded history, Theo stopped playing a computer game unbidden. He flung the controller on the couch and ran up to her, smiling and talking all at once.

"Slow down, Theo, I can't understand you," Penelope said, running her finger lightly over the abrasions that ran down both cheeks. They weren't as bad as they looked from a distance.

"I did it, Mom. I finally did it."

"Did what?"

"Took Alex down. Took him down hard."

"On the bus? Wow. I can't believe it."

"No, not on the bus. I told you, you can get in big trouble for fighting on school property."

Theo, as he often did while telling a story, got sidetracked. He was now detailing instances—many of them sounding like urban legends—where kids were disciplined for bus infractions. He seemed to have forgotten the point to his story.

"Theo, back to you and Alex."

"Oh yeah. So I told myself last night before I went to sleep that if he did anything today, I wasn't going to just take it. I was going to *let it rip* like you said. He bugged me on the way to school, doing all the Fart Boy stuff, but I ignored him. Then on the way home, he sits right beside me and keeps flicking my ear. Like twenty times. And he kept saying *wait till I see you at the pool* and that kind of stuff."

Her son was the worst storyteller ever. She wanted to shout for him to get to the point but didn't have the heart. He was awfully proud of himself.

"So I made my decision. I didn't say a word or do anything the whole time he's flicking my ear, but you should have seen Alex's face when I followed him off the bus. I thought the driver would notice and maybe ask why I was getting off at that stop, but he wasn't paying attention. A bunch of kids get off there. So then I just walked up to Alex and tapped him on the shoulder and said, *You're not going to do anything to me at the pool. Or next year either.* He pushed me, and then I tackled him into some people's yard. I used both a reversal and a half nelson like we practiced. Anyway, I held his face down in the grass until he promised to leave me alone. A lot of the kids were cheering. That kind of surprised me. I was going to try a full nelson but he was already crying by then. You were right about bullies. They are babies. And then I walked home. It didn't take that long. You want to play Mario Kart?"

Penelope couldn't believe what she was hearing. Her only thought was: In your face, Karate James.

"Theo, I am so proud of you," she said, thinking not just of this but also of the sweet essay he'd written. "I can't believe you this past week. What's come over you?"

"YOLO."

"What?"

"You don't know YOLO? Then I am definitely SMH."

"Just tell me what it means."

"Truer words were never spoken. YOLO."

"Tell me, Theo."

"You only live once."

"YOLO? People say that? That's even worse than *smeh*. Seriously. YOLO makes me weep for the future."

"LOL."

"Are you trying to get on my nerves so I'll play you in Mario Kart? I can still take you down. Remember that. I haven't taught you half the stuff I know."

Theo made the motion with his hands of someone yakking and repeated LOL several more times. Penelope rued the day she'd first said OMG just to irritate her son. She was getting paid back in spades now. She'd have to be more careful about teaching him all her *messing-with* tricks in the future. She didn't want to be tortured—like a spider caught in its own web—by her own psychological ploys when Theo was a teen. That would be too much to take.

"All right, one game before supper," she said. "Just one, seriously. I pick the track. And after I kick your butt, I am going to LOL. Hard."

31

Penelope lay on her bed in the basement, disbelieving the recent turn of her luck. Actually, she wasn't too surprised. Her luck had always been streaky, with long runs, both good and bad. Still, this was all kinds of fortuitous and all kinds of awesome. She'd pay George back, one way or another. If he wouldn't take cash once she got her financial house in order, she'd get him that Weber grill he'd been lusting over at Lowe's for the last year and a half. She'd surprise him with it on the back patio. What a sweetie he was.

Unbelievable as it would have seemed that morning, she could start looking for apartments right away. Maybe Rachel or Sandy would help if they weren't posing for Norman Rockwell or lovemaking with their husbands beside picturesque mountain streams. Yes, certainly one of them would be free sometime over the weekend.

On her nightstand, *The Stranger Within* was beckoning. When she'd left off, Sebastian had just enticed Melinda into a quick trip to Vancouver in his private jet, which he piloted himself for his polo matches and international business affairs. Penelope wasn't sure how this flight would turn sexual, but felt sure it would. From what she'd seen so far, Sebastian was the kind of man who could take full advantage of the autopilot.

Before she dove into her book, however, there was that one loose end to take care of. She picked up her phone to do just that, then found herself, before she realized she was doing it, staring at James's Facebook page. Good God. Her fingers were truly addicted. What did they hope to find? It was too early for James to post hanging-at-the-dojo shots. He would eventually, of course. And once that happened she might not be able to resist a peek, especially if she was drinking a little vino with Rachel and Sandy. How could she not? She owed herself that much.

Still, until sufficient time had passed, she'd have to work on muscle memory to retrain her surfing fingers. She was through, once and for all, playing cyber-detective on her ex.

She went now to her Divote account, where once again things had exploded, and not just with young guys. She was being candied from all directions. Ignoring all this stickiness, she searched for an opt-out button, but had no luck. She couldn't even find contact information—an e-mail or a phone number—so she could reach another human about cancelling the subscription. After five minutes, she threw in the towel. It was unlikely her mother would get any money back anyway. She'd just remove the app from her phone and call it a day.

Before she did that, she scrolled through her messages till she found the most recent one from BrettCorinthians2:2, sent only an hour before. The message was simple and to the point: Come on, just call. You know you want to.

Feeling immediately pissed, she hit the respond button and typed: Brett, that shark in your dreams is going to bite your weenie off if you keep sending naked photos to people.

She laughed at this, then erased it. She tried again: Brett, please tell Satan that if he really wanted me to lead you down the primrose path to SIN, he'd give you better advice than suggesting a DONG ShOT. Frankly, I thought that old goat would know me better than that by now. Do you think he's losing a step?

She erased this one too, feeling unclean for even typing the word *dong*, especially in all CAPS, which made it look even *dongier*. Finally, she wrote this: Brett, desperate, aggressive, and uncool is no way to get a date. The shark in your dream is probably trying to tell you something. Good luck discovering what that is, but in the meantime, stop bugging me. I'm not going to go out with you. Today, tomorrow, or ever. Seriously.

It was less pithy than the others, but she was tired of messing with BrettCorinthians2:2. He'd occupied too much of her gray matter as it was.

Okay, now it really was time to get acquainted with *The Stranger Within*. Sebastian would have the jet juiced up by now, and Melinda as well. Melinda, poor girl, couldn't help herself. She knew Sebastian was no long-term deal, and knew as well that the trip to Vancouver would bring surprises—perhaps some of them dark—that she'd never before experienced. Why did this intrigue Melinda so? The dark surprises perhaps most of all? Who could have imagined that a small-town girl from Iowa would end up here, doing that, thirty thousand feet above terra firma?

32

Things were steaming up nicely in the cockpit when the phone rang. What the hey? Who could be calling at 10:30? Looking again, she realized she knew that number. But what was the HHR doing awake at this hour? There were weeds to be eaten in the morning, lands to be scaped.

She answered with a hesitant *Hello?*

"Penelope, I'm sorry to be calling so late. I had a four-wheeler bust an axle on the way back from jug-fishing on the river, and I'm just now getting back to my place. Jake Shifflet, the dumbass, forgot where we were supposed to meet up and went to the marina instead of the dam, so I had to swim out to this buoy until I could wave down a passing boat and catch a ride in. Don't know how I'm going to get my four-wheeler out of there, but that's a problem for another day. Anyway, I had a hell of a day fishing—got one cat that must run thirty-six, thirty-seven pounds."

Penelope could tell he'd forgotten the original purpose of his call, his short-term memory floating pleasantly above the river he'd just fished in a tidy one-hitter cloud.

"Were you calling about anything else?"

"Oh yeah. Got you. Sorry. Well, it's done. That picture's gone. Weasel tried the intellectual property angle on 'em first, but they had no idea what he was talking about. Then he went with the invasion-of-privacy thing, and they just laughed at him. That got him all worked up so he threatened to sue the *ushanka* right off em."

"The what?"

"The *ushanka*. Those furry hats Russians wear."

"I have no idea what you're talking about."

"Penelope, come on. All these outfits are run by the Russian mafia. Everybody knows that. Weasel was just calling them on their Russian bullshit."

The HHR took a break here to blaze a fresh fattie. She could tell it was a joint instead of one of his multitude of pipes because he had to flick the lighter a number of times before she heard the inhale and cough. Actually, it was probably a roach left over from his day of jug-fishing on the river. Penelope paused to consider how she knew so much about the particulars of the HHR's cannabis habit. With a gun to her head or a perjury charge in the balance, she'd be forced to admit that back in the day she'd gotten reasonably acquainted with most of his smoking apparatus. And most of his leaf blowers too. It seemed like a thousand years ago.

"Hold on," she said. "Weasel was talking to someone who runs Paybacks Are Heaven on the phone? How in the world did he get their number?"

"Are you kidding?" said the HHR as if it was as obvious as the nose on her face. "He pays for one of those services where you can look up anything on anybody. I mean anything: arrests, bankruptcies, restraining orders, liens on your house. All that crap. Getting a little phone number is nothing for that service he's got. It probably took him like three seconds."

The HHR paused here to let that sink in, accustomed, one would guess, to a fair amount of oohing and aahhing around the hookah-hazed coffee table over this nugget of information. When none was forthcoming, he continued:

"Anyway, this guy was laughing at Weasel when he threatened to sue, just laughing right in his face. So Weasel all of a sudden starts crying, I mean really blubbering. You wouldn't believe how quick he changed personas. That Russian didn't know what hit him. Weasel starts going on about how in reality you were his ex-wife first love, and that he didn't know how to handle the situation so he pretended to be a lawyer when in fact he was a simple soybean farmer from Alabama. And he came up with this genius bit about you being not just his ex-wife and first love but also deceased, and that some creep had stolen the photo in a burglary of his secret lockbox where he kept all his prized possessions. And he kept talking about how you were the only gal he'd ever loved and how nice you were and that your son was your spitting image, right down to the long legs you display in the photo in question. I wouldn't have guessed it from a porn mogul, much less a Russian mafia capo, but he ended up feeling sorry for Weasel and said he'd take it off. His exact words when he hung up were: *Your wife sleeps with the angels.*"

Penelope couldn't believe what she was hearing. It seemed too good to be true.

"Weasel started fake-crying?" she asked. "Just like that?"

"No, he was really crying. He was so into the role, especially when he switched to that widower dude with the perfect hot dead wife. You know he's one of those method actors. I was there. I got a little teary myself."

"So it's gone?"

"Well, a few folks might have downloaded the image before we could get it off. I mean you can't blame them. You're throwing some serious flame. But maybe not. That Russian dude took care of business almost as soon as he got off the phone. Weasel really did a number on him. Poor guy didn't know what hit him."

"I can't believe Weasel pulled it off," she said. "What a relief. I'll call him tomorrow to thank him."

The HHR now cleared his throat, always a prelude to a serious thought or question. She braced herself.

"I know it's inappropriate to ask, and I figure you'll say no, and that's fine, but I was wondering how you'd feel if you knew that this ole ex-husband of yours downloaded that picture himself right before Weasel got it taken down for good?"

"What do you mean how would I feel?"

"I mean would you think I was a weirdo if I kept it, just for old times' sake? I promise I won't show it to anyone else. I never have in all these years. It's just a little something to remind me of a really good time in my life. But if you object, I'll delete it. You have my word."

Penelope pondered this for a full thirty seconds. It was an unusual request, but then again, did she really care? She'd known the HHR since she was eighteen. And she'd be lying if she said that she didn't think fondly—on occasion—of those days when she was footloose and fancy-free.

"No, it's okay. You can keep it. I don't mind."

"I thank you, Penelope, I really do."

There was another pause here where it seemed like the HHR had something else to say. Again she heard the lighter, again inhalation and hoarse coughing. She could tell he was working toward some state of mind. Eventually, his thoughts congealed and he was ready to speak.

"Hey, I've been reading up a lot on this, and I'm pretty intrigued. I'm wondering if you've ever heard of something called Bitcoin . . ."

"I have to go," Penelope said. "I've got work tomorrow."

There was a long exhale and then a clearing of throat. He would have to call Weasel or Jake Shifflet or some other of his fellow stoners on this Bitcoin thing.

"All right, Penelope, I'll talk to you later on."

"Okay. Thanks for taking care of that."

"Had to be done. It was my fault to begin with. If I'd known about it beforehand, I would have taken care of it without you asking."

And thus saying, the HHR hung up.

Penelope lay there, staring disbelievingly at the phone, feeling pretty darn good. Forces were at work beyond her control or depth of understanding. The universe was trying to tell her something. She thought maybe she should check her LoveSynch page after all.

There wasn't the bounty of contacts from interested men that she'd encountered the last time she'd visited the site, only one computer *blend* and two *flirts*. She'd been blanked on the *Eiffel Tower* front, which she found a touch disappointing. On the other hand, she had received a message from one Fitzwilliam Darcy of Pemberley by way of Derbyshire.

My Dearest TheosMom75,

I feel perhaps that I have moved too swiftly in regards to my suggestion that we consider meeting face to face. I had hoped it would be construed as a *modest* proposal (please forgive the pun—I'm congenitally incapable of passing one up, even when I know they should often earn the punster a Swift kick in the arse), but if you found it too hasty or forward, I do beg of you a thousand pardons. I am more than happy to continue our correspondence via the LoveSynch message board, though one of these days I hope to write a real letter, on real paper, with my real Montblanc fountain pen. (Yes, I am one of those Luddites who still write long letters. Not to worry, however, on the ecological front—I am a fervent recycler, though I have been accused—but never convicted—of keeping every single letter I have received in the course of my life.)

Please write back whenever time affords and the muse is caressing you with literary favors. No, strike that!

The muse can be most unpredictable. Please write back
even if your muse is away on a well-earned sojourn. Any
words from you at all would be appreciated.

With sincerest wishes for a reply,
FD

Penelope took a moment to reflect on this and then put her phone
away. She was tired and could hear the expensive hum of Sebastian's
jet calling her name. It was time for the return trip from Vancouver.

33

A good portion of the day had been spent listening to Missy analyze why Dimwit's visits now lasted five minutes longer than before. She'd sat beside Penelope at the computer, passing notes and miming—via grimace and gesticulation—a number of scenarios she imagined happening behind the closed bathroom door, all of them improbable if not physically impossible. But Penelope hadn't reciprocated. With few exceptions, the less you thought about bad stuff, the less bad it got. It was Psychology 101. So as far she was concerned, what happened in Dimwit's lavatory—no matter how morbid or pagan or Confederate-themed it might be—should remain there, and not sully the beautiful, bountiful, and independent summer that was currently taking shape in her mind.

It was Thursday, and James, in a surprise move, had taken the day off to celebrate the start of summer with Theo. He'd even offered to take him to baseball practice that evening. Penelope knew he was minding his Ps and Qs after her discovery of the Ms. Dunleavy affair, but felt no need to look gift horses in the mouth. A free afternoon was a free afternoon.

She was now en route to Sandy's house, in her softly purring car, with Van Halen cranking on the stereo, mentally tallying her financial ledger. She would receive her first paycheck from Rolling Acres Estates on Friday. And she had discovered, via online banking, that she still had $27 of wiggle room left on her credit card. She felt positively flush. Not only that, but George had filled up her car on the way home from the mechanic. Life was good—so good that she'd stopped at the 7-Eleven for the first time in forever without needing gas. It still felt unnatural to be driving without lights on the dash taunting her, but she hoped to get used to the feeling. Man, she wouldn't miss those yellow assholes.

She currently had a brain freeze from drinking her blueberry Slurpee too fast, but this too would pass. She reached for the volume knob, but it was already as loud as she could get it. How could anyone not like Eddie Van and David Lee? No one rocked harder. She'd bought dollar personality bracelets at 7-Eleven—SOPHISTICATED for Sandy, INTELLECTUAL for Rachel—and her friends would love them as much as she loved the bright-pink bauble on her own wrist, which confirmed what everyone already knew: she was CLASSY with a capital C. It felt luxurious to splurge on silly stuff, and she couldn't wait to see the gals.

She pulled into Sandy's driveway with her phone buzzing. She parked and snagged her phone from her purse, impatient to get inside and get the party rolling with her pals. It was her employer:

Please tell about the can of whoop-ass you opened on Ms. D.
Penelope replied: Like I told you. Situation is handled.
Missy: I hope you at least rapped her knuckles like the nuns did
    to me when I got sassy, which was every single friggin day.
Penelope responded with a smiley-face emoticon.
Missy: Just confirming one more time that you will definitely work
    six months. You promised.
Penelope: Yes. I told you. Six months. I swear.
Missy: I have it in writing now.
Penelope smiled and wrote: Send a copy to my attorney.
Missy: I bet we can come up with a scheme for Dimwit. I'm about
    whacked out.

Penelope: Glad to help anyway I can. Six months. Then I'm off to Wall Street. ☺ Have to run now.

She turned off the phone and grabbed the 7-Eleven bag with the bracelets, smiling at all the dirt she had to dish to her friends.

Dimwit, for starters. That freak would blow their minds. And the new job. Theo and the bully. James and the teacher. They'd go crazy on that one. James and his dojo. James and the return of Shorty Robe. *Escape from Neti Pot Island.* She was chock-full of material, and it would be nice to enjoy a glass of wine or several and talk about apartment-hunting and the upward trajectory of her life.

She thought she'd tell an expurgated version of the BrettCorinthians2:2/Paybacks Are Heaven/hot tub at Missy's episode, and not mention the HHR at all. They would stroke out over the HHR—her own personal catnip, according to Sandy—and send her home with a sack full of knitting needles and a chastity belt.

She also wasn't sure if she'd tell them about Fitzwilliam, or that she'd messaged him just an hour ago, agreeing to meet up for a lunch date next week. His age and yet-to-be-determined career/job/financial situation would just get them unduly riled up, Sandy especially.

Then again, it was pretty fun to rouse them on occasion. A good lathering was just what someone like Sandy needed every so often to rinse off the suburban sheen.

Penelope smiled as she got out of the car and started down Sandy's sidewalk, already hearing—and ignoring—the very good advice of her friends.

ACKNOWLEDGMENTS

All of my books have been a collaborative effort, enlisting close friends and family to act as first readers and editors, often of very rough initial drafts. This novel is no exception. Christy performed yeoman duty this go-round, reading the entire manuscript multiple times and offering plot suggestions, characterization ideas, and editing tips. The book couldn't have been written without her help and support. She, along with her partners in crime—Kristi Cross and Jen Feller—inform this book. Their bonhomie around our kitchen table about the foibles of men, high school misadventures, and the crazy things that all mothers go through proved a bounty of information. I am in their debt for the times they let me sit in on wine-time. My aunt Betty, to whom this book is dedicated, was the original inspiration for this story about a smart, single gal just trying to get by, and it is her appreciation for the comically absurd that gives *Penelope Lemon* its spirit and tone. Her wry humor and sharp tongue will be sorely missed.

Reid Oechslin and Chris Vescovo read early versions of the manuscript and offered feedback and support. Also lending a supporting hand were Anna Vescovo, Jason Hottel, and Frank Majors. Thanks to all for your assistance.

David Jeffrey, my dean at James Madison University, has been a stalwart in my corner for the past thirteen years. There aren't adequate words to describe what he's meant to my writing career, and the life I now have. I'm forever grateful for all he's done on my behalf. I'd also need to thank my former provost, Jerry Benson, Michael Speight, and the James Madison University Foundation and its Creative Development Fund, which allowed me the time and resources to complete the book and get started on its sequel. Mark Parker, Rose Gray, Dabney Bankert, and Bob Hoskins are others at JMU who have gone beyond the call of duty. I value the encouragement and friendship they've offered, and the smiles along the way. Finally, I'd like to give a nod to my fine, fun, talented students. I've enjoyed every class I've taught at JMU and have been well treated by students and administration alike. I'm grateful to have the job I do.

For a host of reasons, it will be six years between books for me, and I'd like to thank the following for various acts of kindness and support during this often trying time, especially those who helped out my family during my extended illness: Frank Majors, Chris Vescovo, Nancy and Stan Braun, Jeff and Karen Pickering, Steve and Becky Elkins, Jen and Eric Peifer, Wayne and Skip Smith, Don and Jeanmarie Sharretts, Liz Barnes, Mollie Bryan, Whitney Barker, Justin Rogers, Bruce Dorries, Nicole Oechslin, Kelly Flanders, Ed Fowler and Wendy Carlton, Karen Moran and Wistar Morris, and David Strasburg and Dania Chastain. There are many others who chipped in with phone calls and emails or giving a kid a ride. Thanks to all.

These folks offered much appreciated encouragement and advice: Bryan Di Salvatore, Allen Wier, Kim Trevathan, and Kathie Lang. The members of the Charlottesville Hung Jury Lunch Club—John Grisham, Corban Addison, and John Hart—were especially invaluable and supportive. I value your camaraderie and hope we can continue our literary roundtable for years to come.

Julie Stevenson, my champion of a literary agent, hustled like nobody's business for this book. Her patience, tenacity, faith, and good humor mean the world to me. She is the opposite of a front-runner, and the kind of advocate that every writer hopes for.

Michael Griffith, my editor, selected this book for his "Yellow Shoe Fiction" series and—frankly—saved my bacon. I will never be able to repay him for bringing my fifth book into the world when it was a little too this, a little too that, for others. He is also the best line editor I've witnessed firsthand, a great writer, and an all-round dude. I feel fortunate to have worked with a writer/editor who treated my work with the same painstaking care he shows his own. I had more fun revising than should be legal.

Everyone at LSU Press has been a dream to work with, and I'm proud to be publishing with people like MaryKatherine Calloway, James Long, Erin Rolfs, Lee Sioles, Neal Novak, M'Bilia Meekers, and Michelle Neustrom. My copy editor, Susan Murray, was fantastic as well.

Thanks to Mom and Stan, who have been in my corner since the beginning. The same can be said of my grandmother, Nina Winton, who will be 100 when the book comes out. My brother Frank is the kind of sibling we should all be lucky enough to have. He's not just my sounding block for every tough decision I've ever had to make, but also my oldest and truest friend. All of my books could be rightfully dedicated to him or to Christy. The help he gave me and my family during my illness meant so much.

Finally, thanks to my daughter Tess and my son Maxwell. Having two smart, cool kids in the house has kept me sharp and on my toes. All along you guys knew the score with this book—as did your mom— and never lost the faith. Your encouragement and good humor kept me going.